The Widow's Tale

By the same author

THE NOVICE'S TALE
THE PRIORESS' TALE
THE MURDERER'S TALE
THE MAIDEN'S TALE
THE REEVE'S TALE
THE SQUIRE'S TALE
THE CLERK'S TALE
THE BASTARD'S TALE
THE HUNTER'S TALE
THE SERVANT'S TALE
THE OUTLAW'S TALE
THE BISHOP'S TALE
THE BOY'S TALE

The Widow's Tale

Margaret Frazer

ROBERT HALE · LONDON

© Gail Frazer, 2004
First published in Great Britain 2006

ISBN-10: 0-7090-7908-7
ISBN-13: 978-0-7090-7908-8

Robert Hale Limited
Clerkenwell House
Clerkenwell Green
London EC1R 0HT

The right of Gail Frazer to be identified as author
of this work has been asserted by her
in accordance with the
Copyright, Designs and Patents Act 1988

2 4 6 8 10 9 7 5 3 1

This is a work of fiction. Names, characters, places and incidents
either are the product of the author's imagination or are used
fictitiously. Any resemblance to actual persons, living or dead,
business establishments, events, or locales is entirely coincidental.

Typeset in 10½/13pt Classical Garamond Roman
by Derek Doyle & Associates, Shaw Heath
Printed in Great Britain by St Edmundsbury Press
Bury St Edmunds, Suffolk
Bound by Woolnough Bookbinding Limited

But wel he knew that next hymself, certayn,
She loved hir children best in every wyse . . .
What koude a sturdy housbounde moore devyse
To preeve hir wyfhod and hir stedefastnesse . . .

—G. CHAUCER
The Clerk's Tale

Chapter 1

Heads back, the bright-clad gathering of riders swung their horses around and watched the hawk's climbing spiral into the clear sky of the warm spring noontide of this year of God's grace 1449. At the marshy edge of the meadow a huntsman loosed three spaniels into the green reeds, the tall rustle and sway betraying their going until half a dozen ducks burst up in a clatter of flailing wings. The hawk stooped from the sky onto the rising ducks and came down with one not a bowshot away along the meadow. Edward and Gerveys cheered, Cristiana laughed, and there were satisfied shouts among the other riders while a servant ran to fetch back the hawk and add the dead bird to the dozen already in the bag.

'You see?' Gerveys said. 'Not a lot of choice between yours and mine. Have you ever seen a finer pair?'

Edward willingly granted, 'Not this side of my Lord Bourchier's mews.'

The friendship between her husband and her brother Gerveys was one of the pleasures of Cristiana's life, but even as she smiled at them both, one of her least pleasures rode up on Edward's other side – his cousin Laurence Helyngton, who said, 'You've never seen the duke of Suffolk's best hawks then. He has a peregrine that matches any of the king's.'

'He would,' said Gerveys, adjusting the hood on the hawk on his fist and not bothering to keep disdain from his voice. 'Suffolk matches the king in almost everything and out-matches him in the rest.'

'Don't start it, you two,' Edward said.

Gerveys laughed. Laurence curled his lip and reined his horse away. His father and Edward's had been brothers, with Edward's father the older and therefore inheriting somewhat more of the family lands than did Laurence's. Edward as an only child had in his turn inherited all of his father's properties, but Laurence had two sisters, Milisent and Ankaret, and the dowers given with their marriages had cut his inheritance down still further, leaving him in seemingly constant irk at life. Not that Laurence was left poor. He was far from poor – except in patience – Cristiana thought, while saying, 'Don't goad him, Gerveys. Let this be a pleasant day.'

Her brother smiled at her. 'He's the one making for unpleasant, bringing up Suffolk. I've not brought up my lord of York, have I?'

'Your forbearance has been beyond reproach,' Cristiana said, making int praise of it. But her smile met his, neither of them taking the other seriously. She was too glad to have him with her this while, on leave from the duke of York's household, to much care if he vexed Laurence. She did not like Laurence.

But even while she smiled at Gerveys, her gaze slid to Edward with the worry she had been trying to hide ever since he last came home from court. These past ten years he had served as a gentleman of the royal household, leaving to her, for months at a time, the running of their manor here in Hertfordshire. It meant they saw too little of each other, but Edward's homecomings were all the sweeter for that.

Only this last one, a little over a month ago in mid-March had been not so well. Edward had been far more tired than he should have been from the one day's ride from court and much too pale, even allowing for winter pallor. He had taken to his bed and wanted nothing more to eat than strong beef broth. Cristiana, hovering and tending to him, had been relieved beyond measure when finally he said that was enough of lying about and, well wrapped in his furred robe, had moved to his chair beside the fire and asked for his daughters. When Cristiana brought them, he had taken eight-year-old Jane on his lap while Mary – twelve years old and grown too big for laps – had sat on a low stool, leaning against his knees where he could stroke her hair. Jane had showed him how well she could read now and her embroidery of a bright yellow popinjay perched on a green branch against a red sky, and he had admired Mary's newly won skill at reckoning sums. 'So I can help Mother with the household accounts now,' she had said proudly.

Edward had leaned over to kiss her and said, 'I could not be more proud of my two bright girls. They're worthy of their mother.'

He had smiled across the hearth at Cristiana then, and she had smiled back; and that night she and Edward had made slow and most satisfying love, the first time since he had come home; and afterward they had lain in each other's arms and she had known he was going to be well.

But he was not, and lately she had gone more than once to St Augustine's church in nearby Broxbourne to give a candle and pray before the Virgin's statue for him, as yet to no avail. He was still pale and his appetite still failed; he was losing weight and strength, and today had ridden his older, quieter palfrey to the hawking rather than the gold chestnut gelding he had bought for himself last autumn and was so proud of, giving it to Gerveys instead, saying, 'Let your horse have a rest,' although Gerveys had come all of two days ago and only from Clare, not far enough to tire any horse.

But if Edward was determined to keep the shadows at bay, then so would she, for today and tomorrow anyway, because this was May Eve and by long Helyngton family tradition, family and friends gathered to the Helyngton family manor of Highmeade to hawk in the river meadows below the green rise of hills along the River Lea and afterward to feast before most of them went home to their own manors' May Eve bonfires. Cristiana's secret hope had been that this year Laurence and his sisters and their families would not come but come they had, husbands and children and all, leaving her to make the best of it. Worse, they would all be staying the night, but at least Edward was enjoying himself, and Mary and Jane seemed happy enough, kept with their six cousins at the river meadows' edge where servants were watching over the tables set out with food and drink for when the hawking ended. Even Laurence, Milisent, and Ankaret were, for them, on good behavior. Ankaret *would* ignore her husband and ride too close to Gerveys and cast dove-eyes at him whenever there was chance, but Gerveys mostly ignored her and Master Petyt either did not notice or did not mind. A wealthy clothier from Waltham Cross, he was older enough that he should have known better than to fall for a pretty face and well-breasted body and not be over surprised if she led him in the old dance of cuckoldry. Their son looked neither like him nor at all like Ankaret.

On the other hand, Milisent's boy and girl looked very much like their father, Master Colles, and in its way that was a pity, he being blunt faced and fleshy, with hard little eyes. Not that taking after sharp-faced Milisent would have been better. There were no dove-eyes or winning ways about her. She and Laurence were much alike – and much like the hawks they were flying today, come to that – the both of them constantly on the watch for prey, Cristiana had often thought.

She had pitied Laurence's wife, a colorless woman who had grown more colorless as the years went by. After she had provided him with three sons, Laurence had mostly seemed to forget she was there, until a few years ago when a fever had carried her off and she was truly no longer there he was able to forget her entirely. Cristiana had once said something to Gerveys about Laurence's neglect and Gerveys had answered cheerily, 'At a guess, I'd say being forgotten by Laurence is better than being remembered by him, wouldn't you?'

There was, as the saying went, no love lost between Laurence and Gerveys. As long ago as Cristiana's wedding, Gerveys had said, 'I'd not trust him or Milisent so far as they'd fall if they tripped.'

Nor Edward did trust them. 'But they're family,' he always said. 'We won't be rid of them by wishing.'

Laurence's hawk was on the rise now. It had barely reached its pitch when the dogs set up a heron from the reeds, and like a plummeting stone, the hawk dropped and brought the heron cleanly down. With triumphant cheers, most of the company set heels to horses and cantered away to admire the kill. The servant bringing back Edward's hawk reached him just then. With that for an excuse, he stayed where he was, and Cristiana and Gerveys stayed with him, and holding up his arm while his hawk sidled and settled on his thick-gloved hand, he said, 'This is as fine a lannier as I've ever seen, Gerveys. Thank you yet again. The wonder is you were able to bring them both back in such good form all the way from France.' Where Gerveys had lately been about business for the duke of York.

'That was Pers's doing.' Gerveys' squire since they were boys in training together. 'He said that if I'd tend to myself on the crossing, he'd tend to the hawks. I did and he did and here we are. Though I'm not likely to hear the end of it any time soon, "Very full of himself for it, is Pers," ' he mock-grumbled, stroking his own hawk, blind in its red-plumed hood but turning its head side to side, alert to what might be happening around it.

Slipping on his own hawk's hood, Edward laughed at him and he joined in and Cristiana's heart rose. Edward's ready laughter surely meant he was more well than she feared and that her greatest worry need be only how soon tomorrow Laurence, Milisent, and Ankaret would go away.

Only too briefly was she quit of her fear. Toward the afternoon's end, with the feast done but only a few guests yet departed, all the rest were still standing about in talk in Highmeade's great hall – a dozen and more friends and neighbors besides the Helyngton cousins, with half a score of children busy among them and servants passing out wine and small cakes to stave off whatever hunger pangs might still be possible. Because Cristiana would not be able to avoid Laurence, Milisent, Ankaret, and their families later, she was avoiding them now, moving among her other guests – asking after Beth Say's little daughter who had been ailing lately; discussing this year's probable wool prices with Master Tendale; promising Mistress Norbury word when they would sell some of their timber; laying a quieting hand on Mary's shoulder when things began to be too loud among the children. She saw several of the young unmarried women had gathered to Gerveys – a thing not unexpected, he being young and unmarried and comely. To judge by his smiling talk he did not mind in the least, but his luck in avoiding Ankaret had run out. She was there, too, standing too close to him, plainly determined that he notice her, despite how he was plainly refusing to see her.

He could rescue himself if need be, Cristiana supposed. In more need of help was Beth Say's husband John, cornered near the dais by Laurence and Milisent. When John had come into the king's household as a yeoman a few years ago, Edward had befriended him. It had turned into a mutual liking, but with more ambition to rise than Edward had, John was since then become an esquire of the king's chamber, now held various royal offices, and in the present session of Parliament been chosen Speaker of the Commons. It made his friendship a valuable thing to have, which was surely where Laurence and Milisent's interest lay, but his friendship with Edward remained as it had been, and last year when John had acquired the nearby manor of Baas, Cristiana had found in his wife Beth a good friend for herself.

The only thing about John that somewhat ill-eased Cristiana was that his rapid rise in royal favor was much because of the duke of Suffolk. There was too much being said – and said not only by people like Gerveys who served Suffolk's rival the duke of York – against Suffolk and how he used, or misused, his place of power close to the king. Even Edward, usually silent on such matters, had begun to speak against him.

That did not mean John should be left to Laurence, though, and Cristiana looked around for Edward to rescue him. He was in talk with old Sir Andrew from Hoddesdon at the hall's far end, near the door to the parlor, and she threaded her way toward them with smiles and brief words among her guests, pausing to share Master Foxton's hope for a fine summer and rapping Laurence's middle son James on the head with her knuckles to make him let go of the long plait of a little girl who looked about to cry. 'Trouble someone your own size,' she told him, with the silent hope he'd try it with Mary. When his older brother Clement would not leave off poking her in the arm on the Helyngtons' last visit, she had stomped on his foot. Mary's boldness sometimes worried Cristiana, but sometimes boldness was needed and certainly against the Helyngton cousins.

She joined Edward and Sir Andrew as Edward was saying something about how Suffolk continued to encourage the queen in her grand spending of wealth King Henry no longer had.

'And Suffolk is among the reasons he no longer has it,' Sir Andrew grumbled.

If Suffolk sank into the sea tomorrow and never rose again, Cristiana would not mind, she was so weary of hearing about him; and she instantly forgot him at sight of Edward's face. Whatever strength he had called on today was gone. He was frighteningly gray around his eyes and mouth, and Cristiana interrupted his talk with, 'Edward, you must rest.'

Sir Andrew immediately said, 'I was thinking that myself. You don't look well, man.'

With effort, Edward made a smile. 'When everyone is gone, I'll—'

'Now would be better than then,' Sir Andrew said. 'I'll see you into the parlor to sit while your good lady sees to your guests.'

Cristiana would rather have seen to Edward herself, but he said, 'That might be best,' with such sudden weakness that she did not argue but thanked Sir Andrew and turned away to see what else needed doing. John Say had rescued himself from Laurence and Milisent. He and Beth and others were readying to leave, and Cristiana went, smiling, to make Edward's apologies, saying to everyone what she wanted to believe – that he had come home somewhat ill this last time, was much better. 'Just not so much better as he tries to believe he is,' she smiled, making light of it until even Sir Andrew had gone and only family was left. On them she turned her back and went to Edward in the parlor.

It was a southward-facing room and the one most used by her and Edward and the girls together. The walls were plastered a warm red. The square table in the middle was covered by a Bruges-woven cloth patterned in intertwining yellows and blues and greens, her gift from Edward when Mary was born. There was Edward's tall-backed chair and a plain chair for her and short stools for the girls; and a long bench under the window with embroidered cushions where she usually sat with the girls to work at their sewing; and another chest along one wall where various things were kept, from the household's few books to various accounts and records to the gameboard and pieces for merels. Edward was seated at the window, leaning against the sill, gazing out toward the fresh green of the rye and barley fields in the light gathering gold toward sunset. Without turning his head, he said quietly, 'The harvest looks to be good this year.'

Sitting at the bench's other end, Cristiana agreed, 'It does,' looking not out but at him.

With the evening light giving his face warm color, he looked himself, her well-beloved husband, and she let herself believe that in a moment he would turn his head and smile at her and they would talk about how well the day had gone and enjoy each other's company for the little while until time to gather up the girls and deal with Laurence and the others and go out to the bonfire piled and waiting in the pasture for darkness to come.

Then Edward turned to look at her, and Cristiana knew that for him there would be no going out to the bonfire tonight and on the beginning of anguish, she said, 'Edward. . . .'

He put out a hand, stopping her. She took his hand in both of hers and they looked at each other long and deeply and in silence before she said, 'I love you,' so quietly it hardly stirred the stillness between them.

As quietly back, Edward said, 'You are my heart.'

There was no need for more. Still holding each other's hands, they sat in silence, for the little while until a faint knock at the room's door was followed by Gerveys putting in his head to ask, 'May I come in?'

Without loosing Cristiana's hand, Edward said, 'Of course. No one could be more welcome.'

'It was either Laurence or I,' Gerveys said. He shut the door behind himself. 'I thought I would be better.'

'By miles and miles,' Edward said. 'I'll have to see him, though. I told him we'd talk before the bonfire.'

'Talk?' Cristiana asked quickly. 'About what?'

'He didn't say.' Edward let go of her hand, laced his fingers behind his neck, and leaned his head back into them, easing some weary ache.

'It need not be now,' Cristiana protested.

'If I talk with him now, I won't have to talk with him later.'

'Then I'm going to be here,' said Cristiana, ready to argue over it if need be.

But Edward said, 'That might be best.'

'And Gerveys, too,' Cristiana pressed.

Edward considered that a moment before asking, 'If you would?' of Gerveys who answered, 'If you want me to, then gladly.'

Edward pulled himself around to face the room, drew himself up straight, and said, 'Let's be done with it, then.'

Cristiana rose and moved aside to her chair as Gerveys opened the door and called in Laurence, who frowned with displeasure when Gerveys closed the door behind him without first going out of it. By his look he was unpleased to have Cristiana there, too, but said nothing about it, only took his stand in front of Edward and said with the firmness of a man sure of his ground, 'Well, Edward, it's time we talked, don't you think?'

From where she now sat, Cristiana could guess why Edward had chosen to stay with his back to the window: with the light behind him, his face was shadowed, less easy to read than Laurence's. Not that Laurence was ever difficult to read; just now he looked and sounded ready to argue something he was sure of winning.

'Talk about what, Laurence?' Edward asked in a level voice.

'You. What's going to happen. Your daughters.'

Cristiana tensed at mention of Mary and Jane. Come to stand beside her, Gerveys laid a hand lightly on her shoulder in unspoken reassurance while Edward said evenly, 'I don't see any need to talk about anything between us.'

'Oh, come, Ned. You're not a well man. Everyone can see it. It's time to talk about what happens if you die.'

Except he meant 'when', not 'if', and Cristiana wanted him dead instead – there and then, for preference. But Edward only said, still evenly, 'What happens when I die doesn't concern you, Laurence. My will is made. Everything and everyone is seen to. Let you content yourself with your own business.'

'What happens to our family's lands *is* my business.'

'*Your* lands are your business. *My* lands are not.'

'They *are*. It's bad enough the Helyngton lands were divided once, between your father and mine. Dividing them again between your two girls will only diminish them the more. We—'

'My lands are no concern of yours.'

'They *are*. Look at the way the world is going. The little man hasn't a chance. It's all big fish in the world today. Little fish are no more than a meal to them. Even you can surely see it's better to be a big fish than someone else's meal.'

With less patience than he usually had for his cousin, Edward said, 'Laurence, come what may, you'll never be a big fish.'

Cristiana felt Gerveys' small twitch of contained laughter but she did not see the jest, nor did Laurence, who insisted, 'With your lands added to mine—'

'Which they will not be. I have two heirs.'

Laurence dragged Edward's tall-backed chair around and closer to Edward, sat down impatiently, and said, 'That's the point. As it stands, your lands and all will be split between them. What I'm trying to make you see is that they don't have to be. Put Jane into a nunnery with the least dowry they'll take, and let everything else go with Mary to whomever she marries.'

'Meaning one of your sons,' Edward said.

'Meaning Clement. Yes,' Laurence said, triumphant that Edward understood.

Only Gerveys' hand heavy on her shoulder and her trust in Edward kept Cristiana quiet at thought of bright and laughing Jane put into a nunnery and Mary given to Clement, that Laurence-faced lout.

'No,' said Edward.

Ignoring or not hearing the flat refusal in that, Laurence said, 'If you think Mary would be better for the nunnery, well enough. It will be a few years longer before Jane is ready to bear but—'

'No,' Edward said again. 'Give over, Laurence. If nothing else, they're cousins.'

'A dispensation will take care of that. I'll see to it. I'll even pay for it.'

'Neither Mary nor Jane are going to marry Clement or any other of your sons, Laurence. Let it go.'

'Don't be a fool, Ned,' Laurence snapped. 'You're going to die soon. What's going to happen then, do you think?'

Cristiana jammed a fist against her mouth to stop her outcry. Edward without wavering said, 'What happens is that Cristiana will have keeping of our daughters. That's settled in my will.'

Laurence's face darkened with displeasure. 'Your will,' he scoffed. 'You. . . .'

Before he could say more, Edward added, 'Moreover, I've made Sir Gerveys overseer of my will.'

'And I have my lord Richard, duke of York, to back me in it, if it comes to trouble,' Gerveys said.

Laurence sent him a poisonous look. 'Within these two months your duke of York will finally be gone to Ireland with bag, baggage, wife, and all his whelps, well out of everyone's way. Not that his lordship is worth all that much these days anyway, he's so far out of favor with the king.'

'Meaning with Suffolk,' Gerveys returned. 'Whose power can't last forever.'

'Meaning your York will not be coming back any time soon,' Laurence snapped and turned back to Edward.

Gerveys' fingers tightened into Cristiana's shoulder but he made no answer. Laurence had only said what everyone, including York, well knew – that he had been given Ireland to govern for the sake of having him out of England and because he could not be sent back to France. He had governed too well there, in sorry comparison with the present mess Suffolk and his ally the duke of Somerset were making of it. Besides that, York was too royal-blooded, was arguably heir to the crown until such time as King Henry had a son and meanwhile openly no friend to Suffolk and the other court favorites around the king.

None of which mattered here and now as Edward said, before Laurence could go on, 'Laurence, you don't need this marriage. You're well off and comfortable. Forget—'

'I'm talking more than only comfortable! I'm talking about making us strong enough to matter in things!'

With laughter under his words, Edward said, 'Somehow that doesn't much interest me at present.'

'It's never much interested you,' Laurence complained. 'But it does me. With the Helyngton lands joined again—'

'No,' Edward said flatly.

Laurence started to answer that.

Edward cut him off with, 'I'm not selling my daughters' lives for the sake of your ambition, Laurence. You're not likely to be anything more than one of the little men around the duke of Suffolk. With my lands or without them. And as it happens,' Edward's voice hardened, 'it's going to be without them.'

Laurence stood up. 'If you're depending on Cristiana or Sir Gerveys, you're a fool. She's a woman and he's away to Ireland with York, who's worth nothing to anyone anymore.'

'I doubt you're wise to discount my lord of York, Laurence,' Edward said.

'York is finished. Don't threaten me with York.'

'That wasn't a threat, only something that "little fish" like ourselves would do well to remember.'

Laurence made a disgusted sound and started for the door, but as he reached it, he swung around, pointed at Edward, and said angrily. 'You're dying. When you're dead, I'll still be here. Just you think on that.'

Gerveys took an angry step toward him, but Laurence wrenched open the door and went out, slamming it behind him. Cristiana, more quickly than her tears could come, rose from her chair and went to Edward, sat beside him and put her arms around him. He wrapped his around her, too, and they held tightly to each other, Cristiana not knowing whether the tears on her cheek pressed to his were all her own or not.

Only when Gerveys made quietly to leave them, Edward drew back from Cristiana without letting go of her and said, 'Stay, please. There's something I must tell you both.'

Gerveys's answer was forestalled by an eager knocking at the door and Mary calling, 'It's time to go for the bonfire!'

Cristiana straightened farther out of Edward's arms, wiping her face dry as Gerveys went to open the door. Smiling, he said to his niece, 'The bonfire? Surely you don't want to go to that old thing, do you?'

Mary seized his arm and tugged. 'Yes, I do, and so does Jane. It's time.'

From the shadows stretched long outside the window, the sun must be sunk well toward sunset. Everywhere around the manor all the hearth and kitchen fires would be out by now and folk be gathering to the high-piled wood waiting unlighted in the pasture beyond the orchard. From all the other years, Cristiana knew there would be merriment there now, talk and laughter, but a hush would come as the darkness deepened until everyone was waiting, silent, while this year's chosen man set to work with flint and steel to make the year's new fire out of nothing, silence and darkness deepening around him until the struck sparks finally caught in the waiting tinder. The flames would creep then along twigs, growing until it leaped into the larger branches and burst crackling among the piled logs. Then there would be cheering, followed by dancing and drinking well into the night.

Everywhere it would be the same, in manors, villages, and towns: the breathless wait in the darkness, as if this year maybe the needfire would not happen and all the cold hearths and kitchen fires stay unlighted. That the fire always came never changed that almost fearful waiting. Without that brief fear, the triumph and merriment afterwards would have been less, and Cristiana, like Mary, had never willingly missed a May Eve bonfire. But this year Edward would not go to it. And next year he. . . .

She shivered the thought away before it had fully formed.

'Mary, come here,' Edward said, beckoning.

Reluctantly she gave up her hold on her uncle and crossed the parlor. 'It's time,' she pleaded.

Edward put an arm around her waist and drew her to his other side from Cristiana. 'I know,' he said gently. 'But I fear I'm not feeling well enough to go.'

Mary burrowed her head against his shoulder. 'We thought you were feeling better, Jane and I.'

'I am, but I still tire too easily.' He lifted her head by her chin and kissed the tip of her nose. 'I'd hoped to hold together until after the bonfire, but I have to rest instead. Even worse, I need to talk with your mother and Uncle Gerveys a while longer. They'll come later but it will have to be Ivetta who takes you and Jane.'

'Ivetta?' Mary protested. Ivetta had been both girls' nurse since they were small and lately Mary had begun a revolt against having a nurse at all. 'Oh, please, not Ivetta.'

'What about Pers?' Gerveys asked, offering his squire. 'How if Pers takes you and Jane, with Ivetta merely along?' He lowered his voice to conspiracy level. 'She and Pers like each other, you know.'

Mary's dismay sparkled into delight. 'I know! If he comes, she won't heed us much at all!'

'Off you go then.' Gerveys opened the door for her as she gave her parents each quick kisses. 'And no pushing anybody into the fire. Including your cousins,' he added as she went happily to kiss him, too. When she was gone and the door shut, Gerveys looked to Edward and Cristiana. 'Well enough?'

'Very well,' said Edward. 'Now come sit here.'

He pointed to the chair Laurence had left. Cristiana wanted to tell him that he should go to bed, not talk more, but contented herself with taking one of his hands to hold in her lap while Gerveys came to sit. He looked ready to protest, too, except Edward forestalled him with, 'Don't say it. I know. But I need to tell you and Cristiana something, not leave it any longer.' He smiled at them both, squeezed Cristiana's hand, and said to Gerveys, 'Laurence is, alas, right about things on the whole. Suffolk is riding with a high hand these days and there's nearly no one left to stand out against him. I wish from the heart that York wasn't going to Ireland just now, or else that you weren't going with him.'

'So do I,' said Gerveys.

'But since you are, I mean to change my will. At present, Cristiana and Sir Andrew are my executors, with you as overseer. I'm going to change that, make you an executor with Cristiana, with John Say as overseer in your stead. How does that seem to you?'

Gerveys was slow to answer, but finally said, 'I can see the point of not having me as overseer, but why Say? I like him in himself well enough, but he's Suffolk's man much deeper than Laurence is.' Which was a way of saying Gerveys did not trust him.

'He's not Suffolk's man in the way you mean it. Suffolk has made thorough use of his abilities, and if it comes to trouble with Laurence, he'll have Suffolk's backing far more than Laurence ever could. But John is first and foremost the king's man and therein is the difference. You see?'

Cristiana did not. Since Suffolk controlled everything around the king, didn't being the king's man come to the same as being Suffolk's? But after a moment Gerveys said, 'Good enough. I'll trust your judgment of him.'

Satisfied, Edward shut his eyes and, still holding tightly to Cristiana's hand, leaned his head back against the window frame, looking ready now to be helped to bed. But after a moment he said, not much above a whisper, 'There's something more,' and opened his eyes. He looked at her and then at Gerveys. 'I have something that, certain as Hell, will ruin Suffolk if ever it's made known.'

Gerveys had sat forward to hear him better but now jerked upright, drawing in a harsh breath before asking, even more harshly, 'Ruin him? How?'

'It's a letter,' Edward said softly. 'A rough copy of a letter. Not the final, fair copy but plain enough in its meaning. Written by Suffolk and others. To the duke of Somerset in France.'

Gerveys leaned forward again, matching Edward's low voice. 'What does it say?'

Edward moved his head heavily from side to side, refusing answer. 'Unless you have to use it, better you don't know. It's too dangerous.'

'If it's against Suffolk, I can give it to York. He'll use it.'

Edward pulled himself straight and reached out with his free hand to grip Gerveys' arm. 'Believe me, this is something even York won't want to use. Not unless he's looking for war here in England.'

'God's great mercy, Edward.' Gerveys sounded half disbelieving, half appalled. 'How did you come by this . . . this letter?'

'The king had mislaid an embroidered and pearled glove. I was looking for it, was in the privy council chamber, thinking he might have been there earlier that day. Suffolk and some others had been, anyway, and no one had been yet to clear things away. This was lying on top of a scatter of other papers and some of the words caught my eye. It's crossed over and rewritten. Probably everyone who had a hand in it thought someone else among them had destroyed it once a fair copy was made from it. I read it. Then I took it.'

'When was this?' Gerveys asked.

'Late this February last past.'

Gerveys held silent, calculating something, Cristiana thought. Then his eyes widened. 'Edward. Is this thing . . . you're not saying it's about Brittany? About Surienne and Fougères?'

That meant only a little to Cristiana. She knew there was lately some new outbreak of the war in France, but the war in France had been going on her whole life. The only time it had mattered to her was when Gerveys had been with the duke of York's household in

Normandy, so what he said now meant nothing to her; but Edward answered sharply, 'Better you don't wonder about it, Gerveys. At all. Better you forget the thing altogether unless there's need of it.'

'Need of it for what?' Gerveys demanded.

'Once I'm dead, I don't trust Laurence to leave matters alone. He and Milisent. Thieves aren't thicker than those two. She'll be neck deep in whatever he gets up to, and so will that husband of hers. The three of them are all bent the same way – all ambition and not much sense.'

'You don't think John Say in their way will be enough?' Gerveys asked.

'I want even more between Cristiana and them. This letter is the more. But understand me, Gerveys, it's to be used only if things have gone so direly wrong there's no way else to stop whatever Laurence tries.' The fierceness Edward put into that took suddenly its toll. He closed his eyes and slumped back and Cristiana tightened her hold on his hand, willing him not to leave her, please, please, not to leave her. Without opening his eyes, Edward whispered, 'I can't tell you how to use it, if the time comes. Too much will depend on how the world stands. Who holds power and who doesn't. Just remember, both of you' – he squeezed Cristiana's hand – 'it's to be used for Cristiana and the girls' safety before anything else.' He opened his eyes, looking first at Cristiana, then at Gerveys. 'Give me your oath on that, the both of you.'

More because it mattered to him than because she fully understood, Cristiana vowed by St Anne to obey him. Gerveys gave his own oath more reluctantly but sealed it past breaking with, 'By Christ's body and St Martin.'

Satisfied, Edward said, 'Thank you,' and closed his eyes again.

Gerveys leaned toward him. 'But where is it? You haven't told us that.'

Eyes still shut, Edward said, 'I've given it to someone who doesn't know what it is, only that it's to be kept until you or Cristiana gives him the right words to recover it. I'm going to tell you who has it, Gerveys. Later I'll tell Cristiana the words.' With effort he opened his eyes. His breathing was shallow and rapid, but he forced out, struggling against his own weakness, 'Swear to me, on your oaths already given, not to tell each other what the other knows until the time comes you're both agreed on the necessity of having this thing.'

21

Willing to do anything so that Edward would let them put him to bed, Cristiana readily gave her promise again and so did Gerveys; but then he asked, 'What if one of us, God forbid it, dies? Have you thought of that, Edward?'

'The man who has this thing will hear if either of you dies. He's charged, in that need, to find out the other of you who lives and give the thing over to you.'

'But if there's after all no need to use it against Laurence, can I have it to give to York?'

Edward gazed at him a long moment, considering, then answered in a whisper so faint that Cristiana barely heard him. 'Yes.' He gathered strength, drew himself a little straighter, and said, 'Now, Cristiana, leave us, please, so I may tell Gerveys what he must know.'

Cristiana obediently let go of his hand, leaned to kiss his cheek, rose, and left the room. Not until she had shut the door behind her and was crossing down the empty hall, alone, with no one to see her, did she let the tears at last scald down her face.

Chapter 2

The day had started well, clear-skied and warm after two days of rain. The Oxfordshire fields around St Frideswide's nunnery were in the full flourish of a fine summer, green with thick-grown peas and beans and full-headed wheat and rye and barley and oats, with the hayfields' yellow stubble and high haycocks telling that midsummer was prosperously past. There was a month yet to the beginning of harvest but everything promised a good year for the nunnery, and Dame Frevisse – taking her turn again as hosteler, in charge of the nunnery's guesthall and guests – took pleasure in the days going simply past in a quiet flow of duties and the eight daily Offices of prayers and psalms. By the Benedictine Rule, the nunnery was required to give food and shelter to any traveler who asked for them, but St Frideswide's was a small priory, well away from everywhere, and travelers were not so frequent as to be a burden or much bother. Last night there had been only a franklin who often came this way with a servant, stayed the night, and rode off in the morning after Mass, always leaving a coin in thanks-gift that more than repaid the nunnery's cost of his brief keep.

'If they were all so good, we could turn a pretty profit at this,' old Ela, head of the guesthall servants, had said when she gave the coin over to Frevisse.

'If they were all so good,' Frevisse had answered, 'we would hardly be doing the charity the Rule requires of us. Unless we claimed,' she added thoughtfully, 'that we did them charity by giving them the chance to do their souls good by alms to us.'

Old Ela had said, 'Humph,' and limped away.

Frevisse, smiling to herself, had gone back across the cobbled yard to the cloister. In expectation she would not be needed at the guesthall again until late afternoon when she would go to be sure all was in readiness for any wayfarers who might wish shelter and supper tonight, she had settled contentedly to her other work, presently the copying out in a fair hand the *Livre de chevalrie*. The nunnery's small scrivening business, taken up to help pay off debts, had thrived of late; this book was wanted by a landowning squire as a gift to one of his sons, while Dame Juliana and Sister Johane were working on a prayer book for a cordwainer's wife in Banbury, and Dame Perpetua was copying out a translation of Boethius' *Consolation of Philosophy* for Abbot Gilberd of St Bartholomew's near Northampton.

These pleasant summer afternoons they were usually able to work at their desks in the cloister's north walk for an undisturbed hour or more, with no more than the scratch of pens on paper and some- times the soft-soled footfall of another nun passing along the cloister walk to stir the quiet. So the sudden rapping at the cloister's outer door broke in unwelcomely, and because St Frideswide's was so small, with no porter kept at its door, Sister Johane rose from her desk muttering something that was probably not a prayer and went to answer it. Frevisse, determined not to be disturbed, kept at her work, not looking up at the following busyness of footsteps as Sister Johane hurried back from the door and up the stairs from the clois- ter walk to Domina Elisabeth's parlor, then shortly came down again and to the door, only to return a moment later with – to guess from their heavier tread – two men she led up the stairs to the prioress.

That was not unusual. People often came with need to see Domina Elisabeth, but it meant Sister Johane would not be back to her desk soon, would have to stay with Domina Elisabeth and her guests, it being unseemly for any nun to be alone with a man or men. Frevisse, quite happy it was Sister Johane and not her trapped to that duty, was less happy a moment later to hear old Ela's limping shuffle along the cloister walk and – resigned – had already stoppered her inkpot and was cleaning her penpoint when Ela bobbed a curtsy beside her desk and whispered, 'I think you might best come to the guesthall, my lady, if it please you.'

To leave Dame Perpetua and Dame Juliana undisturbed, Frevisse waited until she and Ela were outside the cloister, crossing the courtyard toward the guesthall, to ask why Ela wanted her, but Ela only answered, 'Something's not right. I don't like it. There's two women come with those men. You'll see. There's that, too.'

She jerked her chin toward a curtained litter at the gateway into the nunnery's outer yard, the two horses between its forward and rear shafts standing with the head-lowered weariness of having come far and hard. A travel-dressed man, standing much like the horses, was holding six other saddled, equally wearied horses nearby. Since there were priory servants who would have seen to watering them at least, even if the travelers did not intend to stay, why were they all standing there like that? Added to Ela's dislike of whatever was going on, the question brought so many possibilities to Frevisse's mind – ranging from unpleasant to unlawful – that she held off asking anything more.

The priory's guesthall, though it had a few rooms kept for travelers of the better sort, such as last night's franklin, was mostly a wide, long, open-raftered room where trestle tables could be set up for meals, then taken down and set against the wall at night, clearing the floor for bedding to be laid out for lesser guests and poorer travelers. At this mid-hour of the afternoon neither tables were set up nor bedding laid out and certainly there was no fire in the fireplace at the near end of the hall, but one of the low, backless wooden benches was set beside it, and on it sat the two women. Two men stood a little beyond them, obviously travel fellows to the one waiting with the horses but only servants, and Frevisse no more than noted them, then ignored them. It was the women who were – as Ela had sideways given her to understand – troubling.

One of them was dressed in a dark green, low collared riding gown of summer-weight linen, her headdress a light veil over a close-fitted coif to cover her hair. She would not have been unlovely, save for the hard set of her mouth and her hawk stare at the woman beside her, as if daring the other to move or speak.

There seemed small likelihood that the other woman would do either. She was altogether a slighter person, pale and huddled in on herself in a way that made Frevisse think of ill-health and utter weariness. To judge by the black veil over the white wimple that tightly circled her face and completely covered her hair and throat, and the

25

starkly plain, black, sleeveless, open-sided gown she wore over an equally stark, gray, straight-sleeved undergown, she was a widow. It was hardly clothing in which to travel, though, not even in that waiting litter. She looked to have slept in her gown, too, and more than once.

A prisoner with her guard, was Frevisse's thought in looking at her. The way the two men stood watchfully behind them made the thought stronger, but Frevisse approached the women showing no more than a mild smile of greeting and in a voice mild to match asked, 'My ladies, have you been made welcome? May I ask someone to bring you something to drink, or are you hungry? You or your men?'

The huddled woman made no move, did not look up from her hands clasped tightly in her lap. One of the men shifted from foot to foot, looking like he would not mind something to eat or drink, but the hawk-eyed woman said curtly, 'No.' Only belatedly adding, still curtly, 'Thank you.'

'My lady,' Frevisse started to the other woman, 'would you—'

'She needs nothing,' the first woman cut in dismissively. 'Thank you.'

Frevisse did not dismiss that easily. Still mildly, as if noting nothing amiss, she asked, 'Have you been long on the road? Have you come far?'

The first woman looked more than ready to send her bluntly away, then seemed to think better of it and said with tolerable politeness, 'Not far today, but we've been several days on the road, yes.'

'The weather has been good for travel,' Frevisse suggested.

'Very good, yes.'

'For where are you bound?'

'Here,' the woman just short of snapped. And added before Frevisse could ask, 'We're not staying though. We'll be leaving shortly.' She gave the woman beside her a hard glance. 'Most of us.'

A small tremor passed through the huddled woman and still she did not raise her head. The other woman, looking past Frevisse, said, 'Henry,' and stood up. 'Is it settled?'

Frevisse looked back over her shoulder to see a burly man entering the hall, as well-dressed for long travel as the woman and his fleshy face as hard-set as her own. Ignoring Frevisse as thoroughly as if she had not been there, he closed on the women, saying, 'All's settled. I'm to take her in.' He grabbed the huddled woman by one upper arm and hauled her to her feet, ordering at her, 'No trouble, you. There's no one to care if you make it, so don't.' He added, 'This won't take long,' to the first woman and shoved the other woman roughly away with him, gone before Frevisse could think of anything to say. The harsh-faced woman suddenly smiled, sat down, and said, 'I should very much like something to drink now, thank you. And to eat, if that's possible. Will you join me, my lady?'

Not liking her any the better for her sudden change, Frevisse nodded to Ela to bring something from the guesthall kitchen, sat down at the bench's end, and said with a very feigned mildness, 'Your companion seems an unfortunate creature.'

'She's not my "companion". She's my charge. Though I suppose she would say she was my prisoner. My late cousin's widow. It's all very regrettable.' She did not feign so well as Frevisse did; she sounded less regretful than very satisfied. 'Even before our cousin died, we had our suspicions of her, my brother and I and my husband. That was my husband who took her just now. We feared several things, and since our cousin's death, they've all come to pass. She was never stable. She went half-mad with grief when he died. She wept and screamed and wouldn't eat. We feared she'd do herself harm. She couldn't be trusted alone, nor did we dare let her near the children, she so frightened them. Two sweet little girls. And then, well, then. . . .'

Ela had wasted no time in the kitchen. She was back already with a tray with four mugs of ale. She offered them to Frevisse first, then to the woman. Though it would have been more courteous to do it the other way around, Frevisse did not chide her, not feeling particularly courteous to the woman herself. While the woman took a deep drink, Ela served the two waiting men and would have lingered but the woman began again.

'Well, there are things she did that a nun shouldn't hear and I won't tell you,' but she was going to, and Frevisse waved Ela away, out of hearing. Ela made a face and shuffled away, while the woman went on, 'Believe me, I daily, hourly pray that my cousin in heaven, God keep his soul, doesn't know what she's done. You've heard of 'wanton widows'? Wanton hardly touches it.'

Frevisse put aside any thought of trying to stop her; put aside, too, any thought of simply believing her. The woman was too much enjoying her tale, going on, 'She was so openly beyond all seemliness that we appealed to the bishop and anyone else we could think of, for help in curbing her. It was even being said she and her brother were, well, what sister and brother shouldn't be together. But that I will *not* believe,' she said in a way that said she very much did believe it. Or else that she wanted Frevisse to.

Frevisse stood abruptly up, ready to excuse herself, but the man Henry reappeared at the guesthall door, said across the hall, 'We're done. Let's go,' and disappeared again. Setting her emptied mug on the bench, the woman rose, saying, 'That's done, then. Thank you for your hospitality, my lady.'

She said that with a scorning curl of her lip, and admittedly it had been scant hospitality and very weak ale – a sign that Ela had taken dislike to the woman, nor did Frevisse mean to chide Ela for that and did no more herself than bend her head in token courtesy and make no haste after the woman as she swept out of the hall, her two servants behind her, so that by the time Frevisse reached the guesthall doorway, the woman's husband was helping her into her saddle while another man, already mounted, was saying something at them and gathering up his reins. Then, with a clatter of hoofs on cobbles, they were all gone – woman, men, servants, horses, and horse-litter – and afternoon quiet came back to the courtyard. The whole business had taken hardly the time it took to say the short Office of Compline, and not once had any name, save Henry's, been given. Even the bishop had been nameless. Nor had any place been mentioned. They had come nameless from nowhere and were now gone back there, leaving an allegedly wanton widow behind them.

Frevisse admitted to herself that she very much looked forward to hearing what Domina Elisabeth would tell the nuns about it all, and was pleased, when she came out of the passage from the cloister's outer door into the cloister walk, to find she did not have to wait. Along the leftward side of the cloister the desks were deserted and there were several nuns crowding eagerly through the door into the church. Nearer to hand, Dame Claire, the nunnery's infirmarian, and Sister Johane were coming from the direction of the infirmary. Sister Johane nearly stumbling over her own feet in her eagerness to get on but held back by Dame Claire's more deliberate pace, until at sight of Frevisse coming from the doorward passage, Dame Claire freed her with, 'Go ahead,' and the younger woman hurried on, leaving Frevisse to fall into step beside Dame Claire, matching her longer stride to the shorter woman's with the unthinking ease of long familiarity as she asked, 'What's toward?'

'Domina Elisabeth wants to tell us something about someone who's come. Do you know anything about it?'

'Not enough to guess what she'll say.' Unwilling to repeat what she had been told in the guesthall – the more especially because repeating it was probably what the woman had wanted her to do.

'We'll hear soon enough,' Dame Claire said, resigned. 'Just so it takes only a little while. I want to finish hanging the feverfew to dry.' A much greater matter to her than whyever they were called to the church. 'If we have much in the way of rheums and coughing come winter, we'll need it, the horehound is growing so poorly this year.'

The door from the cloister walk brought them into the church's south side, near the choir stalls where the nuns sat for the Offices, facing each other in a double row. The nuns were standing now, though, in the open space between the stalls, looking toward the altar where Domina Elisabeth stood with the widow. St Frideswide's presently had only nine nuns and no novices, but clustered together, a dark gathering in their Benedictine black gowns and veils, they were probably daunting enough to the woman standing slight and pale beside Domina Elisabeth's firm presence. Her wimple and veil and outer gown had been taken from her since Frevisse first saw her, leaving her in only her plain gray undergown and with a simple headkerchief tied to hide her hair the plain way a servant would. Despite that shame, she was no longer huddled but standing stiffly straight, her hands behind her, her head raised, her wide eyes staring blankly into nothingness far away and over the heads of the women all looking at her and murmuring to each other.

'This,' Domina Elisabeth said in her clear, certain voice, 'is Cristiana. She has Christ in her name but not in her behaving. She has been brought to us that we may keep her safe from her sins and, if God wills, bring her into her right mind and heart.'

The woman jerked slightly, as if a lash had been laid across her back, and began to tremble.

Quelling with voice and gaze the stir and murmurs rising again among her nuns, Domina Elisabeth went on, 'What her sins have been need not concern you. Let it suffice that they were sufficient that at our Abbot Gilberd's request I have agreed to have her here in our keeping.'

Because St Frideswide's was only a priory, not an abbey, it was under the care and protection of St Bartholomew's Abbey near Northampton, whose present abbot was Domina Elisabeth's own brother, making more tight the tie between the two houses. That meant that Abbot Gilberd's 'request' carried the same weight as an order. Domina Elisabeth's 'agreement' had been beyond question, but she did not show that as she went on, 'Because of the depth of corruption in her, none of you is to speak with her except on the most immediate of matters. To give her direction at her tasks or to warn her when she is in the wrong. You are not to ask who she is or from where she came. If she tries to speak to you without you speak to her first, you are to warn her to silence and tell me of her disobedience.'

Heads were turning among the nuns, everyone looking at everyone else in wordless wonder at what sort of woman was being put among them. Only Sister Thomasine stood with bowed head, probably in prayer for the woman.

'She is here not as servant but as penitent,' Domina Elisabeth said. 'Her relatives harbor hope that in the fullness of time she may find it in her heart to become a nun among us.'

At that, the woman turned her head to stare at Domina Elisabeth.

'For her better keeping, she will sleep in the dorter with you, eat in the refectory but apart from us, and attend all the Offices.'

Cristiana went back to staring away at nothing.

'During the Offices she will lie on the floor before the altar in penitent fashion, facedown and arms wide. When she has no tasks in hand, she is to be here in the church, on her knees before the altar, that she may pray for her salvation from her grievous sins. She is never to go out of the cloister. Ever. Sister Margrett, you'll see to the servants being informed of all of this.'

Sister Margrett, presently the nunnery's cellarer, charged with overseeing the cloister's servants among many other duties, nodded wide-eyed agreement.

'That she never go out is most especially important,' Domina Elisabeth said. 'Make sure they understand that. I will so inform

Master Naylor' – the nunnery's steward, who saw to the outward matters that supported the nunnery's inward life – 'that he may likewise order and warn all his folk that if ever she is seen abroad, she is to be brought back. We can talk more of this in chapter meeting tomorrow morning, if need be. For now, she will begin her penance, kneeling here until Vespers.' Domina Elisabeth took the woman by one shoulder, turned her around, and pushed her downward. The woman sank to her knees and bent her head, maybe relieved just then to be facing God instead of so many staring nuns. 'You may all return to your duties,' Domina Elisabeth said.

Most of the nuns obeyed in a hurried bustle, though probably less in ready obedience than in desire to be out of the church, away from Domina Elisabeth and free to burst into talk. Unable to wait even that long, Dame Emma exclaimed as she went, inapt as ever with a proverb, 'Didn't the vile woman ever hear how it's a great virtue to abstain from pleasant things?'

Not joining the rush, leaving more slowly, Frevisse saw that Sister Thomasine still stood with bowed head, then paused in her own going to watch Dame Claire, ignoring her prioress' order, go forward, past Domina Elisabeth to the kneeling woman and lean over her, looking at something. Then she said something to Domina Elisabeth, who looked, too, and after a moment gave a terse nod of agreement.

Dame Claire came briskly away then, and Frevisse joined her but waited until they were in the cloister walk, heading toward the infirmary, before asking, 'What is it?'

Dame Claire was openly furious. 'Her wrists. She's been tied with a rope and must have fought it. Her wrists are rubbed raw. They've even bled. There are new sores on top of some several days old and no one has done anything for any of them. It's a wonder they haven't festered. I think she was gagged, too. There are sores at the corners of her mouth. Didn't you see? She must have fought the gag, too. I'm going for water to clean them, and an ointment.'

Frevisse stopped, letting Dame Claire go on alone. On the other side of the cloister walk, most of the nuns were tightly gathered in busy talk that barely faded as Domina Elisabeth came from the church, going the other way, around to the stairs to her own rooms. She would have passed Frevisse but Frevisse did not wait to meet her, instead went into the passage toward the outer door. It was time to see that all was ready in the guesthall should any travelers come to stay, but she took with her irk at herself for not having seen the hurts on the woman. This Cristiana had not come quietly to her penance. She was quiet now, but she had struggled against it hard enough to hurt herself. How much trouble was this woman going to make here?

Chapter 3

The stone-paved floor was cold under Cristiana's cheek; cold under her hands laid flat against it at the full outstretch of her arms; cold under the whole length of her body through the linen of her chemise and gown.

She had not known how painful it would be to lie face-down like this for so long. The arch of her back was wrong; it ached. Her breasts, pressed against the stone, hurt. By most careful holding of her neck at a certain angle she could keep it from pain but the effort was mortally tiring and six times a day she had to lie like this in front of the altar, through the Offices of Prime, Tierce, Sext, None, Vespers, and Compline; and then again in the middle of the night, through the two long Offices of Matins and Lauds. She ached with the need for more sleep as well as with the pain of lying there, but even when abed, she slept too little. Her narrow cell was like all the nuns' cells in the long dorter, wide enough for a washtable and a bed with a blanket that must have been new fifty years ago, a lean pillow, and a mattress so barely stuffed with straw she could feel every strand of the rope strung through the bedframe to hold it up. She was only allowed there at night, but it was the one place she was ever alone, unseen, able to grieve, and it was there, with the bed's thin pillow pressed to her face to stifle the sounds of her weeping, that she cried all the tears she held in through every day. If anyone heard her crying, no one ever spoke of it. Probably because they thought her misery was well-deserved, Cristiana bitterly supposed.

She shifted her neck slightly, trying for ease that was not there. Over her head the nuns' chant went on, untroubled. '*Clamavi in toto corde meo. Exaudi me, Domine. Clamavi.*' The sweetness of voices utterly at variance with everything else in this horrible place. Cristiana neither understood the words nor cared. How long had she been here? The days lurched past so senselessly, one into another, that she could recognize Sunday only by the Offices' greater length, by the drawing out of her pain, and she was not sure how many Sundays there had been. Several, she thought.

With a soft and downward grace, the nuns ended the Office. '*Fidelium animae per misericordiam Dei requiescant in pace. Amen.*' May the souls of the faithful through the mercy of God rest in peace. That much Latin she knew and began stiffly to lift her aching body to its knees even before the nuns – and most of them were quick enough about it – had risen to their feet. They would go about their work now but she was expected to stay here the while until dinner for more penance. Just as she stayed on her knees during the nuns' morning Chapter meeting; and again at midday between Nones and dinner; and again through the nuns' hour of recreation between supper and Compline, until finally she was allowed to bed.

Between those whiles, the nuns kept an unrelenting distance from her, no one speaking to her except to give an order and no word wanted from her at all. They talked *about* her, though. She knew that by things she sometimes heard in talk broken off when she came near, and she could guess more by the looks some of the nuns had given her in her first days here – divided between horror and vast curiosity. What she didn't know was how much more of Laurence's lies their prioress had told them when she was not there to hear them. Or maybe they'd been told nothing else and were making things up to suit themselves. It didn't matter. All that mattered was how she would escape from here, but thus far she had seen no way. Her one poor hope was Gerveys – that somehow he had heard she was disappeared, no one knew where; that he was searching for her and would some-how find her. *That*, rather than for any forgiveness of sins, was what she prayed for desperately in the painful hours of supposed penance.

The nuns were filing from their choir stalls now. Slowly, with diffi-culty, Cristiana finished raising herself to her knees, pulled to her the small pad lying nearby, and eased it under her knees. On her second day here, a thin little nun with a young-old face and almost perpetu-ally downcast eyes had brought that pad to her after her morning penance; had held it out without looking at her and said, 'Domina Elisabeth says I may give you this,' and hurried away as soon as

Cristiana had taken it from her.

That was the one kindness anyone had given Cristiana here. She was still grateful for it, but she had to wonder at that nun – someone had called to her once as Sister Thomasine – who, Cristiana had since seen, spent much of her time in the church praying, seemingly of her free will, on her knees with no pad at all. That was a degree of piety Cristiana neither understood nor desired, as with head bowed over her clasped hands, she listened to the nuns leaving the church. Because sometimes someone would come to be sure of her, she had to keep up the semblence of prayer, but lying flat on the floor always roused the pain in her breastbone and she huddled her shoulders forward to lessen it the little that she could until it faded into its usual dull ache again. She had strained the muscles along the bone there, she told herself. Probably while struggling against Laurence and the others. Her hatred-hurt she called it and knew she should pray to be freed from both the hatred and the pain; but the hatred and the pain kept the fear at bay and she did not dare to lose them. She feared that without them her fear for Mary and Jane would drive her mad. Better the pain and the hatred than madness, because someday, somehow, she would be free of here, able to come at Laurence and Milisent. That and her daughters' safety and Gerveys' return were the things for which she *did* pray with her whole heart.

And for Edward's soul. Always and always for Edward's soul.

From May Day onward he had steadily faded out of life, in no pain but less alive each day. For as long as she could, Cristiana had pretended his dying was not happening. Only almost too late had she finally faced it; had sat beside his bed – their bed, except that by then she was sleeping on a servant's truckle bed beside it at night, that he might rest better – and held his hand, he being too weak to hold hers, and gazed and gazed upon his face, wanting to beg him not to go, not to leave her. She had had the courage not to trouble him with hopeless words, had simply let all her love for him show in her eyes, there for him whenever he awakened and looked at her; and at the last he had found somewhere the strength to say, 'I'll be there. Waiting. When you come. In heaven.' His eyes had closed then, but his last whisper was clear. 'My dear-heart.'

He did not open his eyes or speak again, though it was another day more before he altogether ceased to breathe, so gently that Cristiana did not know when it happened despite she was sitting at his side. She had simply, slowly, come to know he was no longer there; had lifted her gaze to the priest whose murmuring on the other side of the bed broke off at the same moment with the same knowing. Then Gerveys and Ivetta had come from the far side of the room and between them lifted her from the chair and led her away as she began to sob.

She had of course drawn herself together and done what needed to be done about the funeral and the funeral feast and all. There had been help from everyone around her – Gerveys quiet and unfailing in his strength; Beth Say best among the neighbor women at giving help without making a burden of it; Ivetta seeing to Mary and Jane – and through it all she had kept hold of her sense that it was all unreal. Even the burial in the Broxbourne churchyard had seemed to have nothing to do with Edward. She had done all the necessary things without letting herself think about why. Only afterward, when all was over and she went alone to their bed that was now only hers, had the completeness of Edward being gone swept over her. He was not simply gone for a time. He was gone. Completely. Never again in all her life would she see him, touch him, hear his voice.

When her crying was at its worst that night, Ivetta and Gerveys had come quietly into the room, unasked and unbidden. They had probably been waiting for her grief to finally break free, afraid for her while it did not. Ivetta had sat on the bed holding her the way she would have held Mary or Jane, rocking and rocking her while she wept. And when Cristiana had worn out at last, Gerveys had sat with his arm around her while Ivetta had washed her face with cool water, then tucked her into bed and sat beside her until she slept.

Four days later he had left to join York's household in Wales on their way to Ireland.

And four days after that, early in an afternoon, Laurence and Milisent had come.

Cristiana had been in the parlor with Mary and Jane. Through the past days she had found comfort in comforting their own bewildered grieving and they had been sitting all together on the floor, choosing bits of cloth from her cloth-scraps bag to sew into gowns for their two dolls, the little heaps of reds and greens and blues and even some expensive saffron-dyed linen – 'We'll share that for collars and decorating hems,' Cristiana had ruled before there could be a quarrel about it – a pleasure to the eyes against their own black mourning gowns.

She and Mary had been planning a gown half of red and half of blue and Jane simply playing happily with all the colors when, with a single short knock at the door, Laurence had walked in, Milisent behind him, Master Colles behind her, and lastly Ankaret, who closed the door and stayed beside it while the other three crossed the room to Cristiana. Too surprised and offended by their abrupt appearance to do them the courtesy of rising to her feet, Cristiana had demanded at then, 'Why are you here? Go away.'

Laurence had thrust a folded paper at her, a wax seal hanging from it. 'We've come to show you this.'

She had taken it, opened it, read it. Had needed to read it again, then slowly stood up, a vast, cold pit opening in her stomach. Lifting her gaze from the paper, she found them all watching her: Laurence with harsh satisfaction; Milisent with much the pleasure of a cat with a trapped mouse; Master Colles with his usual blankness; Ankaret both excited and uncertain.

'What,' Cristiana asked, 'is this?'

'It's what it says,' Laurence snapped. 'A grant to me, their uncle, of the wardships of Mary and Jane Helyngton, heiresses of Edward Helyngton, along with keeping of their properties and the right to determine their marriages. A royal grant, as you can see, sealed with the king's own signet ring.'

'But . . .' Cristiana had been barely able to find air enough to speak. 'Edward's will. He gave all that to me in his will.' Taking hold on her stumbling wits and beginning to be angry, she lifted her chin and held the paper out at Laurence. 'Besides, Edward didn't hold any lands from the king. The king has no say in my daughters' wardships or marriages.'

'Not to judge by this,' Laurence said with a hard gleam of triumph.

The same triumph, cruel with a pleasure, was in Milisent's smile and even in Master Colles' narrow stare.

Cristiana let the paper go. It fell with the wax seal's heavy thud to the floor. 'It's worthless,' she said.

'Then there's this.' Milisent held out another folded paper, hung with a seal like the first one.

Cristiana did not take it, demanded instead, 'What is it?'

Smiling, the document still held out toward her, Milisent said, 'It says that because of the breakdown of her wits upon her husband's death, making her a danger to herself and her husband's heiresses, the keeping of Edward Helyngton's widow is given into my hands and those of my brother Laurence Helyngton until such time as Cristiana Helyngton may be found to be in her right mind again.'

'No.' Cristiana heard her voice rise with protest, disbelief, and sudden, sharp fear. Mary and Jane surely did not fully understand what was happening but frightened by her fear, scrambled to their feet on either side of her. She reached out and put her arms around their shoulders, pulling them close to her. 'That's all a lie! You can't have me and you can't have my daughters! Go away!'

Not raising his voice, Laurence said, 'Ankaret.'

Ankaret immediately opened the door and there were men – four men Cristiana did not know – on the other side. 'Now,' said Laurence, and they came in, two of them straight at Cristiana, two to either side of her. The first two grabbed hold of her even as she started to draw back from them. The other two grabbed Mary and Jane away, picked them up and were carrying them from the room before Cristiana fully understood what they were doing and began to scream and struggle to follow them. Mary began to scream, too, but the men went out and Ankaret followed them, slamming the door shut behind herself as Laurence said, 'There,' pointing to Edward's tall-backed, heavy chair.

Cristiana's struggle against the two men holding her was as wasted as if she never made it. They shoved her to the chair and into it and one of them held her there, ignoring her cries for Mary and Jane while the other took a rope from his belt and tied her by her arms to the armrests and around her waist to the back. Then they stood aside and Milisent came forward and began to unpin Cristiana's heavy widow's veil. Cristiana twisted and tried to keep her head away, but tied as she was, that was as useless as her struggle against the men. Milisent stripped off first her veil and then her wimple, baring Cristiana's head and neck in a way she had not been exposed before so many men since she was married. It brought her to gasping silence. But she drew breath and would have started to scream again for Mary and Jane because someone had to hear her, the house was full of servants, why didn't someone—

'Shut her up,' Laurence ordered.

Milisent was already taking a long cloth out of her sleeve. Cristiana instantly understood what it was for and tried to turn her head away, but Milisent forced it into her mouth like a bridle into a horse's, gagging her outcry even before Milisent twisted the ends behind her head with a jerk and said, tying it tightly, 'You can't know how long I've wanted to do this.'

'Your screaming was no good anyway,' Laurence said. 'Your servants are penned in the kitchen under guard by now and Ankaret is seeing to your girls.'

Some part of Cristiana's mind refused all of that. None of it was happening. It was too wrong to be happening. She was in a nightmare and she would wake up. . . .

But from the hall, growing fainter, Mary's cries and now Jane's, too, brought her wrenching forward against the ropes, fighting them, twisting her head from side to side to be rid of the gag. Only when she saw Laurence, Milisent, and Colles watching her, pleased by her useless fighting, did she stop and fall back in the chair, tears starting.

Laurence leaned toward her. 'There's being sensible. You'll only hurt yourself or else make it so we have to do worse to you. You being a madwoman, no one can object if we do whatever we must to restrain you.'

Cristiana made a protesting sound.

'There, there,' Milisent mocked her. 'We'll see to you well enough, never worry. Shall I tell you how?'

'No,' Colles said. 'Let her wonder.'

'If Edward hadn't been so stupidly stubborn,' Laurence said, 'it wouldn't have to go this way.'

Cristiana twisted her head, trying to loosen the gag. Milisent took hold of her chin, carefully digging in her fingernails to hold Cristiana still while she leaned close to say into her face, 'We're putting you some place where you'll be safe. If you're good, it won't be forever. If you stay put and make no trouble, then when your girls are safely seen to – marriage for Mary, a nunnery for Jane is what we have in mind – we'll let you out. Until then' – the nails dug deeper in and Milisent's breath was hot on Cristiana's face – 'you be good, or I'll see to it you hurt far more than you do now.'

They kept her there, tied, all that afternoon. Helpless, she had to watch Laurence and Milisent go thoroughly through everything in the chest where Edward kept his less valuable documents about the manor. 'Not that there's any need to see it all now,' Laurence said as he dumped a handful of scrolls on the table. 'The place is mine until the wardships run out.'

Less easily satisfied, Milisent took the household keys from

Cristiana's belt, saying, 'I want to see the rest. Edward gave her some pretty things, as I recall.'

'Ankaret will want her share,' Laurence warned. He left off shifting through the papers. 'I`ll come with you. Edward's money-chest is somewhere. I want it.'

Colles, from where he had sat himself down at the window, called after them as they went out the door, 'Send someone with wine. This waiting is dull.'

Waiting for what? Cristiana shut her eyes and tried to find some corner of her mind she could crawl into and hide until she awoke from all of this, but no awakening came. Instead, hours later, as the room was darkening with early evening and Laurence and Milisent had been drinking for a while with Colles and talking over how well they were going to do here, Laurence finally gave order for her to be loosed from the chair. By then she was too stiffened to move on her own, unable to resist at all as the same two men untied her, dragged her to her feet and dragged her hands behind her to tie them again, careless that they hurt her. She made an unwilling sound of pain but no one heeded it.

A cloth like the one still jammed in her mouth was tied over her eyes and, held again by a man on either side, she was led blind from the room into the great hall. She strained to hear anything at all – some sign that someone was there to see what was happening to her – but all she heard was nothing.

Then she was outside, was lifted astride a horse, with a man immediately swinging into the saddle behind her and other people mounting other horses around her. She tried to tell which way they rode from the manor and for how long, but she wasn't sure. It was night, though, when they finally stopped and she was dragged down from the horse and into a building and through a room that smelled unclean. She was bumped carelessly against a doorframe, into another room, and a door was shut heavily behind her before, at last, someone took off the blindfold.

She did not know where she was. The room was poor and bare, with a small, battered table with a single candle burning on it, two stools, a bed, a shuttered window. An inn somewhere? Someone's house? Neither Laurence nor Colles were there, only Milisent and one of the men who had bound and blindfolded her in the parlor. When another man soon brought food – cold beef and bread and some thin ale – she was untied and ungagged so she could eat while Milisent did. She was too stiff beyond hope of making any move to escape nor did she try to cry out for help. Neither Laurence or Milisent was so careless as to have anyone near who would heed her if she did. Finished eating, she was allowed to see to her bodily necessities in a small, windowless side chamber with Milisent standing in the doorway to be sure she tried nothing foolish. What could I possibly try, Cristiana wondered dazedly. She could think of nothing. She could barely think at all by then, even when Milisent led her to the bed and shoved her down on its edge, for the man to tie her by both wrists to one bedpost, leaving her able to sit on the bed's edge or uncomfortably lie down.

The man left the room. Milisent readied for bed and – far more comfortably than Cristiana – lay down on the bed's far side, saying, 'Don't think I'm enjoying having to keep you company,' before she rolled over and, by her breathing, was soon asleep.

Cristiana did not have that mercy. Held by the rope, afraid of waking Milisent if she moved, her mind beating wildly from one thought to another, all of them desperate, all of them useless, it was a long while before – crying inwardly to Edward to make all this not be happening – she finally fell into something like sleep, though it brought her neither rest nor peace.

The morning reversed the night. Milisent awoke, one of the men came in, Cristiana was untied, allowed her body's needs, fed, then gagged and blindfolded again. To her shame she whimpered slightly. Milisent laughed. Again held firmly between two men but her hands unbound, she was led outside, where Milisent said, 'You're going to be put in a horse-carried litter today.' Cristiana had a brief hope that with her hands free she might find some way of escape; but when a hand at the back of her head bent her over and shoved her forward to grope her way onto the litter – finding it a small one meant for one person – she had no more than eased her way around and into the cushioned seat than her arms were seized from either side and her wrists bound to the litter's sides. Then her ankles were grabbed and likewise tied to something fixed that did not move when she tried to kick loose from it. Thwarted, tears coming anew at her helplessness, she flung her head backward hard against the end wall of the litter. It, too, was cushioned, and as she heard curtains drawn closed with the rattle of metal rings on both sides of the litter, she knew that – tied, gagged, and cushioned as she was – there would be no way to make anyone know she was in need of help.

Through that day and two more she was carried in the litter, kept always gagged and blindfolded, loosed only to be hurried into some place for each night. Milisent warned her that the people wherever they stayed were told she was a madwoman, that crying out for help would do her no good, would only get her gagged at night, too. Afraid of that, Cristiana kept silent. She never saw Laurence or Colles but during the days heard them and Milisent talking as they rode. They were careful, though, never to be near enough for her to hear what they were saying and the guards must have been forbidden to talk at all. No one betrayed where they were or where they were going, and the first day and second must have been overcast because she had not even sun-warmth on one side of the litter or the other to tell her the direction they traveled. But none of the towns through which they passed were big enough to be London, nor did they cross a river large enough to be the Thames, and if they had gone east, surely they would have reached the coast in less than three days. So they were set north or west. Or northwest or southwest. Or. . . .

At some point and time Cristiana gave up even that wondering. Numb with fear and despair, she curled into a corner of her mind and stayed there, accepting there was nothing she could do to help herself and nothing she could do to help Mary and Jane. There was nothing she could do except cease to feel and think, and she did; let herself be bound and unbound and told what to do without thinking to resist. When there was nothing to be done, all she could do was nothing.

It was the third night, when she had been bound to yet another bed but Milisent was still up, that Laurence came into their room. Neither he nor Milisent looked the worse for their journey. In truth, he looked so sleek with satisfaction that Cristiana stirred enough out of her numbness to remember how much she loathed him as he crossed the room, stood staring down at her, and said to Milisent, 'You'll have to make her presentable tomorrow. We want them to think she's been cared for.'

'She'll be presentable,' Milisent said impatiently. 'There'll be no cause to complain against us.'

Laurence went on considering Cristiana. She read his look and went rigid even before he put out a hand and stroked her, deliberate and slow, the length of her body from throat to hips, saying, 'A waste, in a way, to put you into a nunnery unused. Edward seemed to enjoy you so much.'

Milisent laughed. 'Take her. Who's to know?'

In worse terror than any until now, Cristiana stared up into Laurence's face through the long and horrible moment before he took his hand away from her, turned away with, 'I think I can do without Edward's leavings,' and left the room.

It was in the morning while roughly combing out Cristiana's tangled and matted hair, untended these three nights, that Milisent told her, 'It's a nunnery we're taking you to. They'll be told there that you're a wanton widow, so debased and shameless in dishonoring your husband's name that your priest and bishop and lord have agreed you should be kept away from your children and in penitential prison until such time as priest and bishop and lord see fit to bid us take you into our care again or set you free.'

Cristiana fumbled for words of protest.

Milisent jerked on her hair, silencing her. 'We have a warrant that authorizes us to put you away, and another letter from an abbot that assures the nuns that they are to take you in strict charge and keep you for as long as need be.'

Teeth set against the pain of her pulled hair, Cristiana forced out, 'Where?'

'So far away from anywhere you know that there's no chance anyone will find you or that you'll find your way home again. Not with the watch that will be set on you.'

Milisent finished with her, and Cristiana was gagged and blindfolded and tied into the horse-litter yet again; but in the afternoon the litter stopped long enough for one of the men to take off the gag and blindfold and untie her. Cristiana had no more than a useless sight of a hedgerow along a dusty road before the curtain was closed again. With no hope of anywhere to run, she sat with her shaking hands clenched together in her lap until the litter stopped again and she was pulled out and taken into the nunnery's guesthall.

After that she had had to endure Milisent only a little longer. To be unbound and ungagged and rid of Milisent and Laurence was such relief that only when she had been standing in the church, hearing her supposed shame exposed to the nuns and her punishment detailed, had she begun to understand how completely she was still trapped, still helpless.

She had not dared, while Laurence and Milisent held her, to be anything more than afraid, but as these days and nights of enforced silence and false penance went unendingly on, and with the pain of the hours in front of the altar on her face or knees, her understanding grew and her hopelessness deepened into a dark despair. And with the despair, fed by her grief for Edward and her fear for Mary and Jane, came hatred.

Her single hope was that somehow, *somehow*, Gerveys would find her. That he would find out where she was and come for her.

Only please, by all of Heaven's mercy, let him come soon.

Chapter 4

With fair weather and hope for a fine harvest, the easy days of middle summer passed inside St Frideswide's walls in their familiar way, bound around and carried onward by the ever changing, constant pattern of the daily Offices. So many of the Offices' prayers were the same from day to day, but through each week the psalms were spread through the Offices so that all one hundred and fifty were said between one Sunday and the next while other prayers came and went with times of the year and saints' days. To Frevisse it was an unending garland, its strands woven beautifully around each other. She had joined the weaving when she became a nun. Some nuns who had been part of the weaving then were dead now but others were become nuns in their place, just as someday she would be dead and there would be others here instead, the weaving of praise and hope and love going always on, as it had gone on now for a thousand years already and would go on until the World's end came, God willing.

Still, her own handful of years – well, several handfuls – were enough with which to deal for now. This year especially, that was passing so fair among the priory's fields, was fraught with trouble elsewhere. As hosteler she heard more than she might have – and certainly more than she wished – about how the world was going. Worst of the troubles was that the war in France looked likely to break out again. Toward the end of March an English raiding party out of Normandy had seized and plundered a border town in Brittany, directly against the truce there had been since the king's marriage a few years ago. Frevisse gathered from stray bits of talk that both the duke of Brittany and his ally the king of France had first requested and then demanded a withdrawal of the English troops and restitution for stolen goods. That seemed a fair enough demand to Frevisse, but lately in the guesthall she had heard a Coventry merchant complain to another traveler, 'That fool Dorset . . . No, he's been made duke of Somerset, hasn't he? He's still a fool, either way . . . He's refused to give the French anything except rude answers. Have you heard the French have seized some place of ours to show they mean business?'

'Pont de l'Arche, isn't it?' the other man asked. 'Now we'll have to trade Fougères to have it back.'

'What I want to know is how they took the place so easily,' the merchant had grumbled. 'As soon as the truce was broken, every border town of ours should have been on double guard, and the more on guard because Somerset has refused every French offer toward peace.'

'I've heard Suffolk is supposedly gone to Normandy to deal with the whole thing. Someone was saying that in Oxford.'

'Suffolk,' the merchant said with disgust. 'There's setting the cockerel to deal with the fox. What I want to know is why should Suffolk or anyone have to go to Normandy to "deal with it"?' He had thumped a fist down on the wooden tabletop. 'Why doesn't King Henry send Somerset an order to stop being an idiot? I say there's something foul afoot about the whole business and that Suffolk and Somerset are hand in glove in it.'

'I haven't been able to make sense of what's been done in France ever since they pulled York out from being governor,' said the other man. 'And what about this Winnington business?'

The merchant had thrown up his hands. 'Don't start me on the Winnington business!' Another source of ongoing anger across the country. Late in May one Robert Winnington – charged by the crown with safekeeping of the sea – had used the royal fleet to seize over a hundred ships of the Hanseatic League and its allies homeward bound to the Baltic with its yearly cargo of salt and other goods from the south. Because England was not at war with the Hanse, the seizure had been more bold than sensible, and in June a group of pilgrims from Gloucester, staying overnight at the priory on their way to the great shrine at Walsingham, had been full of talk and bitterness about it, one man complaining, 'The Hanse is taking whatever English goods they find abroad, I hear. I've a cousin will be ruined if that's true.'

'He won't be the only one,' someone else said. 'Nor king or council has made any move toward peace or to return the ships or to punish Winnington.'

'And they won't either,' a lean, aggravated woman had said sharply. 'Winnington is their man and if you don't know that you're a fool. Suffolk and those jackals around him run the king and never doubt but they'll all make a pretty profit out of it. God keep King Henry, but where's his wits in this, I ask?'

'Ah, there then,' a plump, easier woman had said soothingly, 'it's not the king's fault, is it? He's hardly to blame, being so young and lacking experience.'

'He's twenty-seven,' one of the men grumbled. 'His father at twenty-seven was winning the battle of Agincourt.'

'Well, we're not all like our fathers, are we?' the plump woman returned.

'True enough,' the first woman snapped, 'but some miss it by more than is good for them.'

Added to that, as the summer went on there was talk and worry of French raids along the south and east coasts, irk at a new tax laid on all wool going into Flanders, speculation on how ill an omen was the sudden star that had burned for a number of spring evenings in the west, report that an outbreak of plague had adjourned the Parliament from Westminster to Winchester, and all of that mixed in with a general seethe of discontent against the king and his council of lords like Frevisse had never heard before.

'And anger,' she said one warm morning in the prioress' parlor in answer to Domina Elisabeth's question about what was being said.

Because a prioress sometimes had to receive particular guests and conduct such business as was not suited to the chapter meetings with all the nuns, the parlor was a more comfortable room than any other in the priory, with glassed windows and a fireplace and a fringed carpet woven in a Spanish pattern laid over the carved-legged table. In Domina Edith's time, when Frevisse had first come to St Frideswide's, there had been an embroidery frame with always some work on it and a small greyhound who slept in a padded basket beside the fire. With Domina Elisabeth there was a slant-topped writing desk near the window where – like her nuns – she copied books to earn much-needed money for St Frideswide's and a sleek white-and-gray cat presently curled on a cushion at one end of the windowseat, regarding Frevisse with a baleful green eye over a tail carefully curled over nose and paws, unforgiving the interruption of his morning nap.

Frevisse tried not to regard him balefully back while she went on, 'Nor is it the usual discontented talk about things "not going well". It's real anger at very certain things and certain people.'

'Such as?' Domina Elisabeth asked, with more than simple curiosity.

Frevisse suspected that the worry came from the letter from Domina Elisabeth's brother Abbot Gilberd, brought yesterday by a passing knight. As nuns they might be removed from the world, but they were not remote from it. Trouble was too often a thing that spread and Frevisse's present unease at things made her answer carefully, 'People are angry at how badly the French war is suddenly going and at the king's people demanding more money when there's no sign that good use has been made of the money already given. They're angry at the lords around the king for their greed and misgoverning and for spoiling the wool trade with Flanders this year.'

'The lords around the king,' Domina Elisabeth repeated. 'That includes the duke of Suffolk?'

Knowing from where that particular question came, Frevisse hesitated over what to say before settling for, 'I would say especially the duke of Suffolk.'

While Domina Elisabeth silently, frowningly, considered that, Frevisse asked in her turn, 'Your brother is at Parliament?' Abbots, like lay lords, being regularly summoned to attend.

'Yes,' Domina Elisabeth said, a weight of worry to the word.

'Did he say how things go there?'

Domina Elisabeth stroked the curve of the cat's back. 'Not well, I gather. Gilberd says the Commons are refusing to give any more tax toward the war and he doesn't think they'll change their minds.'

A merchant from Northampton had put it more bluntly in the guesthall two days ago. 'If Suffolk thinks he's going to get a grant of money for this French war he looks determined to lose, he's damn-all in for a surprise, may the devil rot his bones.'

To which a yeoman had said, 'If Hell gaped open and swallowed Suffolk tomorrow, England would be the better for it, and the devil can take Somerset, too, for better measure.'

'Why wait until tomorrow?' the merchant had answered.

Here in the peaceful parlor, with a dule of doves rising from the guesthall yard below the window with the morning sunlight on their wings, those passions seemed far off, almost unreal; but like an echo to Frevisse's less comfortable thoughts, Domina Elisabeth said, 'You haven't heard from your cousin lately, have you?'

Frevisse had not, as Domina Elisabeth well knew because any message – by word or writing – that came to a nun had to be made known to her prioress. It was with wariness of the unasked question behind the words that Frevisse answered because she knew from where the question came, 'No. I haven't.'

Unlikely as it seemed, given their so different lives, her cousin was the duchess of Suffolk, wife to the much-hated duke. Because of that, Frevisse knew something more of the duke of Suffolk than she wished she did, and because of what she knew, she and her cousin had not been able these few years past to write or send so much as a word to each other. But as if no word from her cousin were a little matter, Frevisse said, 'With Suffolk so busy about the king of late, she's probably too much occupied with seeing to their lands and all else in his place.'

She was saved from more by the cloister bell starting to ring to Tierce. Domina Elisabeth gave a mild sigh and stood up and Frevisse moved aside to let her go ahead from the room. There should be silence now until they began the Office in the church, but Domina Elisabeth had let the Benedictine rule of silence slacken over the years and said as she led the way down the stairs to the cloister walk, 'I meant to ask you, too, what you think of how our widow is doing.'

Frevisse missed the strictly kept silence of her early years as a nun, but even then if the prioress had asked a question, it was answered and after a due moment of thought she made as near to a nothing answer as she could, saying, 'She gives no trouble.'

They had reached the foot of the stairs. Beyond the doorway other nuns were hurrying from all sides of the cloister toward the church, but Domina Elisabeth stopped and turned around. 'Does that bode good or ill, do you think?'

Frevisse hesitated, not happy to be asked, unsure how to answer, settling finally for, 'It's difficult to say.'

'You mean,' Domina Elisabeth said crisply, 'that you can't tell whether she's truly penitent or is merely biding her time until she can be done with us.'

Frevisse hesitated, then said, 'I can't tell, no.'

'Neither can I, and it disturbs me.'

Domina Elisabeth turned away and swept toward the church in a fullness of black skirts and long veil. Frevisse, heavy with thought and following more slowly, was among the last to take her place in the choir, and as she took up her prayer book, she looked from the side of her eyes at Cristiana lying in her penitent's place before the altar. Frevisse knew from experience how uncomfortable she had to be, had seen her sometimes shift a little during an Office but never much. Neither had she ever shown any protest against the long whiles she had to kneel there. In truth, she never showed anything or made any protest. And yet somehow there was no feeling of penitence about her.

'*Laus tibi, Domine, Rex aeternae gloriae* . . .' Praise to you, King of eternal glories . . . The familiar words, leading on to the prayers and praise and psalms that were usually Frevisse's delight, did not catch and hold her mind this morning. She chanted with the others, '*Deus caritas est, et qui manet in caritate, in Deo manet, et Deus in eo.*' God is love, and who lives in love, lives in God, and God in him. But Domina Elisabeth's questions had set further off balance her already unsettled thoughts.

Cristiana was proving to be more than a passing wonder among the nuns. With rarely any scandal among themselves greater than some- one falling asleep during an Office or sometimes a sharp word said over something, and such family news as came usually providing no more than talk for a day or two at best, a sinful widow set among them, doing her penance before their very eyes, was like a god-sent gift. At least that was the impression Frevisse had from listening to the talk about her. Domina Elisabeth kept discipline enough that during the day everyone tended mostly to their own work and business, but during the recreation hour between supper and Compline's prayers before bed, tongues were set free, and even after these few weeks, talk about the woman was still rampant despite they had long ago run out of fresh ground to cover. They had only what Domina Elisabeth had said on the first day – certainly nothing from Cristiana herself, wrapped in her silence – but that did not stop or even slow their spec- ulations. She was a widow who had done something terrible beyond the ordinary, but precisely what she had done had been frustratingly not said, leaving them free to talk over again and again what she might have done; and for women who lived chaste lives apart from the world, they found their way through a surprisingly wide number of possibilities.

Along with Sister Thomasine and, usually, Dame Claire, Frevisse kept aside from the talk. On her own part, she had never repeated to anyone what the woman in the guesthall had said, partly because she did not know the truth or falseness of it, partly because she was certain the woman had viciously meant for her to repeat it, and Frevisse – quite aside from her own unwillingness to such talk – had decided not to oblige her, but wished that Domina Elisabeth, besides forbidding talk *with* Cristiana, would likewise forbid talk *about* her.

'*Domine, miserere mei . . . ne derelinquas me. Neque despicias me, Deus . . .*' Lord, pity me . . . do not abandon me. Nor despise me, God. . . .

Frevisse slid her eyes sideways again to the woman. In her gray gown, lying so still on the gray stones, she seemed hardly there. Indeed, she went so silently and gray through every day that she would have hardly seemed to be in the nunnery at all save for the nuns' talk about her, and even that would have to pall someday. Soon, Frevisse hoped.

During a chill and rainy recreation hour a few days later, she and Dame Claire were walking at a measured pace around and around the roofed, square cloister walk. Because everyone else had chosen to stay in the warming room, save Sister Thomasine, gone, as was her way, to the church to pray, they were alone; and because silence was easy between them, they were silent, until Dame Claire said, 'I'm worried about our widow.'

Frevisse, who had been thinking about her copying work and how many days it might be before she finished with the present book, took a moment to shift her thoughts, then said, 'Worried? Why? Do you think she's ill?'

'When I've asked her,' which would count as necessary talk from Dame Claire as infirmarian, 'she says she isn't.'

'She'd surely tell you if she was, if only to win some ease in her life.'

'Yes,' Dame Claire agreed but sounded no happier. 'Or if she were the monster of sinfulness we've been told she is, she would lie that she was ill, so as to have that ease.'

'*If* she were the monster of sinfulness?'

Dame Claire gestured impatiently. 'If I knew nothing about her, if

I only saw her, watched her as we've all been watching her these days, it's grief I would think of. Not that she was depraved but that she was in deep grief.'

'She might well be in grief. For her sins, if nothing else. Or for having been taken away from her sins unwillingly.'

'Or for both and other things we've no thought of, which aren't my duty to consider but Father Henry's.' The priory's priest. 'It's her health I'm worried for. She's too pale and growing thin.'

'Thin will happen when every other day you have only bread and water,' Frevisse said. 'Can you advise Domina Elisabeth to ease that part of her penance?'

'I've presumed it's by Abbot Gilberd's order.' And therefore not readily ignored.

They walked on in silence, turned the corner near the refectory, and began around the walk again before Frevisse said toward the paving stones, 'Have you noted that Sister Thomasine doesn't avoid her?'

'Yes.'

Dame Claire sounded no more comfortable with that than Frevisse was. Sister Thomasine in her early years in St Frideswide's had been almost cripplingly pious, but over the years her piety had deepened, steadied, was no longer something she forcefully asserted but simply lived in. It made her – for Frevisse at least – far easier to live with. It was only to be expected she would pray for their sinful widow's soul; it was equally expected she would otherwise shun her. Perhaps not so openly as some of the nuns did, gathering their skirts away if Cristiana happened near them, as if her sins were a sickness that might be caught, but surely keeping her distance. Instead, she made no point of it at all and in the church knelt beside her at the altar as easily as if she were another nun.

Frevisse had been disquieted by that, was pleased Dame Claire was, too, and said on a sudden thought, 'What if she made confession to Father Henry? If she did and showed any degree of contrition for her sins, he would be able to ask Domina Elisabeth to allow her more food at least.'

'That might help, yes.' Dame Claire's voice rose with relief. 'He'd do that. Especially if I prompt him that way first. Yes. That might very well help.'

And if it did not, at least they had tried.

Chapter 5

In honor of St Lawrence's day, supper had finished with the rare pleasure of crisply fried wafers dipped in sugar, so that afterward Cristiana on her knees in the church during the nuns' daily hour of recreation gave deep thanks that today had not been one of her bread-and-water days and that for this little while she was not hungry. At most meals the nuns ate far less than she was used to having. She told herself she might have grown used to that, but her bread-and-water days left her so light-headed she was sometimes unsteady on her feet and at night her stomach gnawing at itself kept her awake when she might have slept, now that she no longer cried so much.

In truth, she rarely cried at all anymore. She felt as if her grief had eaten its way into her so deeply it was maybe beyond her tears' reach. Or maybe she was just too tired for crying.

Having given her small prayer of thanks and her other, constant prayers for Mary and Jane and that Gerveys might find her soon, she sat back on her heels, her chin resting on her clasped hands pressed against the base of her throat in at least semblance of prayer. Around her, the church was a-bloom with golden, fading, evening light. She could remember when she would have felt that beauty was like God's embrace made visible. Now all it meant was that she had endured through another day with no sign of any better hope for tomorrow.

If only she wasn't always so hungry she would be able to think more clearly and maybe find some way of escape from this place. She was sorry, too, in a distant way, that she had upset the priest when he took her confession. today. He seemed, all in all, a kindly enough man, with a burly, uncomplicated certainty to him that in another time and place she would have found comforting. He had even been kind enough to tell her his name. Father Henry. But despite that he had asked if she wanted to make confession, he had seemed almost afraid to hear it. Afraid of what depths of sin she would reveal? Afraid he would see hell's mouth gaping behind her and his own soul polluted by her mere words? Even suspecting that was his thought had not curbed Cristiana's gladness at a chance to talk to someone.

She had promptly unsettled the poor man, though, when he began by asking when she had last made confession. 'In Holy Week,' she had answered.

Startled, he had fumbled, 'Not since then? When they . . . after you . . . Surely before they brought you here . . . you didn't make another one?'

'I was seized without warning.' She had let all her bitterness show. 'I was bound and gagged and brought here with no chance for anything.'

Uneasily he had asked what penance she had been given at Easter. She had listed the Aves and Paternosters given her by Father Richard for her numerous small sins and the beeswax candle she had given the church in recompense for her anger at Edward when he bought the chestnut gelding last autumn when they had not needed another horse.

When she stopped, Father Henry had sat silently waiting, then asked, 'Nothing more?'

'There was nothing more.'

Again he had been silent, then bade her go on with what she wished to confess now. With bitter satisfaction, she had confessed to her wrath and her hatred and to her despair, then had waited through another silence from Father Henry before he asked cautiously, 'Is that all?'

'And envy,' she said, belatedly thinking of it. 'Envy of the nuns at their meals on the days when I have only bread and water.'

'And?'

'There's nothing more, Father.'

'No . . . sins of the flesh?'

'On my soul's hope of salvation,' she had said more sharply than she had ever spoken to any priest, 'those are all my sins.'

Father Henry's unhappy silence had drawn out somewhat long before finally he asked, 'Do you repent of these sins?'

She had meant to be humble, because those were sins, however justified, but found herself saying harshly, 'No.' With no urge to take back the word once it was said.

'I can give you neither penance nor God's forgiveness if you're not repentant,' Father Henry had warned. He had sounded as if it hurt him to say it.

Caring nothing for his hurt, Cristiana had said, 'Then don't,' stood up, and walked away.

Afterward she was sorry it had come to that. She knew full well the comfort there was in giving up her sins to a priest and the relief that came with forgiveness and penance. But what use would pretended repentance be? The hunger pains in her stomach would reawaken her envy. Her despair would not give way so long as she was trapped here. And as for her wrath and hatred at Laurence, Milisent, and everyone who had helped them put her here, what use would penance be when her fury at them still seared with actual, burning pain behind her breastbone? It wasn't penance she wanted. What she wanted was out of here and her daughters with her and the chance to pay Laurence and Milisent back for everything.

A flare of her hatred-pain took her with no warning, curled her forward on herself, and then, its warning given, faded. She straightened slowly, wary of waking it again, and was surprised to find tears on her cheeks and – when she opened her eyes – Sister Thomasine kneeling beside her in prayer toward the altar.

Sister Thomasine prayed more intently than anyone Cristiana had ever known. No matter what the hour or how long she knelt, her body was straightly upright from her knees, her hands steepled together palm to palm at her breast, her head deeply bowed, her face shielded from view by the soft fall of her veil to either side of it. Save for when she gave Cristiana the pad for under her knees, she had never spoken to her nor given any sign that Cristiana was there while she was praying. That made it the more startling when now, as Cristiana drew a cautious breath, wary of wakening the pain again, and settled back onto her heels, Sister Thomasine lifted her head and turned to look at her, the first time Cristiana had fully seen her face.

Whatever Sister Thomasine had been when young – pretty or plain or even ugly – was gone. Her face was refined down to fine bones and pallor almost as white as the wimple tightly around it, as if both food and sunlight were things in which she rarely indulged. And yet in her eyes were more of depth and distances than Cristiana had ever seen in anyone's. Cristiana stared into them as Sister Thomasine put out a narrow, white hand and laid it gently on her shoulder with all the tenderness a mother might have given a child.

It was only for a moment. Then Sister Thomasine took back her gaze and her hand and faced the altar again, head bowed to her prayers. Yet for that moment of her touch and look, Cristiana's hatred, angers, and pain had all seemed little things.

A few days after that the church was again softly golden with westering sunlight and Cristiana was again alone in front of the altar in the hour before Compline. As she had come toward the church after supper, she had seen Sister Thomasine among the nuns going through the narrow slype toward the tall-walled garden beyond the cloister to spend their hour's recreation, but now when she heard a slight, soft footfall behind her, she supposed she was come after all, until the nun who stopped beside her did not kneel, instead said, 'Cristiana,' and when Cristiana jerked up her head to look at her, added, 'I want to speak with you.'

Wary both of the nun and her own stiff knees, Cristiana stood up unsteadily.

The nun, her hands tucked into her opposite sleeves, made no move to help her, simply waited until she was standing, then said, 'I'm Dame Frevisse.'

Cristiana had learned a few of the nuns' names by chance, but mostly she knew them as 'the older nun who talked too much,' 'the young nun who stared,' 'the nun with her nose in the air.' This one was 'the tall nun who had been at the guesthall.' Not knowing what lies Milisent had said to her then, Cristiana set her lips tightly together, determined not to be lured into speaking. The nun made a slight nod, accepting her silence, but said, 'Since you confessed to Father Henry, he's been openly unhappy. It seems to be a troubled unhappy rather than weighed-with-sin unhappy. Do you see the difference? Do you understand?'

Cristiana gave a curt nod that she did. Was she supposed to be stupid as well as sinful?

'He of course can say nothing about your confession, but he's asked that your penance of bread and water be eased.'

Cristiana felt hope quicken. If only she weren't so hungry all the time, if only she could think more clearly. . . .

'Domina Elisabeth has agreed to write to Abbot Gilberd about it,' the nun continued.

Cristiana's hope dwindled. Letters took time and permission might well not come, not if this Abbot Gilberd believed all that Laurence must have told him.

'In the meanwhile, since we are allowed to speak to you on necessary and immediate matters, and because as hosteler I have to consider the well-being of our priory's guests – which in some sense you are – I have determined that knowing how you are in both your body and mind is a necessary and immediate matter. Because you are charged not to speak except in answer to questions, I'm asking you if there anything I can do to help you?'

Cristiana gulped for air along with hope, half a score of things racing through her mind before she grabbed at one that had been heavy on her all these days. 'Please,' she said and heard her desperation raw in her voice. 'Where am I?'

Dame Frevisse's eyes narrowed. 'You were never told where they were taking you?'

'No one told me anything. I was taken suddenly and by force in my own house. I was blindfolded and gagged and kept tied in a curtained litter until we were nearly here.' The nightmare of it rose again in a black wave. Her voice shook. 'Three days. And at night I was tied to a bed in a locked inn room. I was never told where I was, where I was going.'

Quickly, almost as if she understood the pain of that, Dame Frevisse said, 'You're in St Frideswide's priory in northern Oxfordshire. You're near to Banbury.'

Oxfordshire, Cristiana thought, dismayed. Three far days' journey west from home.

'Where do you come from?' the nun asked.

'Hertfordshire,' Cristiana said faintly. 'Near a place called Broxbourne.'

'On the main way from London to Walsingham, yes,' Dame Frevisse said. 'I've passed through it, going to Walsingham. A long time ago.'

Tears welled hot in Cristiana's eyes. In this wasteland of hopelessness and strangers, even to know someone knew from where she came was a relief. The tears flowed over and she wiped them from her cheeks almost angrily. She had hoped she was done with crying. What use was she going to be to even herself if such small mercy as this undid her?

Ignoring her tears, Dame Frevisse said, 'You say you were seized without warning. . . .'

'And falsely!' Cristiana said, not heeding that was not yet a question. 'I told the priest and I'll swear on anything you ask that I've done none of the things I'm accused of! My husband died and they took my daughters. They—'

Dame Frevisse stopped her with a quickly lifted hand. 'Abbot Gilberd in his letter—'

'I don't even know this Abbot Gilberd! He can only know what Laurence – he's my husband's cousin, he's the one who's done this – he can only know what Laurence told him. Laurence wants all the Helyngton lands for himself. He's persuaded the duke of Suffolk to give him my daughters and our lands by lying about me, but it's all false! I swear . . .' Something in Dame Frevisse's face stopped her; hope drained out of her to discouragement again and bitterly she said, 'You don't believe any of this, do you?'

Her face shadowed by a frown, Dame Frevisse said, 'I think I rather more believe you than not. But I don't see yet what I can do to help you.'

Cristiana could have wept again, this time with her discouragement.

But Dame Frevisse went on, 'More food and less penance, to begin with. I'll do what I can for that. Try not to despair too deeply.'

Dame Frevisse started to turn away, but Cristiana said urgently, 'Please!'

The nun turned back to her and Cristiana tumbled out, 'If a man named Sir Gerveys should come here – Sir Gerveys Drury – please, for God's mercy, tell him I'm here.' Doubt rose in the nun's face at this sudden mention of a man. More desperately Cristiana said, 'He's my brother. He'll be trying to find me.' She had to believe that or utterly despair. 'If he comes, please, tell him I'm here.'

Considering, Dame Frevisse said slowly, 'No one has forbidden us to say you're here. If anyone comes asking for you, they'll be told.'

'Thank you,' Cristiana whispered.

Dame Frevisse gave a short nod and left her. Cristiana watched her black-gowned back until she was gone, remembering when she had been as certain in herself and place as the nun was. When there had been Edward and Mary and Jane and home and her whole world sure around her.

With her tears burned dry again, she turned back to the altar and knelt to pray for Laurence's death and for Gerveys to come for her. Soon.

Soon.

Frevisse paced alone along the cloister walk, head bowed, watching the paving stones pass beneath her skirts. Should she confess, either to Domina Elisabeth or else to Father Henry, that she had talked with Cristiana? Her justification for it was, at best, of doubtful worth. Still, it had served, however little. She knew more than she had known. But how much of it did she believe? That the woman was from Broxbourne in Hertfordshire was probably true; and that she desperately hoped a man named Gerveys would find her. He might even be her brother. For the rest of it, she had indeed been bound and gagged while being brought here, and while that could have been to keep her under necessary control because she was not fully sane, she had given no sign of either madness or violence while she was here. Although if she were as corrupt as she was accused of being, she *was* mad, even if not violent. Thus far, though, she had been obedient enough, with no sign of anything but grief about her.

And anger, Frevisse amended. Most of what she had said just now had assuredly been bitter and desperate with anger, with no sign at all of penitence. Anger, grief, bitterness, desperation. But no penitence. And yet Father Henry, deeply troubled about something, was apparently not troubled about that.

And as much as anything Cristiana's claim that the duke of Suffolk had helped her husband's cousin in wronging her unsettled Frevisse and gave weight to her protest of innocence. All too well Frevisse knew that William de la Pole, duke of Suffolk was not overly given to honesty or justice if they were in his way to something he wanted. She could believe far too easily that, given reason or money enough, he might well have helped this Laurence as Cristiana claimed.

But none of that solved or settled anything, only raised new questions, and almost Frevisse could have wished she had not started it.

Chapter 6

August was come, the days heavy with heat, the nights thick with warmth, the square garth at the cloister's heart close-grown with flowers and herbs in their full summer flourish. Passing around the cloister walk to the church after her afternoon lesson with Dame Perpetua, Cristiana paused beside the low wall between the walk and the garth to take pleasure in the flaunt of colors in a way she had never done in her garden at home. At home there had been so much else as well to please the eye and pleasure the mind and heart. Here in St Frideswide's there was so little of anything, the nunnery was so small and unwealthy, with no *luxuria* anywhere. In the church the altar cloth and the priest's Mass garments were beautifully embroidered and the silver-plated altar goods were kept faultlessly polished, but the altar goods were old – Cristiana had seen where some of the plating was worn almost through – and the altar steps were bare, with no carpet or decorated tiles, only the same plain stone as the floor she lay on, the stones cool under her even now, so far into summer. When winter came, the cold of those stones would cut through the linen of her chemise and gown into her flesh, into her bones.

Sometimes, in an unguarded moment, she wondered if she would be given a warmer gown come wintertime; then the thought that she would still be here when winter came frightened her as much as thought of the cold. But at least she was no longer left completely alone. Whether by Dame Frevisse's doing or Father Henry's or simply because she had been no trouble thus far, some of the rigor against her had lately eased. She still had three days a week of bread and water, no word having come yet from this Abbot Gilberd, but on the other days her portion of food was greater than it had been. No one had said why; it simply was. And although the silence against her was still

kept, she sometimes had lessons with Dame Perpetua on understanding the Offices. Dame Perpetua enjoyed teaching and was good at it;
sometimes Cristiana now understood some of the things said above
her during the prayers. More than that, though, she was relieved to
be given something other to think about than her fear and anger, and
there was comfort in having someone talk to her.

But if the nuns had begun to have better hope that time would
come when she would become a nun, hope was all they would ever
have of it, she thought bitterly. Standing there beside the garth's low
wall, she looked up from the gaudy yellow of the St John's Wort to
the shiningly blue sky above the cloister's roof-ridges that was all she
ever saw of the world outside the nunnery. Sky and nunnery walls had
become her world and, oh, by St Anne, her own hope was sometimes
hard to hold to. Those walls could so easily outlast her and she was
so weary with waiting.

Head bowed with that thought and her hands folded together over
her hurting heart, she went onward to the church the way she was
supposed to do in any idle time she had and knelt before the altar and
prayed with the desperation that came over her whenever her fear of
never escaping from here was more than usual. How many weeks had
it been now?

She was still rapidly murmuring for release when she heard a nun's
soft step behind her but went on praying until a hand touched her
shoulder. Just loud enough for the nun to hear, she said, 'Amen,' and
looked up to find Sister Amicia there.

Stiffly, being one of the nuns who ever made a point of staying well
away from her, Sister Amicia said, 'There's a man to see you.'

Cristiana's heart lurched. Gerveys.

'Domina Elisabeth says you can see him in the guest parlor. He's
Master Helyngton, she says.'

Christiana's heart lurched again, downward this time. Making no
move to rise, she only stared at Sister Amicia until the nun said impatiently, 'Now,' and walked away.

Stumblingly, Cristiana stood up. Not Gerveys. Laurence.

Her mind went empty, unable to handle the sudden shift to hope
and out of it again into new fear. Through a fog of unthinking she
followed Sister Amicia from the church. Two nuns were working at
the desks along the church wall, their pen scratching loud in the cloister's quiet. The guest parlor was beyond them and around a corner of

the walk, beside the passage from the cloister's outer door, but Sister Amicia was going the other way, and Cristiana stopped, taking time to gather her wits. Was she supposed to see Laurence alone?

Not Gerveys. Laurence.

The understanding that Laurence was here and she was to see him finally took hold on her. She lifted her head. Very well then. Laurence. She was here on his terms. Whyever he was here now, it was on his terms, too. If nothing else – and he had left her nothing else – she would meet him on *her* terms. Even if that meant no more than not going to him immediately. And rather than toward the guest parlor, she went the other way around the cloister walk, to the refectory where the nuns ate. Just inside the door a basin and a water-filled pitcher sat on a bench and a clean linen towel hung on the wall above them, waiting for hands to be washed before and after meals. Steadily, making no haste about it, Cristiana poured some of the marjorem-scented water into the basin, washed her hands, used a dampened corner of the towel to wipe her face, dried her hands and face, and hung the towel carefully straight on its rod. By feel, she made certain her headkerchief was straight, covering as much of her hair as possible. There was nothing to be done about her gown. Besides the gray gown she had worn at first, she had been given this equally gray, more coarsely woven one to wear turn and turnabout when one and then the other was being laundered. All that could be done for it was to shake out the skirts before she folded her hands over each other at her waist and went out and on around the cloister walk to the guest parlor, trying to believe she was ready to face Laurence.

The guest parlor was a small, bare room where nuns were allowed to meet with relatives or others who might come to see them. The white plastered walls were plain, there were a bench, a few joint stools, a small table for use if food and drink were given, nothing else. Stopping in the doorway, Cristiana saw, first, Laurence standing beside the table, his fingers unevenly tapping at it with impatience, and then – to her relief – Dame Frevisse standing against the wall beside the door. She would be why Cristiana had heard no knocking at the outer door; she must have been at the guesthall when Laurence arrived and had seen him into the nunnery herself.

Her presence made Cristiana more bold and she said at Laurence before he could say anything, 'You asked to see me?' ungraciously enough to leave him with no doubt she was not yet broken.

He returned her ungraciousness with his own, a slight lift to his lip as he eyed her before saying, 'You're doing well, I see.'

'Well enough. What do you want?'

'Your help.'

Because neither screaming at him nor damning him to hell would be any use, Cristiana went on staring at him, saying nothing.

'With Mary,' he said.

Knowing he counted on that rousing her, Cristiana kept her face blank. That she could do it so well frightened her. For weeks-lost-count-of she had been praying for her daughters, and here was Laurence offering her word of Mary and she was able to stand there staring at him, showing nothing, saying nothing.

Sharply, not liking her silence, Laurence said, 'We're trying to marry her to Clement as we planned.'

'As *you* planned,' Cristiana said sharply back at him. 'Not Edward or I.'

'Edward and you are beside the point now. The point is she won't do it. She won't even accept betrothal to him. When we try, she screams at us, says she won't say the words and never will. She bit the priest when he took her hand to give it to Clement, and she hit Clement in the face with her fist when he tried to kiss her.'

Warmth spread around Cristiana's heart. Mary was well, then, and being brave. 'And Jane?' she asked, keeping her voice level. 'Is she well, too?'

'She's well, too,' Laurence snapped. 'Better than Mary will be, the way Mary is going, and no, that's not a threat against your miserable daughter. She's doing it to herself. Making herself sick with her glooming and crying and not eating. Milisent says she'll be ill and no use if she goes on this way.'

Hearing that, Cristiana kept her face blank only with difficulty but said with cold satisfaction, 'Nor can you marry Jane to him instead because she's too young. Besides, you'd have to wait that much longer for her to bear your Clement a child, to make the inheritance secure.'

'Yes,' Lawrence agreed tightly. 'That's why I've come for you. To take you back so you can persuade Mary to this marriage.'

Cristiana stared at him, not quite grasping what he was offering her.

Probably impatient at her silence, Laurence snapped, 'Do you understand what I'm telling you? If you'll swear that you'll quiet Mary down, that you'll persuade her to this marriage and see her through the wedding, I'll take you back with me. You'll be out of here today.' His voice dropped into a darker tone. 'Otherwise, we'll have to find a way to *force* her to it. It can't be that difficult a choice, woman. Make it.'

He was right: it was not a difficult choice. Cristiana's heart leaped with her answer; but the cold back part of her mind held her silent a moment longer. She was finding there was something in her that was like the hard cinder left when all lesser matter had been burned away. Her weeks of fear and grief here had done that to her – or *for* her. Had burned away the parts of her that had been simply loving, had simply wanted to care and be cared for; had burned away her simpleness and left her with the unyielding wall of determination to have back what Laurence had taken from her. To have her home and her daughters and her life – and to destroy Laurence, and Milisent, too, if it were at all possible. And here he was, offering her at least hope of that chance somehow to strike against him. Against them.

So, no, her choice was not difficult at all, and letting her shoulders drop and her gaze fall as if she were defeated by his strength, she said in a small voice, 'I'll make all well about the marriage. I swear it.'

'Good woman,' Laurence said, satisfied and triumphant, not even thinking twice whether she meant 'all well about the marriage' the same way he did. She doubted Milisent would have so easily trusted her submission, but Laurence heard only what he expected to hear, accepted her defeat, and made to lay a hand on her shoulder. Cristiana shrank back from him, refusing his touch, trying to make her disgust look like fear. At the same moment Dame Frevisse made a small movement forward and Laurence took back his hand and told her curtly, 'I'll see your prioress now.'

To Cristiana, Dame Frevisse said, 'Go back to what you were doing,' and Cristiana, glad for the chance to be away from Laurence, bowed her head lower in answer and started to leave.

Behind her Laurence said, still triumphing, 'Don't hope your brother is going to help you once you're out of here, either. He sailed with the duke of York for Ireland a month ago.'

Cristiana let her shoulders slump more and went out. His words hurt but did not cripple her. Let him think what he would, she did not mean to wait for someone else's help anymore. Let her be free of here and with her daughters and she would do herself whatever needed to be done for them and her, against Laurence and anyone else.

Chapter 7

The long-slanted light of a rose-and-yellow sunset fell through the wide, westward-facing window of the prioress' parlor, keeping at bay the cool evening shadows gathering elsewhere in the cloister. Overly warm and worried over why she was here, Frevisse sat sipping wine slowly from her goblet while watching Domina Elisabeth seated in the room's other chair turning her own goblet around and around in her hands, looking down into it instead of at Frevisse. Wine was a rare indulgence in St Frideswide's. Almost equally rare was Domina Elisabeth hesitating over what she had to say. Those things, joined with having been summoned here when the other nuns were gone out to the garden for their hour's recreation after supper, made Frevisse warily silent, doubting it was for the pleasure of her company that Domina Elisabeth had summoned her.

'About Cristiana leaving us,' Domina Elisabeth finally said, still looking into her goblet. 'What do you think about it?'

Respectful and cautious, Frevisse ventured, 'It didn't seem my place to think about it.'

Domina Elisabeth looked at her. 'My lady, pardon my saying so, but you think about everything. What do you think of this Master Laurence Helyngton?'

'I didn't like him.'

Domina Elisabeth slightly smiled. 'Nor did I. What do you think Cristiana thought of him?'

'She didn't like him either. She fears him, I think.'

'But she was willing to go with him?'

Frevisse hesitated, then said, 'She wants to be out of here. If it means going with him, she'll go.'

'He's also the reason why she's here at all. I gather the warrant for her to be put away was given at his petition. That same warrant allows him to determine when she may be taken out, too.'

'If he has the authority for that, then we've no concern left in the matter,' Frevisse said, knowing full well it must not be that simple or they'd not be having this talk.

Still twisting the goblet around and around between her hands without ever drinking from it, Domina Elisabeth said, 'The trouble is that I've had no release from Abbot Gilberd.' She rarely referred to her brother by other than his title and name, and yet somehow no one ever forgot it was by his doing she had been made prioress of St Frideswide's almost ten years ago. 'In his letter about this woman he strictly charged me with her care, that she must not be let go or allowed to escape, that I must answer for her in all things. Now this man has come to take her out of our care, but I've had no release from Abbot Gilberd.'

'Isn't the warrant enough to forego any need of release from Abbot Gilberd?'

'It's enough that I've agreed she can go tomorrow.'

'But?'

'But I still feel bound by Abbot Gilberd's bidding that she is mine to answer for. That's why I didn't release her to him today, the way he demanded. That she must go is plain – her daughter's health being endangered, I understand – but I told him she could not go before tomorrow, that I needed to provide for her release.'

'He accepted that quietly?'

'I'd not say quietly, no. Nor happily. Nor was he happy that I won't allow her to go with him unaccompanied. He didn't see fit to bring any woman or women with him, and considering Abbot Gilberd's charge, I've told him – and he has agreed – that when she goes with him tomorrow, I go with her.'

Frevisse had a terrible certainty of what would come next, and inevitable as the coming sunset Domina Elisabeth went on, 'I've chosen you to accompany me.'

Because no nun was supposed to go out of the nunnery unaccompanied, someone had to go with Domina Elisabeth. That was beyond argument. Frevisse simply did not want to be that someone.

'It's ill enough that I be gone,' Domina Elisabeth said. 'To take anyone who's holding one of the great offices at present' – the cellarer, sacrist, and others who saw to the detailed running of necessary parts of St Frideswide's life – 'would make for greater upset. Nor would taking one of the younger nuns be so satisfactory as taking someone on whom I can better depend for help in forestalling or dealing with any trouble Cristiana may make.'

'Do you think she's likely to? She's made none here.'

'She's been obedient here in all outward ways, but do you truly think she's changed inwardly, become truly penitent? Despite that Father Henry has softened toward her, I've seen obedience but nothing else. I have to worry what she may do once she's freed from here. Until Abbot Gilberd releases me, I want all the help I can have in keeping watch on her and, if necessary, curbing her.'

Still looking for reason not to go, Frevisse tried, 'I'm presently hosteler.'

But hosteler was least among the nunnery's officers; she had small hope it would protect her. Nor did it. Her answer ready, Domina Elisabeth said easily, 'Sister Amicia will take your place. Tomorrow in chapter meeting I'll give all the needed orders and give charge of everything to Dame Claire for the while. We'll leave immediately afterward.'

Obedience had been for Frevisse the most difficult of her vows as a nun. She was far better at it than in her younger days but only with difficulty she said, 'Yes, my lady,' and nothing else.

The three-days' journey went unpleasantly. The weather was the best of it, with enough rain at nights to settle the dust of the road without making mud and the sky clearing before they were much on their way each day so that they rode under bright skies through countryside golden with ripened grain and harvested fields. Not the travel but the company was the trouble for Frevisse.

Laurence Helyngton made plain how much he resented the slow pace that was all Domina Elisabeth would allow for Cristiana, weak from fasting. In return, Domina Elisabeth let him know her displeasure at having to come on the journey at all. In answer to that, Master Helyngton was as near to outright discourteous as made no difference and the four men he had brought for escort followed his lead. On her part, Cristiana was tautly silent or – when she spoke at all – snappish. She kept as far away from Master Helyngton as she could and wanted no more to do with Domina Elisabeth or Frevisse than could be helped. Domina Elisabeth thought her ill-natured and ungrateful for Master Helyngton's mercy in bringing her to her daughter at so much trouble and expense for himself, but Frevisse suspected she was hiding anger and fear behind her silence and that both the anger and the fear were possibly very warranted. She had yet to decide whether or not she believed what Cristiana had told her in the church, but even if it had been all lies and Cristiana was what she was accused of being, that only justified Laurence Helyngton's contempt of her, not the cruelty that lay behind it, flicking out from hiding now and again.

Sometime during the first day of riding Frevisse decided that whatever was the truth about Cristiana, she disliked Laurence Helyngton on his own account.

They spent the last night on their way at St Albans where it would have been good to visit the saint's shrine in the abbey church, but Helyngton curtly refused Domina Elisabeth's request. With that, and after another night shared in an inn's bed with Domina Elisabeth and Cristiana and faced with yet another day in constant company with them and Helyngton, Frevisse found herself waking to the next morning in a dark humour and disinclined to hide it. So it was odd that when Cristiana, trying to pin her veil into place and failing, let her hands fall into her lap, defeated, it was Frevisse rather than Domina Elisabeth who went to her and said, 'Here. Let me.'

When Cristiana held up the pins to her, her hands were trembling. Frevisse saw them but said nothing. To ask if Cristiana was all right was pointless: she plainly was not. To ask if there was anything Frevisse could do to help was equally pointless: there was nothing to be done except the small kindness of pinning her veil and seeming not to see the tears brimming in her eyes, ready to fall if she so much as blinked. But Cristiana did not blink. She sat with her back board-stiff and her hands white-gripped together in her lap, and by the time Frevisse had finished with her veil, the tears had sunk from sight and her voice was level when she thanked Frevisse.

Frevisse silently granted that, whatever else Cristiana was, she was brave.

She was noting other things about her, too. Cristiana had been given back her own clothing – laundered and smoothed – before they left St Frideswide's. She was again gowned as a respectable widow, but Frevisse was considering what she had considered before – that it was clothing meant for home, not travel. That gave weight to Cristiana's claim she had been suddenly seized and carried off. Nor had she lied when she said she had a brother who might help her, Helyngton had granted as much by taking the trouble to quell any hope of him.

Following Domina Elisabeth and Cristiana from the bedchamber to their breakfast in the inn's common room, Frevisse had to remind herself that it was not her place to take any side in this. She was here to companion Domina Elisabeth and keep watch on Cristiana. Moreover, she should take heed against favoring Cristiana simply because she so much disliked Laurence Helyngton. That he was dislikeable did not mean Cristiana should be thought innocent. His wrong did not make Cristiana's right. In fact, Frevisse told herself, for all she knew there might be no one in the right in this matter at all – dead husband, vanished brother, in-laws she'd never heard of – they might all be in the wrong, she thought fiercely and shoved out of her mind consideration of anything but the inn's breakfast of thick bread spread with honey and bowls of last night's leftover lamb stew.

The morning went as the ones before it had gone. Miles were ridden with no one having aught to say to anyone else and the countryside changed, with more forest than there had been but still fields rich with harvest and busy with workers. Not far beyond St Albans they left the main way for lesser roads winding between high-hedged fields, and in a while Frevisse realized Cristiana, riding between her and Domina Elisabeth, had straightened in the saddle and was looking around her with almost gladness.

Quietly, not to be overheard by Helyngton riding well ahead of them or the guards around them, Frevisse asked, 'You know where we are?'

'Yes,' Cristiana breathed. 'Finally, yes.'

The road ran level here, with woodland to the left and on the right a low-cut hedge along a slightly downward slope of field with harvesters scything rye. Ahead, the low houses of a village, white and brown among the surrounding fields, lined the road, with five riders just riding out of it toward them. Not the first travelers they had met today. This was a populous part of England and even harvest-time was not enough to keep everyone at home, and probably only because they were nearing Cristiana's own part of the country did Helyngton turn suddenly wary, making a low, backward gesture that told his men to close in around the women while drawing rein himself until he was riding close ahead of them.

From the way Cristiana was staring at the oncoming riders, Frevisse guessed she still held hope of her brother's rescue; and by the way she slackened again almost immediately, Frevisse knew he was not there. Helyngton, to the contrary, lost his sudden wariness as the other riders neared, went easy in his saddle, and raised a hand in greeting at almost the same instant the other lead rider did. They came abreast, and as both drew rein to a stop, Helyngton said with open courtesy, 'Master Say. Well met.'

Despite he was younger than Helyngton by some years Master Say returned the greeting with confident ease, taking off his simple-brimmed hat of a deep red that matched his short riding doublet worn over dark hosen and calf-high leather boots, and bowed from the saddle, answering, 'Well met with you, too, sir.'

'What brings you this way?' Helyngton asked, making easy talk.

Hat on again, resting his hands on his saddle's pommel, Master Say said as easily back, 'To meet you, as it happens.'

Openly surprised, Helyngton said, 'To meet me?'

Master Say nodded past him to Cristiana. 'More particularly, her, in truth.'

There was nothing of threat in the way he said it nor any threat about the four men a little behind him, two to either side, but Helyngton stiffened. Even from behind him Frevisse could see he was readying some protest. But Master Say, without looking away from him, held out a hand out to the man nearest on his left, who had ready a folded paper he immediately gave him. Master Say immediately held it out to Helyngton, saying, 'A grant to me from his grace the duke of Suffolk to take Cristiana Helyngton, widow of Edward Helyngton of Broxbourne, Hertfordshire, into my care and keeping.'

The surge of blood up the back of Helyngton's neck almost matched the red of Master Say's doublet as he made a strangled sound, not taking the paper but finally choking out, 'Into your keep-ing? Yours? But he . . . he. . . .'

'Gave you the wardships and marriage rights of Mary and Jane and keeping of their lands. He did, indeed,' Master Say said, still easily.

'And the keeping of her! He gave her into my keeping, too!' Helyngton clutched at the pouch hanging from his belt. 'I have it here.'

Making a light, dismissing movement with the paper he still held out, Master Say said with calm cheerfulness, 'But this cancels it and gives her into my care.'

'What are you playing at, Say?' Helyngton demanded.

'It's maybe better you ask what his grace of Suffolk is' – Master Say gave the paper a small twitch that suggested Helyngton might do well to take it – ' "playing at".'

Helyngton snatched the paper from him with an oath, flipped it open, and began to read. While he did, Domina Elisabeth urged her horse forward a few steps and raised her voice to say firmly, 'Wherever Mistress Helyngton goes, we go with her. She was put into our priory's keeping on our abbot's order and unless you have counter-mand to that. . . .'

Master Say bowed from his saddle to her, more deeply than he had done to Helyngton. 'If that be the way of it, my lady, then most certainly you must continue in her company and be welcomed. By your leave, I'm John Say of the manor of Baas, Broxbourne.'

Mollified by his courtesy and perhaps not hearing the subtle change of authority from her to himself in his answer, Domina Elisabeth said with matching courtesy who she and Frevisse were and from where, adding, 'Our abbot is Gilberd of St Bartholomew's near Northampton.'

Master Say gave Frevisse a courteous nod and said, still to Domina Elisabeth, 'I saw your abbot only two days ago at Eltham. He was with the king and my lord of Suffolk.'

'Was he?' Domina Elisabeth's voice showed her pleasure, though the news meant the messenger sent to him at Northampton would not find him there. 'He's my brother. How was he?'

'He was very well, my lady.'

Finished with the paper, Helyngton folded it roughly closed and thrust it at Master Say, saying ungraciously, 'It's as you said, so have it your way for now.' He twisted around in his saddle to glare at Cristiana. 'But your daughters are still mine to keep. That hasn't changed.'

'Ah, yes, that.' Master Say handed the paper back to his man without looking away from Helyngton. 'Her grace the duchess of Suffolk sends her hope that you'll let the girls join their mother while she's with me at Baas. Her grace favors them being with her there. Favors it very much.'

As with Domina Elisabeth, Master Say shifted the words' weight, 'favor' becoming something closer to 'order', and Helyngton swung from Cristiana to face him with a sound just short of an open oath.

Not seeming to hear it, Master Say asked graciously, 'You'll bring them today, then?'

Helyngton started to say something but cut it off; gave his men a sharp gesture to ride on instead; and snarled as he jerked his horse aside to go around Master Say and his men, 'I'll bring Mary today. You'll have to wait for Jane. She's away at Waltham Cross in Ankaret's keeping. She'll have to be sent for. Since my lady of Suffolk asks it.'

He kicked his horse viciously into a hard gallop away. Master Say turned in his saddle to watch him and his men out of sight into the village, then turned back, for the first time looked at Cristiana, and said, 'Well met, my lady. How goes it with you?'

Cristiana had been sitting rigidly in her saddle, as if afraid any move or word from her would turn things wrong. Now she pressed a hand to her breast and said unsteadily, 'John. How . . .' but broke off, losing her fight to control her voice.

Master Say rode to her side, between her and Domina Elisabeth, and laid a gentle hand on her arm. 'We'll talk later. When there's better time. First let's get you home to Beth. Are you well enough to ride at more than a walk?'

Cristiana gathered up her reins. 'So long as it's away from Laurence, I can ride as hard as need be.'

Master Say gave her an approving nod but looked to Domina Elisabeth and Frevisse. 'What of you, my ladies? I can leave one of my men with you, if you'd better go more slowly.'

Firmly for both of them, Domina Elisabeth answered, 'We go with her.'

Master Say accepted that without question. Her own increasing questions Frevisse kept to herself, forced to suppose she would some-time have answers to them, gathering up her reins, too, as Master Say swung his horse around and his men drew aside for him and Cristiana side by side to ride ahead, then falling in behind Domina Elisabeth and Frevisse as Master Say urged his horse forward into a canter. They all matched him, covering ground far more quickly than they had been. There were no great steepnesses of road to slow them, only stretches of woods and fields between villages and not far until Master Say slowed their pace to a jog along the ditch and outer wall of a manor yard, then brought his horse to a walk just before they turned to go under a timber and plaster gatehouse and into the wide manor yard itself.

The manor house was directly across it, with a stableyard away to the right, from where stablehands were coming to take the horses before they were even stopped. The house itself was neither over-large nor over-new, built over a high-walled stone cellar that set the great hall almost a full floor above ground level, with stone stairs running straight and steeply up to a penticed porch and the broad, round-arched main doorway where a woman was just coming out, to hurry down the steps, reaching their foot as Master Say drew rein there.

She was pleasant-faced and young, much about his age, plainly dressed in a bright brown linen gown, high-waisted in the present way but simply cut, with straight sleeves and no excess of cloth, and her veil and wimple were plain, too, all meant for home-wear and work, not display, but assuredly not a servant's. She was smiling with welcome and not a little relief as she took Cristiana's horse by the bridle; and said up at her, 'Thank St Anne you're here! I've been praying all the while.' She turned to Master Say, now dismounted and coming to join her. 'He made no trouble?'

Master Say gave her a swift kiss on the cheek. 'None. It all went as hoped.'

Cristiana was making to dismount, slow with weakness. Master Say steadied her to the ground with a hold on her waist, but when she was down, it was to the woman she immediately turned, holding out her hands, saying in a voice raw with tears to which she was at last giving way, 'Beth! Oh, Beth, I never thought to see you or anyone ever again!'

Beth pulled her into a quick embrace. 'We've been so afraid for you. Ever since we heard you were gone.' But she drew back before Cristiana was ready to let her go, turned her toward the stairs, and said, 'Here's someone else you thought even less to see so soon.'

A man was standing in the sunlight at the head of the stairs, cleanly made and well featured, in a short gray doublet trimmed with green at neck and wrists and hem, a sword belted on his hip. Cristiana stared up at him for a startled, silent, disbelieving instant, and the fear crossed Frevisse's mind that this was the man with whom Cristiana had sinned. Domina Elisabeth must have thought the same. She was beginning to dismount in haste as Cristiana unfroze, cried out with joy, and went toward the man now coming down the stairs two at a time. They met at the stairfoot, catching each other into a hard embrace, Cristiana sobbing against his shoulder, 'Gerveys!', to

Frevisse's relief, while Master Say stopped Domina Elisabeth with an out-held hand and, 'He's her brother. She thought he was gone to Ireland.'

'Yes!' Cristiana cried, pulling back without letting go of him to demand, 'Isn't York gone to Ireland? Laurence said he was. How can you be here?'

'York is gone to Ireland, yes,' Gerveys said. 'I can be *here* because I didn't go *with* him.' He gave her a small, affectionate shake. 'You goose.'

Chapter 8

As Cristiana, her brother, Master Say, and the woman Beth all moved toward the stairs, Domina Elisabeth followed, keeping close to Cristiana as if afraid of losing her. Not that Cristiana would escape by her own effort, Frevisse thought, coming behind them all. On only the second step Cristiana stopped as if whatever strength she had been using was gone, and without asking, her brother scooped her into his arms and carried her not simply up the stairs but inside.

Still coming last Frevisse noted the weather-worn stone-work around the doorway and the feet-hollowed stone floor of the shadowed screens passage beyond it, more signs of the house's age. Turning from the passage in the great hall, she found it open-raftered but neither high nor grand and only three bays long, with three narrow windows on each side. Only the two flanking the dais at the hall's upper end, where the master of the house would sit at meals, were glassed, but the others' shutters stood open to the warm day, giving light enough for Frevisse to see that everything was beautifully kept, with wood polished, plastered walls lately painted, and floor swept clean. The place was old beyond the usual and somewhat small but everything else about it accorded with what she had so far seen of Master Say, how everything about him – clothing, horses, men, and this Beth who was, hopefully, his wife – suggested better than narrow means.

Gerveys carried Cristiana the hall's length and through one of the doors behind the dais. Following Domina Elisabeth following all the others, Frevisse came into a room that immediately raised her assessment of Master Say's means to well above narrow. Old the house certainly was, but here it had been gutted to the outer walls and everything made anew, from pale-boarded floor to green-painted ceiling beams to fresh plastered walls painted with swirling vines and bright birds on three sides and on the fourth, beside the door through which they had just come, a tall figure of the goddess Fortune with her Wheel and its tumbling figures. In the leftward wall a door stood open to another room where a green-curtained bed was just to be glimpsed. Ahead, in the far wall, was a wide, stone-mullioned, glassed window with a cushioned seat built into the wall's thickness under it, while set in the rightward wall was a broad fireplace with a deeply carved stone frame and a long, low-backed settle in front of it, facing the room since this time of year there was no fire on the hearth, only a branch of green-leaved holly. Otherwhere were several goodly chairs, several tall candle-stands with creamy beeswax candles waiting for nightfall, and a table with a book and a Venetian glazed pot with fresh flowers.

The woman Beth went hurriedly to pile cushions against one arm of the settle, and Gerveys laid Cristiana carefully down against them. Her sigh and sudden ease as she sank back were probably reward enough for him, but she whispered, 'Thank you,' before putting out a hand to touch the hilt of his sword and ask, 'Why are you armed?'

Most men wore a dagger most times but a sword slung from the hip was a bother and usually worn only for a purpose, and although Gerveys smiled as he said lightly, 'This was if John came back without you and I had to ride to your rescue,' Frevisse thought he meant it: he would have gone to his sister's rescue.

The woman Beth turned to Domina Elisabeth. 'Did John tell you aught of what this is about?'

Gravely, Domina Elisabeth said, 'We know his name and something of where we are and gather you're friends of Cristiana. Nothing more.'

'John,' the woman said, mock-chidingly at Master Say.

'There's hardly been time,' he protested.

The woman clicked her tongue at him and turned back to Domina Elisabeth. 'I'm Elizabeth Say, his wife. It may put you at better ease to know Master Say is an esquire of the king's chamber and lately Speaker of Parliament.'

'Beth,' Master Say said, 'that's beside this point.'

'It is not,' Mistress Say said firmly. 'They'll feel the better knowing they've come into good company, not bad.'

She was right: it did help to know something of Master Say's place in the world, and no little place it was if, besides being an esquire to the king, he had lately been Parliament's Speaker, too. Domina Elisabeth and Frevisse both bent their heads to Mistress and Master Say in acknowledgment before Domina Elisabeth went on, no less gravely and not yet matching Mistress Say's friendliness.

'We're at your manor near Broxbourne and in Hertfordshire, that we know. But where in Hertfordshire? Are we anywhere near Hertford itself? Or Ware? Or Waltham Abbey, perhaps?'

'Hertford is close to six miles north from here,' Mistress Say answered readily. 'Ware is about the same the other side of the river, and Waltham Cross is five miles southward. If you've ever gone the Pilgrims' Way from London to Walsingham, you've likely come near here.'

Domina Elisabeth nodded with understanding. 'We're perhaps a day's ride north of London, then.' She looked toward Gerveys standing beside Cristiana still clinging to his hand. 'And this gentleman is. . . ?'

'Sir Gerveys Drury,' he answered for himself, bowing. 'Of the duke of York's household.' Which made him strange company for someone of the king's household, given how things presently stood between the king and the duke of York.

'We've been near neighbors here and friends to Mistress Helyngton and her late husband,' Master Say said. 'Sir Gerveys asked our help in finding her after she disappeared.'

'That's our part in all of this,' Mistress Say said. 'Now, my lady, who are you, and why are you here?'

That was a fair turnaround of questioning but Domina Elisabeth's beginning of a gracious answer was interrupted by a quick knock at the room's door and the bursting in of a woman in a gentlewoman's kerchief and apron. Her glance took in all of them but it was at Cristiana she gave a wordless cry and immediately rushed toward her at the same moment Cristiana cried out in return, starting to rise, 'Ivetta! Why aren't you with the girls?'

Sir Gerveys put a hand on Cristiana's shoulder, holding her where she was, saying, 'Milisent threw her out, but only yesterday. She was with Mary until then. She came here because she didn't know where else to go and found me here as well.'

Ivetta was on her knees beside Cristiana by then, gripping her hand and searching her face, mourning, 'You're so wasted away. What have they been doing to you?'

Gripping Ivetta's hand in return, Cristiana said, 'How is it with Mary?' while Sir Gerveys went on, 'It was because of her we knew Laurence had gone for you, was expected back, would probably be somewhere on the road near here by now, and John went out in hope of finding you before they had you locked up again.'

'But Mary,' Cristiana said, caring more for that than how she had been rescued. 'And what about Jane? Laurence said Ankaret has her.'

'Jane is surely well enough,' Ivetta assured her. 'Being spoiled and fed too many sweets, like as not. That Ankaret dotes on her that much. But Mary, aye, she's been having a hard go of it, the darling.'

'Laurence said she wasn't eating.' Cristiana let go of Gerveys to grip Ivetta's hands with both her own, her fear showing. 'He said she's made herself sick with refusing to be married to that Clement.'

'That's right so far as *he* knows,' Ivetta said scornfully. 'But it's not so desperate as all that. She's refusing that young louter Clement, right enough, and prettier furies you've never seen than what she has when they've tried to drive her into it.'

'But if she's starving. . . .'

'She's not. She hardly eats what she's given, no, but I was taking food to her that they didn't know about. They've kept most of the servants on, too, and they've helped, not liking what's been done any better than we do. Mary's not starving by any means. That Milisent and Laurence just think she is. We did hope that if Mary seemed desperate enough they might be forced to fetch you back from wherever you'd been taken. And here you are!' Ivetta finished triumphantly.

'But you're not with her now!' Cristiana protested.

'If Mary isn't here by late afternoon,' Master Say said, 'I'll go for her myself.'

'Will he let you have her?' Cristiana asked.

Master Say smiled, but there was hard-edged assurance in his voice as he said, 'I don't think he'll choose to thwart my asking, friendliwise, for this "favor". Not when it was made in the duchess of Suffolk's name. I'm considerably higher in my lord of Suffolk's favor than Laurence is, and Laurence knows it.'

Frevisse held her face from showing the sudden shift of her thoughts at that. In the plays for power around the king, the dukes of Suffolk and York were absolute enemies to each other. If Master Say stood so high in Suffolk's favor as he claimed, how did he and Sir

Gerveys come to be so friendly together? Was one of them a traitor to his lord, a spy working against the man he claimed to serve? Were they together in some sort of power-game wound around with treachery, no matter how much simply friends they seemed to be?

'The trick is,' Master Say was going on, 'I don't actually have the duchess's word that you're to have the girls. I made that up, but Helyngton is unlikely to find it out, and once we have Mary safe and hopefully Jane soon after, he'll have a hard time getting them back, I promise you.'

'John, there's not thanks enough in the world for this,' Cristiana said.

'It will be thanks enough if you tell us everything that's happened to you,' he answered. 'We know next to nothing. Please, let's all be seated. And here's Pers to make the telling go more easily,' he added as a man carrying a pewter pitcher and goblets on a tray came through the doorway Ivetta had left open.

While Sir Gerveys sat on the settle at Cristiana's feet and Mistress Say gestured the nuns to the windowseat and went herself to sit on one of the chairs her husband drew toward Cristiana, the man Pers poured wine and Ivetta carried the goblets one by one to everyone. While they did, Cristiana – her hands white-knuckled together in her lap, her eyes going from face to face – told the same tale she had told Frevisse at St Frideswide's but added things unsaid before and with all her bitterness, anger, and fears laid open now that she could safely give way to them.

Neither Ivetta nor Pers had been explained, but Frevisse guessed she was Cristiana's waiting-woman or else the daughters' nurse. Pers, by the long dagger at his side and the way he had taken up a place near Sir Gerveys, was most probably Sir Gerveys' squire, rather than merely a servant. Having to guess so much about everyone and everything made Frevisse uncomfortable; there were too many gaps in what she knew, too many pieces that went together strangely, leaving her not understanding enough, even with all that Cristiana was now telling.

Save for wordless, distressed exclaims from Ivetta, everyone was listening to her in increasingly grim silence; and when she had finished at Laurence's return to St Frideswide's and why Domina Elisabeth and Frevisse were still with her, everyone looked to Domina Elisabeth as Master Say asked like a judge willing to weigh all sides,

'What have you to say to this?'

Calmly certain of her ground, Domina Elisabeth answered, 'I knew only what Master Helyngton said about her and what was in the letter from Abbot Gilberd. I did as Abbot Gilberd bade me and no more. I have his letter here. If you care to read it?'

She took it from her belt pouch. Pers came for it and handed it to Master Say while Sir Gerveys and Mistress Say both rose and went to read over his shoulder and Cristiana wearily shut her eyes. In the brief silence then, Frevisse caught the look that passed between Pers and Ivetta, warm enough for her to guess at affection between them. Was that something else she had to add to the mix of everything else she was trying to understand here?

Finished with the letter, Master Say folded it closed. Domina Elisabeth held out her hand for it, and while Sir Gerveys brought it to her, Master Say said, 'We can easily see you've done no more than you were bid and no blame lies on you for it. But now?'

'Now that Cristiana . . .' Domina Elisabeth paused, then began again. 'Now that Mistress Helyngton has been given into your care, it's well and good she's here with you. Unfortunately, I have not been released of my responsibility by Abbot Gilberd.'

Sharp with bitterness, Cristiana said, 'You'll surely grant that my brother and the Says are good enough guardians of me.'

'It matters not at all what I grant or do not grant,' Domina Elisabeth said at her most formal and firm. 'What matters is that I was given a charge to keep and have not been relieved of that charge.' She looked to Master Say. 'You said that Abbot Gilberd was at Eltham, yes?'

'I saw him there two days ago, yes. If you wish to let him know how things have changed and ask him for your release, I can have a letter taken to him from you as soon as you've written it, my lady.'

'Thank you. That would serve well. I fear, though, that until my release we must ask your hospitality.'

'No!' Cristiana said fiercely. 'I don't want them anywhere near me.'

Sir Gerveys, at her side again, put a quieting hand on her shoulder. 'Given she was ordered to it, she has no more choice in it than you do.'

Cristiana gathered herself to answer that, but Mistress Say began an efficient, distracting bustle, saying briskly, 'That can all be settled later, after dinner. Cook is not going to be best pleased if we put it off longer. Ivetta, you know the chamber we've readied for Cristiana. Sir Gerveys. . . .'

He was already picking Cristiana up again.

'I can walk!' she protested.

'You maybe can,' he said. 'But you don't look as if you should. Lead on, Ivetta.'

Ivetta did, with Pers following behind Sir Gerveys while Mistress Say said to Domina Elisabeth, 'I'll see to ordering a room readied for you and . . .' She hesitated, looking at Frevisse, ignored by everyone until then.

'Dame Frevisse,' Domina Elisabeth supplied.

'Dame Frevisse.' She and Frevisse bowed their heads to each other, even as Beth went on, 'John, you'll see to my lady having what she needs to her writing?' Adding, 'Dinner will be served soon,' as she swept from the parlor, a lady sure of her household, her duties, and her husband.

Frevisse wondered if Cristiana had been thus before her husband died and everything went wrong around her.

From a small doored space under the table, Master Say set out pen and inkpot and paper, saying as courteously as ever to Domina Elisabeth, 'You may not have time to finish before dinner, but you may make a start, if you wish.'

Domina Elisabeth thanked him with matching courtesy. He bowed to her, bowed to Frevisse, and left the room, shutting the door behind him. And Domina Elisabeth, letting go her dignity, went slack and said to the world at large in open dismay and distress, 'Into the middle of *what* have we fallen?'

Chapter 9

The manor of Baas had been no one's home for a long while, owned by people who lived elsewhere and used it rarely, taking the profits from the land and caring little about the rest. John and Beth in their little while here had begun to undo that neglect. Besides their re-made parlor and bedchamber at one end of the hall, they had turned a long storage chamber above the butlery and pantry at the hall's other end into their children's nursery and a bedchamber for guests.

'Which is not particularly kind to guests,' Beth had said months ago, when showing Cristiana what had been done. 'But it will have to do for now, and we have put in the other stairway,' letting the guest chamber be reached by its own steep stairs at the far end of the screens passage, near the door to the small rearyard with the kitchen and bakehouse. 'And something has to be done about that, too,' Beth had said. 'It is *not* convenient to have the food raced to the house in hopes of it staying warm the while. Surely they could have changed at least that some time in the past hundred years or so.'

But no one had and the Says had not yet and, 'The great hall we'll keep as it is for now. The roof is still sound,' Beth had told Cristiana when they had last sat together in long, good talk.

Sitting on the bed in the guest chamber, leaning against one of the tall bedposts with her eyes closed, too weary to face the trouble of lying down, Cristiana tried to remember when that had been. At Easter? Only four months ago? Was it less than four months since the world had gone all wrong and left her without even her wits, it sometimes seemed? It was so hard to think clearly. But she had to think, and she opened her eyes without lifting her head and stared at her hands lying slack and empty in her lap. Her tiredness was the trouble.

She was too tired to think well. And too worried. When she was rested, when Mary and Jane were with her, safe, then she'd be able to gather her wits toward what needed to be done next.

When she was rested and when she was rid of the nuns, she amended. They reminded her of too much. She wanted them gone.

Small-child sounds came from beyond the wall – scuffling, as from large mice trying to be quiet, and whispers, and someone's smothered laughter. Cristiana raised her head, listening, aware she was smiling. Those were good sounds. Home sounds. Beth and John's Geneffeve would be there, almost two years old now; and Beth's six-year-old daughter from her first marriage, named Elizabeth for her mother but called Betha.

Beth and John seemed so complete together that it was hard to remember she was once married to someone else, that she had been widowed and yet married again and was happy. It happened, Cristiana knew. People remarried and were happy. She had no hope herself though, either for marriage or the kind of happiness it brought. With Edward dead, her only happiness would be what she had when Mary and Jane were safe and with her again.

Beyond the wall someone – probably Nurse – gave a low-voiced order that brought quiet. Beth had surely sent word that quiet should be kept so Cristiana could rest, but Cristiana did not mind if the silence did not last. After the horrible silences of the nunnery – the emptiness where there had been nothing but women's voices – children's sounds were welcome; and the servants' voices in their coming and going across the kitchen yard below the window; and the shifting of dishes and mutter of voices in the butlery under the room, where things were being readied to serve forth dinner in the hall.

Home sounds, familiar and good to hear. But not her home's sounds. She wanted so much to be home again. She hurt with that want, and with the hopelessness of wanting it, because so much of home had been Edward and he was dead.

Knowing Ivetta's footfall on the stairs, she pushed herself away from the bedpost, sat up straight, and braced herself to show no more of her weakness than she could help. She was to eat here rather than in the hall with the household, and here was assuredly a goodly place to be. Beth had made the room a welcoming place, the walls painted dark green with a scrolling border of yellow vines and leaves; the ceiling beams painted yellow with green vines and leaves along them; the bedcurtains and coverlet of plain, dark blue. There was a small chest set at the bedfoot for putting things in and sitting on, a single low-backed chair, a table beside the door with basin and ewer and towel for washing, a wall-pole for hanging clothing. After the barren nunnery, the place was comfort and sanctuary, only tainted by Cristiana's knowing that she had nowhere else to go.

Ivetta came in, carrying a cloth-covered tray, saying while balancing it with hand and hip while she closed the door, 'Here you are and don't tell me you don't feel like eating, because you're skin and bones and need your strength.'

Cristiana had no urge to refuse the food. In truth she felt very much like eating and used the bedpost to pull herself to her feet as Ivetta set the tray on the chest and drew the chair close to it. Cristiana sat there, not minding Ivetta's hand on her arm to steady her, and let Ivetta ply her with slices of cold chicken, fresh bread, new cheese, and, 'Wine,' Cristiana said when Ivetta poured it for her. 'Beth is doing very well by me.' And as easily as that, she started to cry.

That took her by surprise. She had not known she was that near to tears, to be undone by ordinary kindness. Helpless with sobs, she pressed her hands to the ache in her breast that wanted to be pain as she struggled for the breath to go on sobbing. Ivetta came to her, making the same mother-hen sounds she would have made for a child in tears, wrapped Cristiana in her arms and held her until the sobbing stopped, then patted her briskly on the back, said, 'There. That's better out than in. You'll feel better now,' and began to hand her food. 'Just skin and bones. What were those nuns thinking, starving you like that? Have the wine. It's strengthening.'

Still hiccuping from the sobs, Cristiana drank but said as she set the goblet down, 'The nuns did what they were told to do with me. Some of them were even kind.' Fairness came hard, but Cristiana tried for it anyway. 'As far as they were allowed. Dame Frevisse, the one here with her prioress, she was kind.'

'I take it her prioress wasn't,' Ivetta said grimly, not interested in fairness.

'She only knew what she'd been told about me. They live very much by the Rule themselves. They're . . .' It came hard to say it, but if she was going to hate, it was better not to waste her anger where it did no good; better to turn it where it was best deserved – at Laurence and Milisent – and she forced out, 'They're good women.'

'You're not thinking of turning into one yourself, are you?' Ivetta demanded. Ivetta did her duty to the Church but her son had become a priest much against her wishes, nor did it help that all he had from it so far, after scraping out a living tutoring schoolboys in Cambridge, was lately to be made rector of a small parish in Huntingdonshire. 'With never a hope of grandchildren for me now,' Ivetta had complained to Cristiana. 'Nor him likely able to see to me in my old age, the place being all marsh and barely enough to support him alone. Nor is he likely to rise to better, us being nobody and all.'

So Ivetta did not favor lives being given to God, and Cristiana said, smiling and certain, 'No. No nunhood for me.'

She ate enough to satisfy herself and Ivetta both. Only when she was finished did Ivetta say, 'If you've done and you're willing, Sir Gerveys would like to see you.'

'You should have said! Yes, I want to see him!' He had deliberately left her to rest after carrying her here, but she had been waiting for him to return, was angry at Ivetta but heard the anger in her voice and mitigated it with a smile, saying more mildly, 'While he's with me, you can have time with Pers.'

Ivetta blushed, her face bright pink in the white surround of her wimple. 'Yes, my lady,' she murmured, her dimples showing as she fought and failed to hold in a smile.

She left the chamber in a flustered hurry, leaving Cristiana struggling between her own smile and yet more tears. She had been pleased by the affection openly growing between Ivetta and Pers these past two years. Ivetta was a carpenter's widow of Ware. Unable to keep up her husband's trade or their home after his death, she had moved with her son to live with her sister's family in Broxbourne about the time Cristiana lost to illness the woman who had been nurse to Mary and Jane since their births. When word spread – the way word always spread about almost everything – from manor house to village that Highmeade's lady was in need of a new nurse, Ivetta had presented herself at the manor, asking to see Mistress Helyngton. Cristiana had thought well of her courage in daring that, had been impressed, too, by her straightforward manner. Not over-tall, Ivetta had stood four-square and firm in front of Cristiana and said why she was there – that she was an honest widow who wanted honest work and thought she would serve well as nurse to a squire's daughters.

She had brought her son Nicholas with her, a half-grown boy

standing quietly a pace behind his mother. Cristiana had noted he had the good manners she wanted for her own children, and when she had determined that Ivetta could both read and write and had taught Nicholas before he went to grammar school and that he read well, she had said she would consider Ivetta as nurse to Mary and Jane. Edward had then made inquiry in Ware about Ivetta and her late husband, been satisfied with what he heard, and within the week Ivetta and Nicholas had come to Highmeade, to everyone's satisfaction both then and afterward. Ivetta had settled into her duties, while Nicholas with his reading, writing, and reckoning proved useful around the manor, until Edward had taken an interest in him and with help from Father Richard, the priest at St Augustine's in Broxbourne, found a way for him to work his way through an education at Cambridge's University.

The pity was that Edward's influence had stretched only to getting Nicholas the poor rectorship in Huntingdonshire, so that Cristiana had hoped that the growing warmth between Ivetta and Pers would give Ivetta enough pleasure and hope in someone other than her son to ease her disappointment. Besides that, Pers was a good man. That he and Gerveys were here and not gone to Ireland was boon to both Ivetta and herself, Cristiana thought, her smile for Ivetta struggling against her own urge to cry; but hearing Gerveys on the stairs, taking them two at a time, she shook her head, impatient with herself, not wanting him to see her in tears yet again.

He bounded into sight, stopped in the doorway with hands braced on either side of the frame to keep himself from pitching into the room, and looked at her with a questioning tilt to his head. 'You're better?'

Smiling was suddenly easier than tears, and Cristiana held out her hands to him, saying, 'Just seeing you gives me strength enough.'

He crossed the room, shifted the tray from the chest to the foot of the bed, sat down where it had been, caught her hands into his own, and looked hard into her face, to see if she were telling the truth. She looked as searchingly back at him. She felt so changed, so other than she had been when last they were alone together, that she wanted reassurance he was unchanged, that despite her own desperately different self, he was still dearly familiar, still dearly himself

'It was worse than anything you told us in the parlor, wasn't it?' he asked.

Cristiana's hands tightened on his in a spasm of remembrance and her throat constricted, keeping her from answering. Only finally was she able to whisper, 'I was afraid all of the time. I was afraid beyond anything I've ever been before: First, when Laurence and Milisent seized me, then in the nunnery. I was afraid I'd never get out, that I'd never be found, that I'd be there forever.'

That fear rose in her again, not merely the memory of it but a black tide that drove her to her feet and away from Gerveys, not wanting him to see it. Fighting to put something else in her mind in place of it, she went to the window and looked out. The roof of the kitchen across the small, paved yard cut off view of much except its roof-slates, but away over the wall of the kitchen garden beside it she could see a slope of pasture, a stream, a summer-cut hayfield with milch-cows grazing. Peaceful things. Ordinary things. Cristiana leaned against the windowsill, her hands in fists, trying to fill her mind with thoughts about the manor, about life going on its everyday way, not sunk in a black nightmare of fear. Beth's new herb garden, started with help of seeds and slips from Christiana's own. Think of that. And there beyond the kitchen roof were the tops of trees in the old orchard, heavy with apples for eating now or, come autumn, stored for winter or made into cider and cask-stored in the manor's cellars to give sight and taste of golden summer when winter's cold and gray were over everything. And out of her sight the other way from the kitchen was the manor's rearyard with its byres and barns and sheds and dairy, the granary, the poultry-yard. And the fishponds on the slope below them, for fresh fish on fast-days and in Lent. And the fields where harvest was happening – grains and peas and beans to feed the manor's people through the year and, with luck, enough to sell for money to buy those things the manor could not grow. Everything that was everyday life and not a black nightmare of fear. And with that thought, bitterness rose in Cristiana, stronger than the fear. All of those same things had been her life until now. Year in, year out, she had lived their rhythm, sometimes with Edward there, often on her own but always making a home for him, for Mary and Jane, for herself. And now *her* harvest that she had planned and seen planted, *her* orchard, her house, her *everything* were in Laurence's hold. And in Milisent's, along with her cur-husband Colles. They were there and she was here and she *hated* them.

In fury now instead of fear, Cristiana pushed herself away from the window. She wanted to have back her life. She wanted to have back her children. She wanted to have back everything Laurence had stolen from her; and she swung around to Gerveys and asked fiercely, 'You've told no one about Edward's secret?'

Gerveys stood up. 'No one. Not even John. Not yet.'

Cristiana returned to stand in front of him. 'Not yet?' she echoed. 'You mean you're thinking of it?'

'If we need to trust someone in this before we're done, who better?'

'He's maybe too near the duke of Suffolk. Edward said this thing, whatever it is, is against Suffolk.'

'I think Edward was right in saying John is King Henry's man before ever he's Suffolk's. The trouble is that presently Suffolk holds almost all the power around the king and to serve King Henry means to serve Suffolk, too.'

'Edward never had more to do with Suffolk than he could help.'

'Edward's ambition reached no further than his family and Highmeade. John's ambitions go beyond that, and that presently means serving the king by way of the duke of Suffolk.'

'Then it wouldn't be safe to tell him this secret against Suffolk. Not if it's anything so bad as Edward thought it was. At best, even if his first loyalty is to the king, it would be unfair to put him between his friendship for us and his service to Suffolk, wouldn't it?'

'Fair or unfair, I still trust John,' Gerveys said. 'Without him, I wouldn't even know you were missing. I'd be in Ireland and thinking all was well with you.'

Guilty with a sudden thought, Cristiana sat down abruptly on the chest and pressed her hands to her forehead. 'Gerveys, I'm sorry. I haven't asked you anything. Why *are* you here? Why didn't you go with York? How did John get leave to take me from Laurence? Where are my wits gone? It's as if I can't think at all anymore.'

Gerveys took her hands from her forehead and gently kissed her there, the way he would have kissed Mary or Jane over a small hurt. 'You've been somewhat busy surviving,' he pointed out, kindly.

'But why didn't you go with York? How did John and Beth come into this business at all?'

'Someone doesn't disappear the way you did without there's talk. Laurence gave out his story, but the servants had their own of what happened at Highmeade the day you were taken. Beth heard both.

She didn't believe what Laurence said and what else she heard made her afraid for you. She wasn't certain who around here she could depend on against Laurence, and John and I were gone. John was at Parliament at Winchester, remember, and I was in Wales. Laurence probably counted on my being gone without ever hearing about you. If he thought of John at all, he probably thought that by the time John returned, the trail to you would be cold. He may not even have thought that. He seems to have supposed no one would trouble over you disappearing. But Beth sent a messenger to John and a man to find me. He did, two days before we would have sailed. He gave me Beth's message that you were gone and Laurence had taken over Highmeade and the girls. I asked leave from my lord of York and he gave it. I'm to follow him when I can.'

'Laurence thought you'd gone. He didn't know you'd come back.'

'I took care he shouldn't. I came to Baas after dark, talked with Beth, agreed John was our best help, and left that same night for Winchester. Being Speaker, John had to see Parliament through to its end and that didn't come until mid-July. Since then we've been trying one way and another to find out what happened to you, where you were, what Laurence might be planning for Mary and Jane, all the time trying to keep secret I wasn't gone to Ireland. As things went, the Says' servants talked little and your folk at Highmeade talked much. When we'd pieced together what Laurence had done against you, John went to Suffolk and got a grant of your keeping in place of Laurence's. He was going to do what he could about the girls next, while we were still trying to find out where you were. Then Milisent dismissed Ivetta, she came here, and that's how John knew Laurence was bringing you back here. Given all of that, what else can we do except trust John? Besides that he's proved himself a true friend, he's best placed of anyone we know to deal with Suffolk. But handing a mad widow from one man's keeping to another is a little matter. Wardships and marriages mean money. We need something to counter whatever Laurence has paid. Promising Suffolk this paper of Edward's is the surest thing.'

'Edward said it was something that could be used against Suffolk. Wouldn't you rather . . . wouldn't you rather give it to York?'

'I would, but there's little he could do from Ireland.'

'When he comes back?'

'He won't be back. Not any time soon.' Gerveys was both certain and bitter of that. 'Not while Suffolk and his kind have their way around the king. This governorship of Ireland was as close as they could come to outright exile for him. With him gone, there's no one left in England who's both willing and with the power to stand against Suffolk.'

Cristiana suddenly, overwhelmingly longed for Edward. For him here to decide this thing for her. For him to be holding her. For him . . . simply for him. She bent her head under the weight of that longing but refused more tears. There was no more use in either tears or wanting Edward. She had to decide, herself, how best to save herself and Mary and Jane, and the only way she saw was what Gerveys now offered – the buying of their safety from Suffolk.

Gerveys' hands holding hers were the only warmth and steadiness left in the world and she lifted her head and said, 'We'll ask John's help, then.'

'If I saw another way, I'd offer it,' Gerveys said.

Cristiana forced a smile, trying to be confident for him. 'The purpose is to stop Laurence. To *ruin* him, if we can. This should do that. We must needs leave it to someone else to ruin Suffolk.'

Someone came thumping up the stairs lead-footed as an ox. Cristiana and Gerveys sat back from each other, both turning toward the door as a servingman thrust his head in even while rapping at the doorframe and said, 'I've come for the tray, if you're done with it, my lady.'

Cristiana made a small beckon at the tray. The man came, took it, and went nimbly out, his easiness so far from their tightly wrought dealings that behind his back Cristiana choked on a surprised laugh that she knew was nothing more than her own fear taking what release it could. The servant said something to someone at the foot of the stairs. Then there was the familiar bustle of Ivetta coming up, a home-sound even here, and Gerveys leaned quickly toward Cristiana, asking in a lowered voice, 'Then we're agreed? I ask John to deal with Suffolk for us? But ask him to do nothing about it until we have Mary and Jane safely here, away from Laurence, even if that takes a few days for Jane to be brought. Yes?'

Her throat tight at mention of Mary and Jane, Cristiana forced out, 'Yes.'

Chapter 10

That afternoon only Frevisse and Domina Elisabeth were with Mistress Say in the parlor when a servant brought word of riders coming. 'That had better be Laurence with Mary,' Mistress Say said and left the parlor. Domina Elisabeth hesitated to follow, then did, and Frevisse went with her, through the great hall and outside to the head of the stairs down to the foreyard, only barely in time to see the back of two riders already riding out of the yard where a small girl now stood with a cloth-wrapped bundle clutched to herself. Mistress Say called out, 'Mary!' and the girl started toward the stairs. Mistress Say made move to meet her but Cristiana was suddenly there, rushing down the stairs, and with a cry of 'Momma!' the girl dropped her bundle and ran, too. They met and clung to each other, Mary's head pressed to the curve of her mother's shoulder, Cristiana's face to the top of the little girl's head. Watching them, Frevisse thought that – whatever else was uncertain about all of this – Cristiana very much loved her daughter and very much had her daughter's love in return.

Sir Gerveys and Master Say appeared around the parlor-end corner of the house, with Sir Gerveys leaving Master Say behind, coming long-strided to his sister and niece and throwing his arms around them both while they were still holding each other. At the same moment the woman Ivetta burst through the doorway behind Frevisse and hurried down the stairs with a glad outcry. The squire Pers followed her less wildly but widely smiling.

Servants were come out, too, to see. As Mistress Say began to shoo them back to their work, Domina Elisabeth murmured to Frevisse that they would do well to be out of the way themselves, and they returned to the parlor. They had nowhere else to go yet at Baas, and the best they could do when soon the Says, Cristiana, Mary, and Sir Gerveys came into the room all talking and laughing together with

Ivetta and Pers close behind them, was to draw aside to the window seat, somewhat out of the way. Cristiana and Sir Gerveys had Mary between them, their arms around her shoulders, and they sat together on the long-backed settle while the Says drew chairs toward them and Ivetta and Pers followed to stand close behind them.

'They didn't tell me anything,' Mary said, answering something. 'When Uncle Laurence came back without you, all I heard was Aunt Milisent yelling at him, I couldn't hear about what, but then Aunt Milisent came and grabbed my hair.' Mary touched the side of her head, remembering pain, and Cristiana held her fiercely closer. 'She said I had to swear now I'd marry Clement and I said I wouldn't and then she twisted my arm and said she'd hurt me worse if I didn't.'

'My lamb!' Ivetta cried. 'Oh, my poor lamb!'

Mary did not look like a lamb. She looked like a small, fierce lion and said with pardonable pride, 'But I said I never would and she shoved me down and left me and nobody came again at all until one of the maids came with some of my things wrapped in one of my dresses and took me out to the yard and put me on a horse behind one of those men and they brought me here!'

Cristiana squeezed her closer and Sir Gerveys held them both. But suddenly Mary twisted a little away to say up at them in distress, 'But I lost Jane. Did Ivetta tell you? Aunt Ankaret took her away and there wasn't anything I could do. I'm sorry!'

Sir Gerveys gave her a shove on the shoulder. 'Gudgeon. That's as if I said I was sorry I'd not kept fifty soldiers from coming over a wall all by myself. I'd be sorry for it but it wouldn't be my fault. Not letting them marry you to Clement is more than victory enough. Don't be so greedy for glory, girl.'

Mary brightened under his words. 'I made them angry. Uncle Laurence and Aunt Milisent and Clement. Uncle Laurence got red in the face and Clement stamped his foot at me.'

'You were very brave,' Cristiana said. She began to run her fingers through her daughter's hair, combing out the tangles a few days' neglect had made. 'Now, though, you don't have to be brave anymore, because we'll keep you safe from Laurence after this.'

'And get Jane back?' Mary asked.

'And get Jane back,' said Master Say firmly. 'Then, with Jane safely here, I'll see to my lord the duke of Suffolk giving your wardships to me instead of him.'

Mary snuggled closer to her mother with a contented sigh. Frevisse guessed that because everything was already so much better, she easily believed all could be made right. She did not see – but Frevisse did – the look that fixed for a moment between Sir Gerveys and Master Say, full of things unsaid aloud. Mistress Say saw it, though. Frevisse saw her gaze go from one man to the other questioningly; but a maidservant come to the doorway, made a curtsy mostly to Mistress Say and said, 'The nuns' chamber is ready, my lady. You said to tell you when it was.'

Domina Elisabeth immediately stood up from the window seat. 'We'll withdraw then, by your leaves.'

Sir Gerveys and Master Say stood up, too, and bowed her and Frevisse from the parlor as Mistress Say gestured to the maidservant to show them the way.

The way proved to be no further than out the parlor door and along the dais to its other end, where a tight twist of stairs curved them up to a long chamber that stretched the house's width above both the Says' bedchamber and the parlor. The chamber was unfinished, with bare floorboards, walls, and rafters, and the small windows at either end unglassed, their shutters open to the warm afternoon.

'It's purposed there'll be rooms here for the children,' the maidservant said, 'but with them still only nursery-age there's been no haste to finish it. Still, we've made it comfortable as may be.'

They had. There were no more than three low joint stools, one of them with an unlighted candle and two books on it, and for beds two straw-stuffed mattresses on the floor, but when the maidservant was gone, Domina Elisabeth found there was a feather mattress laid on each of the straw-filled ones, and the beds were made up with crisp, fresh linen sheets and pillow-slips and new blankets. That was far better than Frevisse's bed in her sleeping cell at St Frideswide's; but she was already looking to see what the books were, finding to her pleasure John Gower's *Confessio Amantis* and a *Life of St Birgitta of Sweden*.

For guests unexpected and probably unwelcome, Mistress Say had done very well by them, but more than that, the room gave them something they sorely needed – somewhere away from everyone else where they could be alone and talk freely, and the first thing Domina Elisabeth said was, 'I think Laurence Helyngton badly misled us about how things stand with Cristiana.'

'Either that,' Frevisse said dryly, 'or her whole family and the Says are very subtly corrupt, too.'

'Which is possible,' Domina Elisabeth said seriously. 'My feeling, though, is that they're not.' She went to the window over the fore-yard and looked out. 'Master Say has promised my letter to Abbot Gilberd will go off tomorrow. If he's still at Eltham, we could be away from here in three days' time, which would be to the good. I want free of this business as soon as may be.'

With that, Frevisse could only agree.

But there were still the days to be gone through until Abbot Gilberd's release came and not many ways to pass their time. Some they spent by going to Mass in Broxbourne village every morning. The church was hardly more than a mile away but, 'There's somewhat of a hill,' Master Say warned when Domina Elisabeth asked about going. 'It will be a steep walk on your way back.' He offered to have their horses saddled for them whenever they wished to go but Domina Elisabeth refused with thanks, claiming the walk would be good. She did not add it would also use up some of their too-long days. Even saying the Offices at their due hours took up not nearly enough of their idle time. Neither she nor Frevisse were used to being either idle or as constrained as they were here, keeping much to their chamber since Cristiana made plain she did not like either of them anywhere near her.

It helped that when the weather was fair Cristiana and Mistress Say and their daughters were mostly in the garden that lay below the parlor's window and that Frevisse and Domina Elisabeth could be in the parlor then; but in the evenings and through much of the second afternoon, when there was rain, they stayed in their chamber, read-ing. The *Life of St Birgitta* was new to both of them and *Confessio Amantis* familiar but still pleasurable. And Domina Elisabeth found that the maidservant who attended on them, coming sometimes to ask if they needed anything, sometimes bringing them wine and small cakes, was willing to linger and answer Domina Elisabeth's carefully light questions. From that and from what could be overheard at meals, Frevisse began to gather some knowledge of the Says. For one thing, Master Say had not inherited the manor of Baas but acquired it only a few years ago, with several others near here.

'It's Mistress Say's money that's helped them along,' the maid said easily. 'Before she was widowed, Master Say was friends with her husband. He got their daughter's wardship from the king and then he and Mistress Say – Mistress Cheyne as she was then – came together natural-like. Of course, he's done fine on his own, too, being in the king's household and all. More days than not, he sees King Henry and the queen. Talks to them, even.'

And another time, proudly: 'He went to France with the duke of Suffolk and all to bring back the queen to marry King Henry.'

And: 'The duke of Suffolk favors him, you know. It was the duke of Suffolk saw to it he was made Speaker for the Commons in this past Parliament.' She seemed to feel that triumph was her own. 'He's someone now, is Master Say.'

'It means he's gone a great deal, doesn't it?' Domina Elisabeth tried.

'He's here as much as may be, he is.' The maidservant lowered her voice, as if giving away a great secret. 'He and Mistress Say are as happy in each other's company as you ever hope to see. Still in love and there's thought she may be bearing again. Early days yet to be certain, though.'

Once Domina Elisabeth said to Frevisse, 'Should we tell Master Say that the duke of Suffolk is your. . . .'

'Please,' Frevisse said instantly. 'Don't.' But because there had to be a reason not to take advantage of being related to so powerful a man, even if only by a cousin's marriage, she added, 'Things are so entangled here already. And what more can the Says do for us than they are?'

Domina Elisabeth had let the matter go with a regretful, 'I suppose it's better to not,' and went back to reading about St Birgitta, leaving Frevisse to thoughts that were less comfortable than her words. If the Says' prosperity came by way of Master Say's success at court and what Mistress Say had brought to the marriage, it would seem Master Say had had no inheritance of his own worth mentioning, save his wits, and although those had served him well thus far, it meant the prosperity here had only shallow roots, with much depending on Master Say keeping in favor with the king. Or, more truly, in favor with Suffolk.

Knowing what she did of Suffolk besides the general travelers' talk and other news that reached St Frideswide's about the ill-government and greed now attached to Suffolk's near-followers, Frevisse could not help wondering how tainted Master Say might truly be.

The third tedious day came. Besides the man sent with Domina Elisabeth's letter, Frevisse gathered Master Say had also sent a reminder to Laurence Helyngton that Cristiana's younger daughter was expected here as soon as might be, but nothing was yet heard from either Abbot Gilberd or Helyngton, and by late in the third day's morning, when a light rain again meant Domina Elisabeth and Frevisse were in their chamber, Domina Elisabeth chafed openly with, 'Why haven't I heard? There's been time and enough to go to Eltham and back.'

'Mayhap he'd left there before your letter came and the messenger has to find him out where's he's gone.'

'He can't be hard to find. He's an abbot. You don't lose abbots.' She picked up the *Life of St Birgitta* again. 'I want to go home.'

Silently agreeing, Frevisse went back to Gower's tale of the king of Hungary's Trumpet of Death. She found little to settle her thoughts in the king telling his brother, 'Dread god with all your heart more, for all shall die and all shall pass, as well a Lion as an ass, as well a beggar as a lord. . . .'

Time for midday's dinner came and Domina Elisabeth and Frevisse went down to it. Despite Cristiana, there was no fault to the Says' courtesy. Domina Elisabeth and Frevisse dined as welcomed guests at the high table in the hall, while the lesser members of the household sat along the two long tables running the hall's length from dais to wooden screens. At the high table, turns were taken for who sat beside Master and Mistress Say. This dinnertime Frevisse was seated at Master Say's right and she waited only until they were past his polite inquiry after her comfort and a brief exchange of comments on the weather and he was spooning a well-seasoned mutton stew thick with meat and young onions onto Frevisse's plate from a broad bowl set between them before she said mildly, 'There's one thing that's puzzled me these few days you've so kindly had us here.'

'Is there?' Master Say smiled at her as he began to serve himself. 'What?'

Frevisse looked past him to his wife and Sir Gerveys in talk together on his other side, with Cristiana listening beyond them, smiling at something. To Frevisse's other side Father Richard, Broxbourne's priest, was in talk with Domina Elisabeth. Fairly sure of not being overheard, she said, 'It's your friendship with Sir Gerveys.

With all the distrust I've heard there is between York and the king' – meaning Suffolk but not saying so – 'your friendship with Sir Gerveys would seem to be . . . unlikely?'

'It would,' Master Say agreed easily. 'But Sir Gerveys and I became friends long since, before things went so far to the bad. In France as it happened, during the queen's wedding journey.' He asked with a gesture if Frevisse wanted him to cut her another slice of bread from the loaf sitting in front of him and went on when she had nodded, 'It was by way of him I heard of this manor when I began to look for land.'

'And by way of him you came to know Master and Mistress Helyngton after you moved here?' Frevisse guessed.

'I knew Edward – Master Helyngton – a little already. He was a gentleman of the king's household when I started there. But, yes, we only became fully friends after I moved here.' Master Say saddened. 'Edward and Cristiana were happier together than almost anyone I've ever known. They were truly glad in each other's company. It was good to see.'

Soaking the bread in the stew's thick gravy, looking at that instead of him, Frevisse said, 'You're very kind to help her the way you are.'

'Mistress Say would have the hair from my head if I didn't,' Master Say laughed.

Wary of making her questions go too obviously all one way, Frevisse changed direction with, 'I understand you were Speaker in this last Parliament. It was a long one, wasn't it?'

'Into three sessions. I thought we'd never be done with it.'

'There must have been a very great amount of business.'

Master Say made a slight sound just short of a snort. 'Only one business, really. The king wanted more money and the Commons didn't want to give it. Not that anyone denies he needs it, that his household needs it, the government needs it, the war in France needs it.' He reached out with knife and spoon to serve her with a slice of roast pork in sage sauce from the platter just set on the table in front of them. 'But the Commons are tired of the war in France. . . .'

Along the table talk had paused while Sir Gerveys likewise served Mistress Say and – overhearing – he said, 'It's not the war in France they're tired of. It's Suffolk's and Somerset's mishandling of it.'

'No,' Mistress Say said mock-sternly at him. She swung around and held a silencing finger up at her husband. 'Nor you. We are *not* having talk about the war. Stop before you even think of starting.'

Both men froze as they were, and then they and Mistress Say all burst into laughter as at some long-standing jest among them. Even Cristiana slightly smiled. The men returned to the business of dinner, Master Say still smiling as he put the slice of roast on Frevisse's platter, saying, 'No French war then. Nor you surely don't want to hear about the wherefores and whyfores of loans and grants and moieties and tenths and fifteenths and tunnages and poundages and poll taxes and all the other dealings back and forth there were about ways to pay for things.'

Frevisse most assuredly did not and matched his smile while saying lightly, 'You and Sir Gerveys must stay friends by never talking of your lords and their quarrels to one another.'

'You have it,' Master Say agreed, now serving himself. 'The worse things are between Suffolk and York, the less we talk about them. Friendship is too good a thing to lose because of lordly quarrels above our heads.'

But if the Says' prosperity was rooted in Master Say's service to the duke of Suffolk, how much risk of losing it would he actually take, friendship or not? That not being something she was likely to learn by asking, Frevisse settled for saying, 'I gather, though, that Laurence Helyngton is likewise the duke of Suffolk's man?'

She made it a question deeply laced with uncertainty, knowing how few people could hold back from showing their knowledge in the face of another's ignorance; and most obligingly Master Say answered, 'Laurence wishes he were. In truth, my lord of Suffolk likely doesn't even know he was granted Cristiana's keeping and the girls' wardships.' To Frevisse's startled look he explained with a bluntness that surprised her, 'Laurence probably paid someone a fee to present his petition to Suffolk. If Suffolk even read the thing, I doubt he thought about it at all. At the most, what mattered was that one of his people told him a fee had been paid, so he granted the petition. Or maybe they didn't bother showing it to him at all. The fee was enough.'

A harsh and bitter array of thoughts concerning Suffolk went through Frevisse's mind. Since she could not say them aloud and doubted she kept them from her face, she was glad Master Say had turned back to his meal. She turned back to her own and only after a few moments and some thought asked, 'How did you recover her?'

'I told my lord of Suffolk she was a friend of my wife's and that we wanted her in our care. He told one of his clerks to write the order for it. Then he signed and sealed it and I walked out of the room with it.'

'But what . . .' Frevisse stopped, wary her interest was becoming too open. But she had to know. 'What of Laurence Helyngton's grant? That he paid for.'

'He's lost it and his fee. That's how it works, if you're not close enough to my lord of Suffolk to have his constant favor.'

'And since you serve Suffolk. . . .'

'I serve the king,' Master Say said, a hard edge under his voice's mildness. It was like a steel blade suddenly being slightly slipped from a sheath and then thrust out of sight again as he went on easily on, 'But presently the best way to serve my lord the king is to serve my lord of Suffolk. That far, yes, I suppose I'm Suffolk's man. On the other hand, Laurence Helyngton is a pig who wants to feed in every trough and serves no one but himself.'

Frevisse reached for the goblet they shared between them. Master Say reached more quickly, took it, wiped its rim with his napkin, and handed it to her, his manners faultless; but as she took it from him, he looked directly at her and said, 'You're taking a deep interest in all of this, my lady.'

He made it not quite a question, but Frevisse felt both the question and the deeper asking under it and met his gaze openly as she fairly answered, 'Our nunnery was used for a foul purpose. I want to understand how it happened and I'm curious about what's going to come of it. You'll be able to gain the girls' wardships, too?'

'Soon. It's never good to ask for too much at once. Cristiana's plight seemed the more desperate.'

They were interrupted then by servants bringing cheese fritters to the table and afterward she fell into talk with Father Richard on her other side until the meal's end. Then, while they were all rising from their places, a servant made his way out of the general clearing of tables below the dais, bowed to Master Say, and said, 'Please you, sir, there's riders coming. Master Helyngton, I think, and some women and others.'

Chapter 11

Sit Gerveys turned immediately to Cristiana. 'You can take Mary to your chamber. You don't have to see him or any of them.'

Cristiana, one of Mary's hands clutched in both of hers, shook her head against that. 'No. I won't hide from him. They're maybe bringing Jane.'

'Do *you* want to withdraw, Gerveys?' Master Say asked.

'I'd rather see the cur than have him think I'm hiding from him. He has to know I'm here by now.'

'If we meet them in the yard,' Mistress Say said, 'we can go into the garden, rather than the house. We can be easier rid of them from there.'

'Yes,' Master Say agreed. He turned to Domina Elisabeth. 'Will you come with us? You and Dame Frevisse?'

He asked it less for courtesy than for the sake of adding their nunhood's weight against Helyngton and whoever was with him, Frevisse thought; and felt a spurt of anger at being used as a pawn in this clumsy game's purposes; but Domina Elisabeth said, 'Of course,' and Frevisse bent her head in agreement. If she were going to be a pawn, she would rather be in the game's midst than not.

Whoever had been keeping watch had been keeping it well. Laurence Helyngton and maybe a dozen others were just riding through the gateway when Frevisse came to the head of the stairs behind Domina Elisabeth and the others. The Says were at the stair-foot, Cristiana just behind them still tightly holding Mary's hand, while Sir Gerveys was stopped a few steps above them, putting him at eye level with Helyngton reining in his horse in front of them.

Frevisse could not see Sir Gerveys' face, but Helyngton glared at him, saying, 'You. I'd heard you were here. What happened? Things go wrong between you and your duke?'

'Things change,' Sir Gerveys answered evenly. 'Usually for the worse when you're part of them.'

Helyngton's eyes narrowed but he let that quarrel lie, instead snapped his look to Domina Elisabeth and asked curtly, 'You're still here?'

'Good day to you, too, Helyngton,' Master Say said in pointed reminder of courtesy.

Helyngton shifted his narrowed look to him and said with no particular grace, 'Say. Mistress Say.'

What he would have said to Cristiana was cut off by a little girl's cry of, 'Momma!' from among the riders.

'Jane!' Cristiana cried out in return; said, 'Stay here,' to Mary; and went past the Says and Helyngton toward the little girl wriggling out of the arms and saddle of the woman with whom she was riding. Only barely the woman kept grip on her until Cristiana reached them and then did not so much loose her as had her snatched away by Cristiana, who with the little girl in her arms and the little girl's arms around her neck would have retreated toward the stairs, except Mistress Say with Mary by the hand met her, stopped her, and said past her, 'Mistress Colles. Mistress Petyt. Welcome. We're going to the garden. Will you come with us? The day is too fair for being inside, don't you think?' Despite the day happened to be still overcast and somewhat damp from the morning's rain.

Frevisse recognized one of the women, lowering at Mistress Say with dark-visaged irk, from St Frideswide's. It was the other woman, the one who had held Jane, younger and with a milder face, who asked, 'Laurence?'

'Yes,' he snapped. 'Go on. I have things to talk about with Say.'

Cristiana did not wait while the women dismounted. Taking Mary by the hand again and still carrying Jane, she went away toward the garden, leaving them to Mistress Say. Sir Gerveys went down the rest of the stairs, clearing way for Domina Elisabeth and Frevisse to join Mistress Say and the two women, now dismounted. Maybe not seeing the one woman's glare and the younger woman's long, soft look toward Sir Gerveys, she made them known to each other with, 'Domina Elisabeth, Dame Frevisse, please you to meet Master Helyngton's sisters. Mistress Milisent Colles.' The woman who had been at St Frideswide's. 'It's her husband there with Master

Helyngton.' The man who had been at the priory, too, Frevisse saw. 'And Mistress Ankaret Petyt.' Who was again casting a sideways look toward Sir Gerveys. 'Ankaret,' Mistress Say said, taking her by the arm and starting along the yard toward the garden, 'how does your husband? And your little boy?'

Frevisse guessed that meant she had not missed Ankaret's look.

The half of an hour or so that followed was, to say the least of it, unpleasant. The garden was beyond a green-painted door in a tall, new brick wall that hid it from the yard and enclosed it on one other side, while the third side, opposite the yard, had a low lattice fence with a penticed gateway and a wide view of a gentle-sloped stream valley and its fields, hemmed in only on the right by the long run of the wall enclosing the kitchen yard. The fourth side was made by the manor house itself, overlooked by the parlor window, which was the only place from which Frevisse had seen the garden until now. Like the parlor and its window, it was obviously new, with the squared beds of herbs and flowers fenced with ankle-low trellis-work, the paths cleanly graveled, the grass of the brick-sided, turf-topped bench along the brick wall starred with small daisies.

Cristiana was seated on that bench, one arm holding Mary close to her, the other around Jane on her lap. She did not acknowledge the women when they came into the garden. All her heed was for her daughters, none for Mistress Say, Milisent, and Ankaret, stopped just inside the doorway for Ankaret to make exclaims about the garden, and none for Domina Elisabeth and Frevisse going past them, following the garden's middle path to the gate on its far side.

There, as far as might be from everyone, they stood together, looking out. Beyond the kitchen's roof an orchard's treetops could just be seen, but it was toward the shallow stream valley that Frevisse looked. It sloped mildly away between pasture and hayfield toward the river valley lying out of sight beyond a curve of low hill to the east. Green rushes grew thickly tall along it and from somewhere beyond the kitchen and other buildings a dirt track curved down to the sideless timber bridge to the stream's other side where a girl was grazing a large gaggle of brown-and-white geese along the marshy edge of the reeds. With girl, geese, gently swaying reeds, and peaceful field quiet under the softly clouded sky, it was a contented scene, but Domina Elisabeth said, low-voiced and uncontented, 'Do we want to involve ourselves in this matter or stand aside from it?'

'We're involved,' said Frevisse. 'Nor do I like the people who have involved us.'

'Nor do I. Come with me.'

Mistress Say, Milisent, and Ankaret were just beginning to move from the doorway. Frevisse thought Mistress Say was trying to draw them away from Cristiana and that Milisent was resisting that, but Domina Elisabeth led the way briskly and directly to where Cristiana sat and said on her own behalf and Frevisse's, 'May we sit?' Cristiana stiffened and Domina Elisabeth added, with a slight movement of her head toward the other women, 'So no one else can.'

Cristiana flinched a glance that way, understood, and gave a curt nod. Domina Elisabeth sat down on her left, Frevisse on her right, hands folded into their laps and heads slightly bowed. Helyngton had wanted Cristiana guarded: they were guarding her.

The other women kept away, not without occasional hard looks toward Cristiana; and the men when they came in stayed standing just inside the door, Master Say and Helyngton in heavy talk together with Master Colles hanging close but looking more dogged than comprehending, while Sir Gerveys stayed a few paces aside, saying nothing. Frevisse guessed he supposed – probably correctly – that anything he said would only make trouble. And while Helyngton and Master Colles wore both daggers and swords, Sir Gerveys and Master Say had only their daggers at their belts.

Taken up with her daughters – Jane was happily telling what good things there were to eat at Aunt Ankaret's – Cristiana refused to see any of them. Frevisse, feigning prayer but watching everything from under her lowered lids, wished she were leaving here soon. This very hour, if she could. Whatever the rights, wrongs, goods, and ills here, there was nothing she could do about them. Why didn't Abbot Gilberd's release come?

'Give it over, Helyngton.' Impatience raised Master Say's voice for everyone to hear.

'I paid—' Helyngton began.

'You bribed. You—'

Helyngton abruptly started toward Cristiana, ordering, 'Milisent! Now!'

On the instant Milisent left Mistress Say. Before anyone understood, she and Helyngton were both to Cristiana who barely had time to recoil and hold her daughters more tightly, to no use. As Helyngton snatched Jane from her lap, Milisent grabbed Mary by the arm. Trying to cling to both girls, Cristiana was pulled halfway to her feet, but Helyngton shoved her back onto the bench and Milisent dragged Mary away. Domina Elisabeth and Frevisse both rose to their feet, protesting. Ignoring them, Helyngton and Milisent headed back for the gate, met on the way by Master Colles, who took Mary by the other arm, forcing her more strongly toward the garden door. Sir Gerveys and Master Say moved to block their way but Helyngton snarled, 'I have their wardships. I'm within my rights to take them.'

He was but that might not have stopped Sir Gerveys except Master Say put out an arm to hold him back. Ankaret, hurrying after her brother and sister, cast a pleading look toward Sir Gerveys that he did not see, turning to catch Cristiana now running after her daughters, hindered by her skirts and blinded with tears. Mistress Say joined him, putting her arms around Cristiana, both of them trying to persuade her not to follow further. Except to cling to Sir Gerveys' arm, Cristiana refused their help or comfort, crying out for her daughters and stumbling after Master Say as he followed the Helyngtons out of the garden, back to the foreyard where their men and horses waited.

Unable to stay behind, Domina Elisabeth and Frevisse reached the yard behind them all. By then Master Colles was holding Mary while Milisent swung up to her saddle with no nonsense about a sidesaddle, and Master Say was with Helyngton who was shaking his head, refusing whatever Master Say was saying, Jane still in his arms while he waited for Ankaret to mount. Close to them, Sir Gerveys and Mistress Say held Cristiana back between them, but she was crying out, 'Mary! Jane!' to Mary twisting in Master Colles' rough hold and crying back, 'Momma!' while Jane sobbed and held out her arms over Helyngton's shoulder.

Helplessly watching, Frevisse and Domina Elisabeth were probably first of anyone to see the armed men in buff and blue ride through the gateway into the yard, so suddenly there that Domina Elisabeth exclaimed, 'God keep us!' and crossed herself.

Frevisse was as startled, but in the same moment of surprise that brought everyone in the yard to a frozen stop that would have been fatal if this had been an attack by enemies, she took in that the men were come in three orderly pairs and saw the badges on their shoulders, and her momentary alarm turned to something else even before the riders turned aside from the disordered spread of people and horses in the yard's middle, clearing the gateway for more riders behind them.

First among those was a woman who immediately drew rein, bringing to a stop the two women and more men behind her. Sitting straight-backed in her saddle, her dark blue riding gown lightly dusted with travel, a wide-brimmed green hat over the white wimple encircling her face, she sat taking in everything in front of her. Everyone stared back at her in a stillness broken only by Mary and Jane's sobbing. Then she demanded in a clear, carrying voice, certain of her authority, 'Master Say, what is this?'

Master Say started toward her. Helyngton shoved Jane into Ankaret's hold and followed him, beginning to speak even before Master Say did, while Cristiana cried out, 'My lady, for the love of St Anne, stop them!'

Lady Alice, duchess of Suffolk, confronted by angry men, pleading woman, crying children, and a score of lookers-on all at once and without warning, gave no sign she was set back, only demanded 'Quiet', in a voice and with a look that warned she had better have it. And when she did, when the only sounds were a horse stomping its foot and a jingle of harness, she pointed at Helyngton and said, 'You seem to have the loudest mouth. What have you to say about all this?'

Frevisse wondered whether the man was so self-consumed with his own desires that he did not hear her warning and displeasure. If he did, it made no difference; he stepped forward and said with eager certainty, 'My lady, I've done your pleasure. I've let Mistress Helyngton have time with her daughters. Now I'm claiming them again. Whether she's fit or mad is beside the point. I have the grant of their wardships and the right to have them. I did your pleasure but. . . .'

Knowing Master Say had lied to Helyngton about Alice's part in this, Frevisse fairly guessed none of that was making sense to her; nor did she suppose things would be bettered if Helyngton learned Master Say had lied; and she went forward, away from Domina Elisabeth to Cristiana still held between her brother and Mistress Say, and from behind her put a hand on her shoulder and looked straight at Alice, who was looking from face to face of those in front of her, probably trying to assess what was happening here beyond Helyngton's ongoing flood of words. Her gaze paused on Frevisse for a bare flicker of time but enough, because she looked back to Helyngton, and all smooth and smiling with graciousness, cut him off with, 'I see. Of course you're fully within your rights, but I beg your kindness. Let them stay this while that I'm here. A day or two? You'll well have my thanks for it afterward.'

It was probably less her graciousness than the weight of the dukedom behind it that froze Helyngton to silence. Then he swept her a low bow and said, despite he looked as if his guts were grinding, 'Your pleasure in this is mine, my lady.'

Still smiling, Alice said, 'My thanks, sir. I'll well see you're presented to his grace the king when he's here in three days' time.' She delivered that deliberately, bringing Helyngton upright with a jerk to stare at her along with everyone else while she went gracefully on, 'Now, though, I'm ready to be done with riding and to rest a time. Nor should I keep you. You were about to leave, were you not?'

She favored Milisent and Ankaret with her smile but somehow left no choice but for them all to fulfill her expectation that they would go. Milisent even managed a somewhat curdled smile in return, although Ankaret simply looked bemused, as if not fully grasping what had happened.

Helyngton set Jane down with a nod at Colles to free Mary, who instantly dodged away from him to grab Jane by the hand and run toward Cristiana. Sir Gerveys and Mistress Say had let her go by then and Frevisse was stepped back from her, standing with hands tucked into her opposite sleeves to watch as Cristiana caught her daughters to her and Alice smiled on Helyngton and Master Colles as they mounted their horses.

Alice went on smiling while they and everyone with them rode out of the yard. That cleared way for the rest of her own escort to ride in, and as they did, she said to Mistress Say, 'Don't fear. I'm not going to put all of us on you, Beth. There's baggage and wagons a while behind us on the road with everything needful if you'll but tell Sir Robert here where my pavilion, tents, and all can be set up.'

With a look to her husband to be sure of his agreement, Mistress Say suggested the pasture along the stream below the house, and Master Say called one of his own men to show Sir Robert the way around through a field gate. 'Go with them,' Alice said easily to all her people. 'Master Say will see me safely there when the time comes.'

The Says then escorted Alice inside and through the great hall toward the parlor, with Sir Gerveys and Cristiana still holding her daughters' hands and Domina Elisabeth and Frevisse following and the household servants bowing as they passed. Frevisse glimpsed Pers and Ivetta, his arm firmly around her. Wherever they had been, she must have only belatedly heard what had nearly happened and was still drying tears from her cheeks.

But Alice was saying with bright-voiced cheer for everyone to hear, 'I'm merely a messenger, you see. King Henry is making a short pilgrimage to Ely and to see how his college at Cambridge does. If his plans hold, he does mean to come this way, yes.'

Murmurs and soft exclaims went running among the servants.

Nearing the parlor door, Alice went on, 'What we were wondering, my lord of Suffolk and I, was whether you and Beth could be imposed upon to provide a few hours of hawking along the Lea here. The river meadows being particularly fine for that, we thought it would well divert his grace and the court. And I took advantage of that thought to come ahead, for the chance to visit with Beth.' She linked an arm through Mistress Say's. 'I've missed my lady-in-waiting this while, you know.'

'We'll be pleased beyond measure to do all we can,' Master Say assured her, bowing her and then his wife into the parlor, Sir Gerveys joining him to bow Cristiana, Domina Elisabeth, and Frevisse after them.

But when Master Say had shut the door between them all and the hall Alice dropped Mistress Say's arm, swung around, and demanded at him with no smile, 'John, what is all this about? Who was that obnoxious man and those women with him?' She shifted her look and demand to Sir Gerveys. 'And what are you doing here, my lord of York's man?' Without waiting for his answer either, she looked around for Frevisse and said sharply, 'Come to that, how do *you* come to be here?' She waved an abrupt hand at them all. 'Never mind. We'll come to that later.' She faced Cristiana and said much more gently, beckoning toward the settle, 'You should sit down, I think.'

Cristiana was indeed gray-faced, and Mistress Say and Sir Gerveys both went to her, Mistress Say seeing her to the settle while Sir Gerveys swept his nieces away and toward the parlor door, saying, 'It's time you went to Ivetta. Your faces need washing.'

Ivetta was hovering just outside the parlor door, Pers still with her. Sir Gerveys handed the girls over to them both, shut the door again, and returned to Cristiana as Alice refused Master Say's offer of a chair with, 'I've been sitting over-much today, thank you.'

That meant the rest of them must needs stand, too, since she had only given Cristiana leave to sit; and again she demanded of Master Say, 'In the yard – what was that about?'

In far fewer words than Frevisse would have thought possible, Master Say told her, including why Sir Gerveys was there and the nuns' part in it. His look at Frevisse had questions of his own he did not ask. When he finished, Alice sat down beside Cristiana, laid a hand over hers, and said, 'There's been a misunderstanding on my lord husband's part and a great wrong done you. I'll do what I may to right things.'

Cristiana lifted Alice's hand and kissed it.

'Thank you, my lady,' Sir Gerveys said. 'You'll have our prayers.'

Alice regarded him gravely. 'At least your presence is well-explained, sir. I commend you for your care for your sister, and her daughters.' She looked to Domina Elisabeth. 'You had a duty unfairly put upon you but you've borne it well. Unhappily your Abbot Gilberd must have left Eltham before Master Say's messenger came. The sorting out of things will take a little longer but it will come.' She shifted her gaze to Frevisse and gave way to it smile. 'As for you, I'm right well pleased to see you where I would never have thought to.'

Frevisse smiled back. 'I, too, my lady.'

'We're cousins, you see,' Alice said to everyone. 'Our meetings are rare and we treasure them.'

And this one especially, Frevisse thought, because two years ago Suffolk had forbidden them ever to meet again; but no one here, save themselves, knew that and Frevisse doubted Alice was any more inclined to reveal it than she was. And lightly Alice went on, 'It was because she very pointedly sided with Mistress Helyngton in the yard that I knew which side I should take in whatever was the trouble.'

With everyone looking at her, Frevisse took refuge in a slight, acknowledging bend of her head and lowered eyes. Only when Master Say said, 'You never told us you were my lady of Suffolk's cousin. Why?' did she look to him and answer very mildly, 'There seemed no reason to. What more could you do for us than you were?'

'We were courteously and comfortably kept,' Domina Elisabeth said. 'You've been more than kind enough.'

A scratch at the door announced servants bringing wine and

wafers. Talk fell away to simple courtesies while they were there: Alice asked after Mistress Say's children; Mistress Say asked after hers; Alice asked Domina Elisabeth if the harvest promised to be good in northern Oxfordshire; Domina Elisabeth assured her it did. All was graciousness and pleasantries and Frevisse trusted none of it. Alice had come here with an escort too large and well-armed for no more than a simple ride through peaceful countryside, and in a haste so great no word had been sent ahead of her. Frevisse wanted to know why. And when the Says drew Alice to the window to point out something, Frevisse from where she still stood near the door, head bent to hide how much she was watching rather than listening, saw a questioning look pass warily between Cristiana and her brother. Wary of what? Alice, surely. Questioning what? The same thing Frevisse was – her sudden arrival? Or something more?

Despite the seeming ease they were all showing, Frevisse doubted that – save maybe for Domina Elisabeth – there was any ease here at all.

Chapter 12

When the servants had withdrawn, Alice shifted immediately to talk of the king's purposed hawking. 'He'll stay the night at Waltham Abbey and be here by late mid-morning, very likely,' she said. 'A few hours' hawking, then a meal, and then on his way again to Buntingford for the night, I think.'

Mistress Say gave a hunted look toward the great hall. Less than three days to ready everything for a royal visit and set forth a feast sufficient for king and queen and however many of their court were with them.

Alice saw her look and laughed. 'I know. We'd best pray for fair weather so tables can be set up outside and everyone eat with no cere-mony.'

'But if the weather isn't fair?' Mistress Say asked, her despair only half-feigned.

'Then everyone will ride straight on and dine in Ware,' Alice answered lightly.

Leaving the Says with all the expense of a royal visit without the royal favor that could come from it, as well as far too much readied food on their hands.

'My lady,' Master Say said, 'what have you brought on us?'

'You're to blame, Master Say,' Alice protested, still lightly. 'It's your doing that your good service has gained the king's heed and you live where the hawking is so fine.' Her smile went kind. 'Besides, there are wagons behind me on the road with pavilions and tents enough there'll be no need of your hall even if there's rain, and a tun of wine for come the day is on the way, too.'

Mistress Say laughed with relief. 'My lady, you're kind as ever!'

'I've had royal parties come my way on short warning, too. But I've interrupted your day, Beth, all without warning, and yours, too, John.

You surely have things that want doing and Mistress Helyngton looks as if lying down would do her no harm.' Alice smiled on Cristiana but moved toward Frevisse. 'Therefore, asking your pardon, I'll take my cousin for a walk in the garden, that we may talk together a while and leave the rest of you to what you must.' She linked her arm through Frevisse's, turning them both to the door so that it was over her shoulder she added, 'Dame Frevisse will show me the way to your garden, Beth. My thanks. . . .'

On the waft of her words, Alice had herself and Frevisse from the parlor, everyone else left behind them, but Alice kept up her lightsome word-flow through the hall among the scattering of servants and along the screens passage and out the door – talking of her ride to here, her new horse, the pleasure of seeing Frevisse again, how fortunate they were in this weather for the harvest. Even when they were down the stairs and going along the foreyard toward the garden, she went on murmuring pleasantries about her garden at Ewelme.

Frevisse said nothing all the while, waiting for whatever lay behind Alice's pretense of ease; but in the garden Alice kept on, saying how pleasant it was, until they had crossed to its far side and were looking over the gate. Down the pasture slope a long, canvas-hooped wagon and carriage stood beside an ant-busyness of men setting up Alice's round, blue-and-gold striped pavilion, but it was ahead, toward the green thickness of treetops beyond the kitchen's roof, that Alice pointed, asking, 'That's an orchard there, isn't it?' Without waiting for Frevisse's reply, she opened the gate. 'Let's go there.'

A path went that way from the gate. They took it, Alice falling silent, the only sound between them the swish of their skirts against the grass and summer weeds along the path as it ran along the kitchen yard's wall and then the high withy fence of the kitchen garden and the ends of several timber-sided sheds. Beyond those, a cart-track ran behind the rear buildings of the manor, with the orchard on its other side, encircled by a shallow ditch and low turf wall. The way through was a simple L-stile, to be twisted through rather than gone over. Alice crowded her skirts through the narrowness. Frevisse, with less skirts, followed more easily and trailed after her cousin going farther yet, well into the warm shadows under the apple trees.

It was an old orchard, the trees thick-trunked, the branches gnarled, some of them propped with posts under their weight of ripening apples. There were signs of the neglect there must have been until the Says came but more signs of present well-tending now, and the grass kept short underfoot, pleasant to walk on, by a lone sheep now tethered and steadily eating at the orchard's other end. In the middle, well away from where anyone might have overheard them, Alice stopped, turned to Frevisse, and asked sharply, 'What do you know about this Cristiana Helyngton and her brother?'

'I know about them what you heard in the parlor just now,' Frevisse said, more mildly than she felt at Alice's sharpness. 'Nothing else. I've come into their life unwillingly and will more than willingly go out of it as soon as possible.' With a suddenly terse edge of her own, she asked, 'Why?'

'What?' Alice said. She sounded both surprised and offended at the question.

'Why are you interested in them? Very particularly interested, if I read you aright.'

Alice abruptly turned and moved away from her. 'If you know nothing else about them . . .'

Staying where she was, Frevisse said quietly, 'Alice.' Alice stopped, still with her back turned. Even more quietly, Frevisse said, 'We've started on our wrong feet. May we try again?'

Alice stood staring down at the grass in front of her, then turned around and asked ruefully, 'Is it so very obvious I'm here because of them?'

Relieved that the offended great lady whom no one questioned had returned to being her cousin, Frevisse said, 'Not until now, when you asked me so directly about them. Though I wondered that the king knows his courtiers' lives so well that he knows who lives where and with good hawking.'

'No.' Alice made a small sound that failed to be a laugh. 'His grace the king does not know such things. The hawking was my lord husband's thought. Something to lighten the king's humour, things being somewhat heavy around him these days of late. Do you have any knowing of what's happening in the wide world beyond your convent walls?'

Frevisse was not used to scorn from Alice but there was scorn behind that question and she paused, balancing both her answer and her voice carefully to neutral before answering, 'I've heard a little. In Parliament the Commons were not much agreeable to the king's wishes. There's trouble in France again . . .'

Sharply Alice said, 'There's open war in France for the first time in three years. The truce has fallen into pieces and we look likely to lose all of Normandy.'

Frevisse stared at her, momentarily failing to take in what she had said. The French war had started more than a hundred years ago, near to the time St Frideswide's priory had been founded. There had been reverses and long times of no fighting, but these last thirty and more years – ever since the king's own father, Henry the Fifth, won his great battle at Agincourt – there had been mostly victories. Admittedly, Suffolk had given the counties of Maine and Anjou free-handedly back to the French in return for the king's French marriage, but Normandy was the rich heart of England's lands in France. To lose Normandy was beyond thought.

'And after that,' Alice went bitterly on, 'we'll likely lose England.'

'Lose England?' Frevisse echoed. 'To the French? You mean an invasion?'

Alice gestured impatiently. 'No. *We'll* lose England. Suffolk will. There are always men waiting for a chance to grab a place for themselves around the king. These losses in Normandy could make their chance to shove him out and themselves into power.'

The way Suffolk had probably shoved his own way into power, Frevisse thought but did not say. Instead she asked, 'What's happening in Normandy that's so worse than usual?'

'Some captain made an ill-judged raid on a Breton border town under truce this spring. The French demanded reparation. The duke of Somerset, as the king's governor of Normandy, refused it. Now the French have begun to attack and take our border fortresses in return.'

'I'd heard something of that, but even in truce-time there are raids and suchlike. We've had reverses before this.'

'This is more than a raid. The dauphin . . . oh, let's call him what he is. King Charles of France, seventh of that name. He's set a greater, more competent army against us than the French have had in the field since no one remembers when. Not that it need be much competent. Our border fortresses are mostly simply surrendering to him. One after another.'

'Surrendering? Their captains are simply giving them up? That's treason. What's Somerset doing?'

'Nothing, it seems,' Alice said, bitterly.

Unable yet to grasp fully that it could be as bad as that, Frevisse said, 'And while this goes on, the king goes hawking, visits his new college at Cambridge, and rides out on a small pilgrimage to Ely?' Whose St Etheldreda had been a holy woman and nun. At present a pilgrimage to the warrior king St Edmund at Bury would have made better sense.

'I'm not here because of what the king is doing,' Alice snapped. 'I'm here because of this Cristiana Helyngton and her brother. They have something dangerous to Suffolk. I want to have it from them.'

'Something dangerous? To Suffolk?' Frevisse echoed disbelievingly.

'So I'm told. A document or paper of some kind. I'm here to get it from them.' She forestalled Frevisse's coming question with a quickly lifted hand. 'That's all I know of it – that it's something that could be used against my lord husband. I have to have it. It *must not* come into the hands of men who'd use it against him.'

'How would Cristiana or her brother come by something like that?'

'We don't know. We wish we did. Probably by way of her husband. He served in the king's household for years. But how they have it is less an immediate worry than this Sir Gerveys.'

'He's here because of his sister's need.'

'There's surely more to it than that.' Alice moved away, impatient with her own need to be doing something. Frevisse went with her, finding it difficult to read her face well in the apple shadows and sunlight flickering over it as they walked. 'The woman will probably be easy enough to persuade to give me the thing. I judge she'll agree to anything to have her daughters' wardships back, but her brother may be more trouble. That he hasn't raced off to the duke of York with it already argues he may be less loyal to him than I was afraid of. If so, he can maybe be bought. I have only to find out his price. Or else decide how else to get the thing.'

Despite the warm day, her cousin's words made Frevisse cold. The gap there had always been between her life and Alice's widened with them, and far more careful to keep her voice even, she asked, 'How do you know they have this document?'

'Someone here sent word to my lord husband.'

'Someone here? Who?'

'I don't know.'

'Was it Master Say?' While seeming Sir Gerveys and Cristiana's friend, had he served his own ends and betrayed them to Suffolk?

'I said I don't know. No, not him. They were overheard talking about whatever this thing is by whoever is paid to hear things here and send us word.'

Slowly Frevisse said, 'The Says think you're their friend.'

'I am.'

'But you've set a spy in their household.'

Alice stopped, faced her, said more impatiently, 'Besides that John Say has a high and favored place at court, he was Speaker in the last Parliament. That makes it altogether worth our while to know what he thinks and does away from the court. Things go on in any household, friends or not, that are better to know about than not.'

'And now you're using him against his friends.'

'These "friends" will come to no harm if they deal honestly with me.'

Honestly meaning if they gave Alice what she wanted without making over-much trouble about it, Frevisse thought; and heartsick and giving up discretion, she said, 'Alice, besides knowing you must be spied on, too, how can you live a life that has you spying on people, even friends, and setting out to twist their lives to your own ends?'

'It's necessary,' Alice said curtly. She turned away and began to pace again between the apple trees. 'More necessary all the time. If Suffolk should lose his place near the king, everything will come unbalanced. There's no knowing who would take over governing the realm then.'

'King Henry himself?' Frevisse ventured.

Alice grabbed a low-hanging apple branch as she passed, pulled it with her, then let it snap violently back behind her as she said bitterly, 'King Henry doesn't want to govern. It's the great secret all of us keep. Except it's no secret to those best placed to take advantage of it. An advantage Suffolk doesn't dare lose.'

Behind Alice's bitterness, Frevisse finally heard the fear. Not corroding ambition but plain, deep fear behind everything she was saying. And gently she said, 'Alice, how has it been with you these two years since we last saw each other?' When Alice had only been beginning to see her husband's willingness to treachery.

Alice stopped. For a wordless moment she stood very still, her head bowed, then whispered toward the grass, 'Worse by the month I sometimes think.' She raised her head and looked at Frevisse, not only bitterness but raw pain showing now. 'My lord husband tells me next to nothing anymore. This business. He set me on to it like I was his errand-runner. "Go there". "Do that". Hardly a "because" to it and only when I demanded some reason for it all.'

'But you're doing it anyway.'

'It's necessary.'

'Or so Suffolk says.'

Alice returned suddenly to impatience. 'Frevisse, your prayers for me are valuable and welcome. But there in your nunnery you know nothing about how it is to be in the world, nothing of what has to be done to hold a realm and a government together.'

Frevisse was used to people's thought that living apart from the world was the same as being ignorant of it, but Alice at least should know far better than that and impatient in her turn at such willful simplicity she snapped back, 'You mean I'm ignorant of why "being in the world" requires you to spy and lie and mislead people you call your friends. Because if that's what you mean, I'm not so "ignorant" I don't see you're afraid of more than whatever Cristiana and Sir Gerveys have here. I'll grant you I don't know for certain what you fear, but there are so many possibilities. Is it you're afraid you'll lose Suffolk's love if you don't do what he tells you to do, no matter how treacherous – or that you've already lost his love because he no longer loves anything but his power? Or are you afraid there's nothing left in you yourself except ambition? That friendship and kinship and any love except for power are gone out of you, too? Are *those* the kind of things you mean I know nothing about?'

Alice stared at her, nakedly startled. Then she startled Frevisse in return by abruptly turning her head away and half-whispering, 'Yes. All of that.'

Frevisse's anger vanished. Suddenly uncertain what to say, she looked away, too. They had come to the orchard's eastern edge, with clear view over the low turf bank and across the pasture to Alice's pavilion and the servants now unloading wagon and carriage. The bright, graceful pavilion in the green pasture was beautiful to see there under the shining, cloud-cleared summer sky, and a part of Frevisse ached that mankind could make something so simply pleasing and yet spend such effort of time and thought on ugliness.

'Frevisse,' Alice said softly, regretful but still determined. 'I have to have whatever it is they have.'

Curtly, wanting no part in any of this, Frevisse answered, 'Then ask for it.'

Chapter 13

In the late afternoon's westering sunlight the orchard's shadows lay long and black across the grass, and Cristiana stood staring at her own stretched out among them, the afternoon's warm stillness all around her, no near sound but the late summer whir of insects as Lady Alice waited for her answer. Not near were manor sounds: men's voices calling to each other; a cow lowing in a byre, aggrieved at something; a laden wagon rumbling over a rearyard's cobbles. In the kitchen would be the heat and hurry of readying a supper worthy of the duchess of Suffolk and in the great hall the high table was by now being laid with Beth's best linen and plate. Manor life, and all of it as familiar to Cristiana as the sunlight, because all of it had been her life when she was Edward's wife and making their home. But none of it had to do with her here, with her now. Not now that she was Edward's widow and had no home anymore. All she had was other people's kindness. Or unkindness, if they chose.

With a hand pressed over the ache in her breast, she stared at her shadow laid black across the grass, and wished Edward had not done this to her. Wished with a smothering despair that Edward had not died and left her facing this. Wished Gerveys were here with her. But the nun had come for only her, not him, and it hardly mattered whether he were with her or not. There was only one answer she could make to Lady Alice's demand.

But still she held back from giving it. Because once given, what then?

'Well?' Lady Alice asked, impatient.

She hardly needed to be impatient, Cristiana thought. She had to know Cristiana had no real choice. But with that thought, Cristiana rebelled, and turning not to her but to Dame Frevisse waiting a little aside from them both, demanded at her, 'Can her grace's word be trusted? Would you be able honestly to swear that she'll keep her promise to me if I take it?'

Lady Alice drew in a hissing breath of displeasure, but Dame Frevisse considered the question with neither displeasure nor surprise for a long moment before she answered, 'I've never known her to break her word. Aside from that, I think you can trust her to keep it in this because what she offers in return for you giving her what she asks will cost her very little.'

'A simple "yes",' Lady Alice said tautly, 'would have been enough.'

Biting the words short, Dame Frevisse said back at her, 'Not in this matter.'

Cristiana had sensed Dame Frevisse's anger when the nun fetched her from the house. She was relieved now to know the anger was not at her. That Dame Frevisse was willing to vouch for her cousin even while this angry at her, was to the good, too. But not far enough to the good, and Cristiana asked, 'How can I know to trust you? You might be willing to lie to help her in this.'

'No,' Dame Frevisse said. 'I would *not* be willing to lie to help her in this. I don't care a cat's tail about my cousin's ambitions, or anyone else's. If I thought she wouldn't keep her word, I'd say it.'

Lady Alice's sharp sound of wordless anger at that reassured Cristiana more, and trying to keep tremble from her voice, she said at her, 'You swear then that if I give this paper into your hand you'll see my daughters' wardships and marriages are taken from Laurence Helyngton and given' – she hesitated, took hard hold on her resolve, and said – 'are given to John Say.'

'To John?' Lady Alice said. She and Dame Frevisse were both taken by surprise and showed it. 'But . . . why not to you? Or to your brother?'

Committed to her choice, Cristiana said firmly, 'I couldn't save my daughters before and my brother will soon be in Ireland. John has favor with both the king and your lord husband. Mary and Jane will be safest in his care. Safer than I could hope to keep them.'

That was bitterly the truth and bitterly hard to say, but she was relieved when, after a moment's pause, Lady Alice agreed, 'I'll see it done. Master Say will have their wardships and marriages.'

'Immediately,' Cristiana said.

'As immediately as I can have the necessary documents written out and sealed. Within the week.'

'Swear to it.'

Cold with anger, Lady Alice said, 'God and the blessed Virgin be my witnesses, John Say will have the keeping of your daughters and their marriages if you give me this paper or whatever it is.'

'Then if my brother agrees, too, you'll have it as soon as he can get it.'

'Get it?'Lady Alice snapped, impatient and displeased. 'It isn't here? And why does he have to have anything to do with it at all? They're your daughters. The choice is yours, not his.'

'I can't lay hands on this paper alone,' Cristiana snapped as sharply back at her. 'It takes the both of us.'

'And it's not here?'

'It isn't here. My husband didn't want it easily come by. My brother knows where it is. I know the safe-word that gives it to him.'

'So you both need to agree before I can have it?'

'Yes.'

'Then you'd best see to it that he agrees,' Lady Alice said coldly.

Scorning to answer that, Cristiana gathered her skirts, made a low curtsy, and left without Lady Alice's leave to go.

Finding Mary and Jane and Beth's little daughter Betha in the garden with Ivetta, she was for once not glad to see them. What she wanted was to find Gerveys and make an end of all this as soon as might be. But she smiled and held out her arms as they ran to her, braced herself as they threw their arms around her, and held them to her tightly despite the pain, smiling down as she said, 'There, my darlings. I've been in talk with her grace the duchess of Suffolk and she's promised to make everything well.'

Mary looked up without letting go of her. 'We can go home and I won't have to marry Clement?'

'There'll be no more trouble over Clement. You're going to be Master Say's ward.'

'Master Say's ward? Why can't you keep us?'

'We'll talk it all out later. I promise.' She began to loosen the girls from her. 'But I have to talk to your Uncle Gerveys just now, to settle everything. Ivetta, do you know where he is?'

'I can find him, my lady.'

'Please. Tell him I'll be in my chamber.'

'The girls?'

'They can go back to the nursery. Jane, don't pull. What's the matter?'

Mary had stepped back willingly enough, but Jane was holding to her skirts with both fists and tugging at them, distressed and frowning. Heeded, she stopped pulling but stayed frowning as she asked, 'Don't I get to go home with Aunt Ankaret anymore?'

'Ankaret is your cousin. Your father's cousin,' Cristiana said a little curtly. 'She's not your aunt.'

Jane's frown began to cloud to something darker. 'But don't I get to go home with her anymore?'

Before Cristiana could straightly tell her that no, she would not, Ivetta took firm hold on Jane's wrists and loosed her from Cristiana's skirts, saying, 'There now, that's something to be settled later, not here and now. Your mother is tired. She's going to go lie down while I see you to the nursery and then find your Uncle Gerveys for her.'

Still talking to distract Jane, she took Mary by the hand, too, and bustled them away. Wearily, Cristiana thought that the only fault she had ever found with Ivetta was her constant wish to make things well in the moment, regardless of the trouble that might make later. This time, though, she was merely glad to be rescued and followed her daughters and Ivetta slowly, giving them time to be well ahead of her, long gone inside before she reached the top of the stairs from the yard. That left only the worry she would meet Beth in the screens passage, but she did not, only the household's steward Master Fyncham, who bowed to her as she passed. Otherwise unhindered, she dragged herself up the rear stairs to her chamber.

There, with no need to seem strong for anyone to see, she lay down on the bed with a groan she could not help and curled onto her side, weary with her fear, tired out with trying to seem brave. How much longer until she had to be neither one anymore – neither afraid nor brave? Blessed St Anne, how long until she was free?

Despite of all, she maybe slightly slept. She found her eyes closed, anyway, and did not hear Ivetta come up the stairs, only heard her as she crossed the room and opened her eyes to ask without otherwise moving, 'Where's Gerveys?'

'Coming, mistress. He was in talk with Master Say.' Ivetta laid a gentle hand on her forehead. 'Is it bad, mistress? Is there anything I can do?'

'I'm only tired.' Which was not the whole truth but as much truth as she could deal with now, and despite she wished she never had to move again, she sat up and eased herself toward the head of the bed. Ivetta hurriedly pulled a pillow up at her back. Cristiana sank gratefully against the feathered softness with, 'Thank you.' Then betrayed to herself how much she still distrusted Lady Alice by adding, 'When Gerveys comes, keep guard outside the door while we talk, so we won't be overheard.'

'Of course, mistress.' Ivetta hesitated before saying, 'Are you really going to be able to make all well for Jane and Mary?'

'Yes,' Cristiana said, tired and with her eyes closed again. 'Gerveys and I are going to give Lady Alice something she wants and everything will be well.'

'Give her something?'

'A thing Edward left us that we have no need for except this. Lady Alice wants it, is welcome to it, and in return will give me Mary and Jane. Then . . .' Tiredness and her fears' weight seemed to drag her very bones down into the bed. 'Then I'll be able to rest.'

Gerveys knocked and came in. Ivetta gave him a curtsy and went out. Cristiana heard her speak to someone on the stairs as she closed the door and asked Gerveys, 'Pers is there?'

'Pers is there. You may lose your girls' nurse to Ireland if this goes on.' He sat down on the edge of the bed, his voice light but his gaze worried. 'You don't look well.'

'I'm tired is all. I want all this to be over.'

'What did the nun want with you?'

'She took me to talk with Lady Alice. She knows about Edward's paper.'

'Lady Alice does?' Gerveys said, as alarmed as Cristiana had been. 'How?'

'She wouldn't tell me. She said it was enough she knew I had it.'

'And?'

'If we give it to her, she swears she'll have the girls' wardships and marriages away from Laurence.'

Gerveys held silent, his jaw set in the way that meant he was thinking fast and hard, until finally he said, 'We've already agreed we'd use it this way. That's no trouble. It's how she knows about it that makes me uneasy. That, and whether we can trust her word.'

'Dame Frevisse says we can.'

'Can we trust Dame Frevisse?'

Oddly, that was one thing Cristiana had not doubted until now; but made doubtful by Gerveys' doubt, she said, 'We have to, don't we?'

Slowly, still thinking Gerveys said, 'Let me ask John if we can depend on Lady Alice's word. He's not kin to Lady Alice and I'm still willing to trust that his first loyalty is to the crown, not Suffolk. I'll speak with him after supper, and if he says we can trust Lady Alice's word, then tomorrow at first light Pers and I will ride to Ware for this damnable paper.'

'Is that where it is? Ware?'

'In the Franciscan priory. In the prior's keeping. If Pers and I leave at first light and the weather is fair and the prior is where he should be, we'll be back here by midday. I'll hand the thing over to Lady Alice and all will be well.'

'The safe-word for it is—'

'Save that until we're certain I'm going.'

Through the door Ivetta called, 'They're calling to supper and Pers is here with hot water. Should he come in?'

Gerveys called, 'Come,' leaned over, gave Cristiana a quick kiss on the forehead, and said with a smile, 'By this time tomorrow it will all be done with. So tonight, for once, I want for you to eat a hearty meal instead of seeming like you've forgotten what food is for. Yes?'

Wanting both to believe him and to please him, Cristiana smiled back, agreeing 'Yes.'

Chapter 14

The next morning's light rain was already thinning away when Frevisse and Domina Elisabeth started on their way to Broxbourne's church to say Prime there and afterward hear Mass. They had chosen to ride, not minded to be bothered with the road's mud or to slip and slide on the long hill's wayside grass, and as they went, Domina Elisabeth nodded over a field gate toward Alice's pavilion and the wagon and carriage beside it and said, 'I hope she slept dry. And her people.'

'I've no doubt they did,' Frevisse answered, with the unsaid hope that the quiet pattering of rain on canvas had soothed away some of Alice's sharp displeasure. She had been so short with Frevisse in the parlor last night after supper that Domina Elisabeth had said later, while they readied for bed, 'Your cousin seemed unpleased about something.' Not quite making a question of it.

Mildly, as if both unworried and uninformed, Frevisse had said, 'She must have some worry on her mind,' and Domina Elisabeth had let it lie.

Frevisse's own worry was less obliging and still with her. Alice was not shallow, not governed by each moment's passing humour. Frevisse had seen her put on a smiling, gracious front in seemingly worse times than this. For her to be as she had been yesterday told that something was far more wrong than anything to which she had admitted. Set as high in royal favor as Suffolk was, and holding the power that he did, what threat would be sufficient to unsteady Alice this badly?

Frevisse did not think she wanted to know the answer to that and she was grateful that she and Domina Elisabeth had left the house this morning early enough to see no one but servants, early enough that they finished saying Prime together well before Father Richard came

for the Mass, so that Domina Elisabeth went to sit on the stone bench along the nave's wall and fall into low-voiced talk with the several elderly village women already waiting there, leaving Frevisse alone on her knees before the rood screen, her head bowed over her clasped hands.

Her knees would not be pleased with her but she was in need of the quieting that prayer usually brought to her mind, especially in somewhere like this. St Augustine's was an old church, its nave plain and unpillared, with small, round-headed windows set high in the side walls and a short, round-ended chancel beyond the wooden rood screen. The nave's white-plastered walls were boldly painted with Christ's Passion along one side and a more-than-life-size line of saints along the other, while the Virgin and Child looked down from the chancel. The quiet of the centuries since it was built lay deep between its thick stone walls: the women's murmuring talk was only the ongoing murmuring talk of other women on uncounted other mornings through unnoticed other years – just as all the prayers of the Offices and the Mass had gone on, day around into day, for centuries before St Augustine's stood here and would go on for centuries more, God willing. But that everlasting did not lessen the needs of everyday and Frevisse slipped back to part of this morning's Prime. *Respice in servos tuos, Domine, et in opera tua . . . Et sit splendor Domini Dei nostri super nos, et opera manuum nostrarum dirige super nos, et opus manuum nostrarum dirige . . .* Look at your servants, Lord, and at your workmen . . . And let the brightness of our Lord God come upon us, and guide the work of our hands . . . *Sicut erat in principio, et nunc, et semper, et in saecula saeculorum.* As it was in the beginning, and now, and always, and forever.

There was deep comfort in that blending of the eternal and the now; and when the time came, she was able to give herself to the Mass with its far-reaching into otherness, its going into the mystery of Beyond that was greater than the passing passions of the world. And after it that release and pleasure stayed with her while she and Domina Elisabeth exchanged a few mild comments on the weather with Father Richard, a small, balding, quiet-mannered man who had never yet asked intrusive questions about why they were there and asked none now about Lady Alice though word of her coming was surely all through the neighborhood by now.

Frevisse could not decide whether he was so content with his small corner of the world that he had no curiosity, or if he simply had a servant who informed him of everything, leaving him no need of questions.

The church lay at the east end of Broxbourne's wide green, well away from the broad highway beyond the houses at its far end. It was a road that never lacked for travelers: southward it led to London, hardly a day's ride away; northward it went by way of Ware and a number of other towns to, eventually, the great shrine at Walsingham. Already this morning it was well-flowing with people on foot and horseback when Frevisse and Domina Elizabeth rode onto it and saw Master Say and two servants coming toward them at a jogging trot.

For a moment Frevisse thought that he was come to meet them for some reason, but he only made a small bow of his head as he rode past, and Domina Elisabeth turned in her saddle to watch them away, murmuring, 'How odd.'

They rode on, shortly leaving the highway for the deserted, steeper road to the manor. The morning was still cool but the early clouds and rain were gone, promising a fair and shining late summer day. Frevisse let herself hope that it might be an even fairer day – that today Abbot Gilberd's release would come and she and Domina Elisabeth could leave.

Was it cowardice to want to be away from Alice and her trouble?

She decided it probably was, but she saw no way she was any use here to anyone, and so – cowardice aside – wouldn't it be better to be gone and out of everyone's way?

At the manor, she and Domina Elisabeth gave their horses to a stableman in the yard and went up the stairs and inside, were still in the screens passage when they heard Alice in the great hall demanding with raised voice, '. . . gone where? How long until he's back?'

Frevisse followed Domina Elisabeth into the hall, to find Alice, Mistress Say, and Cristiana were standing in the middle of it, with a scatter of servants frozen and staring at them and Mistress Say taking Cristiana by the arm and beginning to draw her away, saying to Alice, 'My lady, wouldn't this better be done in the parlor?'

'It would be, yes,' Alice snapped and went past them both, leading the way.

From maybe no more than plain curiosity Domina Elisabeth followed them, and Frevisse went with her, less from curiosity than with thought of somehow curbing Alice's too-open anger. At what?

She did not see that Cristiana was as angry until they were into the parlor when, with the door shut against the servants' watching, she pulled free of Mistress Say, spun on Alice, and said in plain rage, 'He had to go to Ware. He'll be back when he gets back.'

'To Ware?' Alice said as sharply. 'No farther? Only to Ware? That's, what, five miles?'

'Six from here,' said Mistress Say.

'Twelve miles to go and come,' Alice said. 'When did he go?'

'At first light, I'm told,' Mistress Say said in a calming voice. 'Even if Sir Gerveys' business takes a while in Ware—'

'It shouldn't,' Cristiana snapped, still glaring at Alice.

'—he could well be back by dinnertime,' Mistress Say ended soothingly.

Unsoothed, Alice said, 'If he'd hurried, he could be back now. If he's decided to take it for himself . . .'

Furious and contemptuous together, Cristiana cried, 'My brother's not treacherous.'

Before Alice could worsen things by answering that, Frevisse broke in, deliberately bland-voiced, 'Has Sir Gerveys gone somewhere?'

'To Ware, it seems,' Alice snapped. 'He and his squire. Early this morning without telling anyone but the man who helped to saddle their horses.'

'And you're helping them return here sooner by raging about it?' Frevisse asked evenly.

Alice turned on her, an angry answer ready, but maybe read in Frevisse's look that she had gone far enough – or too far – because instead of saying more, she made a sharp casting-away gesture with one hand and went away to the window. From there, her back to the room, she said stiff-voiced, 'If you'd be so good as to join me, Dame Frevisse.'

The others all shared quick looks before Frevisse went to Alice's side, where Alice neither looked nor spoke to her but went on staring out the window. Behind them, Domina Elisabeth moved to the settle and began murmured talk about Broxbourne's church being very old. Mistress Say drew Cristiana to sit, too, commenting that the roof was poorly, and under their voices, for only Frevisse to hear but still steadfastly looking out the window rather than at her, Alice said, 'Tell me I've done well to trust these people. Sir Gerveys and his sister.'

Before Frevisse could answer, the door was flung open to the headlong entry of Cristiana's Jane, with somewhere behind her Ivetta call-ing, 'No! You knock first!' But Jane was already in the room, running to her mother's out-held arms as Ivetta, with a firm hold on Mary with one hand and Mistress Say's daughter with the other, reached the doorway. 'If you want me to take them away . . .' Ivetta said breathlessly.

'Of course not,' Mistress Say said before Cristiana could answer. 'Betha, Mary, come here, my dears. Give courtesy to my lady duchess.'

She was making deliberate use of the children for distraction, Frevisse thought. Alice had to turn around and smile and bend her head to their curtsies that were only a little spoiled by small Betha needing Ivetta's hand to steady her. Courtesy satisfied on both sides, Alice returned to looking out the window, and under Betha loudly explaining to her mother that she was sharing her dolls with Jane, asked again, '*Have* I done well to trust them?'

Frevisse took time to consider her answer, then said carefully, 'Cristiana wants her daughters safe. I doubt anything in the world matters to her as much as that. Nor do I think her brother will betray her. I've seen nothing but love and loyalty between them.'

Alice jerked one hand in sharp dismissal of that.

'Alice,' Frevisse said with forced gentleness, 'there *are* people to whom love matters more than worldly power.'

Her cousin's stillness then was, in its way, worse than any answer, because Frevisse could not tell what she was thinking behind it, until very quietly Alice said, 'I know that.'

'But do you believe it?' Frevisse asked quietly back.

And this time the answer was worse than the silence: barely above a whisper, Alice said, 'I used to.'

Frevisse had no answer to that, and the silence drew out between them until Alice said, 'I know I've helped nothing by making show of my thoughts, my fears, just now. Believe me, I'd hide them if I could. Talk to me about something else, please. Just keep me company and take my mind away from this waiting. Because if Sir Gerveys has gone to York with this thing . . .'

Frevisse started in on the first thing that came into her mind, which – strangely – was Domina Elisabeth's cat and its constant interest in the birds Dame Perpetua fed with bread crumbs in the cloister's garden. Dame Perpetua resented the cat's threat to the birds, the cat resented her interference with its business, and more than once protest had been made in Chapter meetings about Dame Perpetua's sudden outcries of 'Shoo! Shoo!' making unseemly disturbance of the cloister's quiet. Frevisse did not greatly care one way or the other about cat, birds, or Dame Perpetua's outcries, and assuredly Alice did not, but it was something to say, something to draw Alice's mind a little aside from other thoughts, and from there Frevisse moved on to the coming marriage between the priory steward's older daughter and the village reeve's younger son, making more a story of it than there truly was until interrupted by a suddenness of raised voices and running footsteps in the great hall.

She and Alice and everyone else looked that way just as someone knocked hard at the parlor door. Starting to rise, Mistress Say called, 'Come in,' even as a maidservant flung open the door and cried, 'The master is back. And Sir Gerveys. There's been a fight! He's hurt!'

Cristiana pushed her daughters away from her and sprang to her feet, only barely behind Mistress Say out of the parlor, with Ivetta on her heels and Alice close behind them. Startled into fright, Jane and little Betha began to cry but Mary would have gone after her mother except Domina Elisabeth caught her by the skirt and pulled her back onto the settle, at the same time putting out an arm to draw Jane and little Betha to her. With no thought of helping Domina Elisabeth, Frevisse went after Alice.

At the hall's far end a fuss of servants were crowding, shifting, falling back, making way for Master Say and one of his men carrying Sir Gerveys between them on their linked arms, his own arms around their necks, his right leg bound around above the knee by a thick, bloodied cloth, his eyes shut, and his teeth set against pain.

To everyone Master Say was declaring loudly, 'A cut with a sword, yes. Get out of the way. Beth!'

Less desperate now that she saw her husband unhurt, Mistress Say caught Cristiana's arm, holding her aside and beginning to give orders, sorting her servants to usefulness with, 'Master Fyncham, my medicines. Kate, fresh yarrow from the garden. You know it. Nol, two basins and a pitcher of hot water, with more hot water after that until I say I need no more. Alice, clean cloths. And wine. The rest of you . . .'

'Pers!' Ivetta shrieked, craning her neck, looking among the crowding servants. 'Where's Pers?'

Nearly to the parlor with Sir Gerveys, Master Say said over his shoulder at her, 'Pers took a blow to the side. He's at the inn in Broxbourne. They're seeing to him there.'

With a wordless cry, Ivetta started toward the outer door. Behind her, Mistress Say ordered, 'Edmund, go with her. Get her a horse and ride with her.'

One of the servants bowed and ran after Ivetta. The others were scattering to their tasks. Master Say and his man had slowed, going carefully through the parlor doorway, watchful of Sir Gerveys' leg, while Cristiana, free of Mistress Say, kept close behind them, silently desperate. In the parlor Domina Elisabeth was guiding the staring girls to the room's other side, away from the settle. Mistress Say circled the men and Cristiana to reach the settle ahead of them, quickly piled up cushions at one end, and stepped aside for the men to set Sir Gerveys carefully down. Not carefully enough. As Frevisse followed Alice back into the parlor, he sank against the cushions with a groan he could not help, and Mary gave a frightened sob.

'Take the children out,' Mistress Say said at Domina Elisabeth. 'Please.'

Domina Elisabeth did, carrying Betha and herding Mary and Jane ahead of her. Cristiana, behind the settle now, as near to Sir Gerveys as she could be without being in the way, was still silent, neither crying nor crying out but wringing her hands, her eyes fixed on his face. Master Say began to ease Sir Gerveys' riding boots off as gently as might be and Mistress Say to unwrap the bloodstained cloth from his thigh. Sir Gerveys opened his eyes, met Cristiana's desperate gaze, and said, short-breathed with pain, 'It's not so bad as it might be. Not deep.'

She made a stiff little nod, willing to believe that, but asked, 'Pers?'

Sir Gerveys shut his eyes again.

Cristiana whispered, 'If he were alive, you wouldn't have left him.'

With pain beyond his body's, Sir Gerveys said, 'He took a sword thrust meant for me.'

'Ivetta,' Cristiana said.

Tersely Master Say said, 'We thought it better she find it out there than here. She would have gone to him either way.'

She would have, and there was enough to do here without adding Ivetta's first storm of grief to it. To send her unknowing to Pers had been a cold decision but a good one, Frevisse thought, keeping with

Alice well aside and out of the way. Mistress Say was ripping Sir Gerveys' hose away to lay bare his thigh and the wound. It was shallow, yes, but also a full six inches long and still somewhat bleeding.

Servants began to come then with all Mistress Say had ordered. When they had been sent out again, she began to see to the wound with the skill every lady of a manor was expected to have; and while Sir Gerveys lay pressed back against the cushions, mouth set and breathing hard against the pain, Master Say told what he knew of what had happened.

'They were just past Hoddesdon, not much beyond Cock Lane, coming back from Ware. I'd just seen them, was raising my hand to wave, when half a dozen riders came at them out of the woods there.'

'They were waiting for us,' Sir Gerveys said. His eyes were tightly closed. 'It was us they wanted. It wasn't chance.'

'I spurred forward with Sawnder and Rafe,' Master Say went on. 'We evened the odds too much for the curs. They broke away, back into the woods, and we couldn't follow them. Not with Gerveys and Pers both hurt.'

Quietly across the room Alice asked, 'Did you know them?'

'They were hooded. I didn't recognize their horses either. Gerveys?'

'No,' Sir Gerveys managed out and nothing more, drawing a quick breath of pain as Mistress Say poured wine into the cleaned wound.

'It was Laurence,' Cristiana burst out bitterly. 'He somehow found out. Someone told him.'

Her look at Alice told who she thought had done that. Alice answered coldly, 'Why would I?'

'To have this thing you want so much without giving up anything in return. To keep Laurence's favor because he's of more use to you than I'll ever be. And to be rid of my brother because he's the duke of York's man.'

'First,' Alice said, her face and voice hard, 'I gave you my word in this matter. Second, I can have Laurence Helyngton's service for the asking, without I play you false. Third, may I be damned if ever I'm party to any man's murder, no matter who he serves. Fourth, if I played you such a trick, I'd likely lose Master Say's loyalty and he's worth far more than Laurence Helyngton.'

'John is hardly likely to give up Suffolk's favor, no matter what,' Cristiana said bitter. 'It's worth far too much to—'

Sir Gerveys jerked up from the pillows, ordering, 'Cristiana! Stop it!'

Cristiana broke off, staring at him, then seemed to hear what she had been saying and cried out in raw distress to Master Say, 'John, I'm sorry! I know better than that. I know . . .'

Master Say went around the settle and laid firm hands on her shoulders. 'It's no matter. That was your fear talking, not you. You've had enough and more to fear with what's happened to you. There's no offense taken.'

'Beth . . .' Cristiana said toward her.

'Not by me and not by Beth,' Master Say assured her.

'Assuredly not,' Mistress Say said without looking from the clean, folded cloth she was pressing over the wound. 'I've said worse things to him myself in anger and with less reason and he's not turned me out yet.' She lifted the cloth. 'Look, Cristiana. It's only a shallow slash. When it's healed, he won't even have a limp to make the ladies pity him.'

As Cristiana bent to look, Alice took hold on Frevisse's elbow and pushed her toward the door to the hall. Frevisse let herself be guided out of the room and – both of them ignoring the servants backing quickly away from too near the door – along the dais to its far end. There, still keeping hold on her, Alice faced her and ordered, 'I want you to find out who betrayed my dealings with these people.'

Keeping a stranglehold on her anger, wanting to hear Alice's answer, Frevisse said, 'The attack might have been merely attempted robbery and no more than ill-fortune that it happened to Sir Gerveys.'

'Don't play simple with me,' Alice snapped. 'Someone here betrayed them to somebody. I want to know who.'

'It was most likely Laurence Helyngton attacked them.'

'Probably. But how did he know Sir Gerveys was gone anywhere? More importantly, did he know what Sir Gerveys had gone *for*? I have to know who here betrayed Sir Gerveys and, in effect, me. I want you to find them out.'

'Maybe your own spy is playing several ways at once.'

'If he is, he'll be very sorry when we find him out.'

At least that reassured Frevisse that Alice had told her the truth about not knowing who the spy was. 'Will my lord of Suffolk tell you who it is, now that this has happened?'

'He'll have to, but it may not be our spy. It could well be someone else. I want you to do what you've done before. Listen. Ask questions. Watch people. You're good at all of that. Find out who betrayed us. I don't like treachery or being accused of it.' She looked past Frevisse and raised her voice. 'John.'

He came toward them along the dais and Frevisse moved a little aside, out of his way. With no bother of courtesy, he held out a small, flat, cloth-wrapped packet bound around with a heavy cord thickly sealed on the knot with wax and said to Alice, 'Here. They want you should have it before it causes more trouble.'

Alice took it. 'Tell them I'll keep my side of our bargain and that I'm sorry for the man Pers's death. John, do you believe this trouble was my doing?'

'No, my lady. Nor, a few months ago, would Mistress Helyngton have thought such a thing. She's ill with the treachery she's lived through of late and frightened of what Master Helyngton may do next.'

'As well she might be, from what I understand of him. John, do you trust my judgment?'

'Always, my lady,' Master Say said with a slight bow.

'At my behest, my cousin here is going to seek for who betrayed Sir Gerveys. It had to be someone here. I'd have you give her whatever help she may need.'

Master Say set a brief, sharply assessing look on Frevisse, then bowed his head again, this time to her, and said, 'My household and I are at your service.'

'Thank you,' Frevisse answered, bowing her head as courteously in return and wondering whether Master Say's intelligence would be an aid to her, or something she would have to work against. Because if more games than Laurence Helyngton's and Alice's were being played here, Master Say very probably had part in them.

Chapter 15

Since, as the saying went, it was best to take chance when chance came, Frevisse took this immediate chance to ask Master Say, 'Why did you bring Sir Gerveys back here with his wound? Isn't there doctor or apothecary to be had in Broxbourne? Or Hoddesdon?'

Straightly, not questioning her sudden question, Master Say answered, 'Given the attack was meant for him, I thought here was a safer place. I know, too, my wife's skill with hurts.'

'From what you said, Pers wasn't killed outright. Why leave him in Broxbourne?'

'Pers was alive but couldn't go further and Sir Gerveys was bleeding. We stopped at the inn and I bandaged Gerveys' hurt while he held Pers until Father Richard came. Father Richard was in time, barely. Afterward, it seemed better to get Gerveys back here.'

'You think there's chance of another attack on him?' Alice asked.

'Not here, my lady. There were only six of them. That's too few for more than an ambush.'

'Unless they gather more men,' Alice said.

'I think that if they could have had more men there they would have.'

'Six men riding together and not on the main road should have been noticed,' Alice said. 'Questions should be asked.'

'They will be,' Master Say said. 'But it's woodland near Cock Lane. If the men didn't ride together but met in the woods and scattered afterward, there'd maybe be no one to note them. But Broxbourne's bailiff has started a search, and word's gone to Hoddesdon; besides what the crowner will do when he comes.' The royal officer charged with looking into violent or unexpected deaths to determine if there were guilt and need for the sheriff or only mischance. Here at least

135

there would be no doubt.

'I have men with me I can spare to the bailiff's use in asking questions through the countryside,' Alice said. And demanded, when Master Say hesitated too long in answering that, 'Why not?'

'You should keep them for your own guard, surely, my lady?' Master Say offered.

'And?' asked Alice more sharply.

Slowly, looking for the right words, Master Say said, 'Men wearing my lord of Suffolk's badge and going about asking questions might not be well welcomed or well answered.'

Alice held frozen-quiet the length of a long-drawn breath, then said stiffly, 'It's gone as bad as that?'

Having been pushed to it Master Say was blunt. 'Yes.'

Alice stood silent for a moment, her face showing nothing, then said calmly, 'Thank you for your honesty. Does Beth expect me to dinner?'

'I believe so.' He looked down the hall at the servants who had begun uncertainly to set up the trestle tables and move the benches, readying the hall for the midday meal. 'It seems we're going to have it, anyway.'

'Once a cook is well along with a meal, very few things will throw him off his task,' Alice said.

'For which we may be thankful,' Master Say responded.

They had retreated into courtliness. Not interested in that, Frevisse said, 'I'd speak to Sir Gerveys now if I might. And Mistress Helyngton.'

'By your leave, it might be better if Gerveys has chance to rest,' Master Say said.

'The sooner the traitor in your household is found out the better. For both Sir Gerveys' better safety and maybe Lady Alice's.'

'Lady Alice is in no . . .' Master Say began but broke off, looked at the packet in her hand, and with an impatient sound at himself, shifted to between her and the servants down the hall, too late though it was. Anyone looking had by now seen what she held.

Alice stared at him, momentarily not understanding, before her eyes a little widened. 'Oh,' she whispered.

To her increasing questions Frevisse added an uneasy wondering how Alice, usually sharp at everything, was presently so slow at grasping the threats around her. Along with that, where was all her skill at wielding gracious manners as both shield and weapon gone to?

But seeing no use for either open pity or gentleness, Frevisse said firmly, 'You might, my lady, want to go to the nursery for now, to reassure both Domina Elisabeth and the children that all is well enough, and bide there until dinner is served.'

Master Say agreed, 'That might do very well, my lady.'

Alice stared at them both, near to offended that they were nearly giving her an order, before understanding surfaced and she said, 'You mean I would be out of your way while you get on with things.'

'Because whoever else wants that' – Master Say nodded at the packet she held – 'might be as willing to take it from you by force as they were from Sir Gerveys. Will you be sending it to my lord of Suffolk?'

By her prompt answer, Alice had already considered that. 'Rather than trust it out of my keeping, I mean to hold it the two days until my lord husband is here.'

'Then you'll have always some of your men with you when you come back and forth to the house?'

'Yes,' Alice said, matching his quiet. 'One of my women and two of my men whenever I go out of my pavilion.'

'It might be better,' Master Say offered, 'if you would stay the nights here.'

'Thank you, no,' Alice said crisply, with warning in her voice that she had reached the limit of what she would hear from anyone about anything. 'I'll not be driven into hiding.'

She left them with a sweep of skirts and head held high. Only when she was well away did Master Say turn to Frevisse and say, 'You'll question Sir Gerveys and Mistress Helyngton now?'

Frevisse bent her head in agreement. 'With no one else there to hear, if you please.'

'I please, of course, to obey my lady of Suffolk,' he answered. Which was not the same as being pleased at having to obey.

But his courtesy hid whatever he thought, one way or the other, and she bent her head to him again and asked, 'If you'll explain me to everyone, then?'

In the parlor, Mistress Say was standing at the window with her arm around Cristiana's shoulders, talking softly to her, while Sir Gerveys still lay half-raised against the arm of the settle, eyes closed but face too taut for sleep. The women turned as Master Say and

Frevisse came in, and as Master Say shut the door, Sir Gerveys opened his eyes and asked, 'She has it?'

'She has it,' Master Say answered.

'Did she read it?' Sir Gerveys asked.

'She means to give it to the duke unopened.'

Sir Gerveys shut his eyes.

'In the meanwhile, toward finding out who set the ambush on you, she's bade me say that Dame Frevisse is to ask questions of whomever she chooses.'

Cristiana started to say something. Mistress Say laid a restraining hand on her arm, but Sir Gerveys, regarding Frevisse with a questioning frown, asked, 'The nun is going to ask questions?'

'At Lady Alice's bidding,' Master Say repeated. 'She'd like to begin with you and Cristiana.'

Mistress Say whispered something, probably comforting, to Cristiana, and left her, going ahead of her husband out of the room. Cristiana with a wary look at Frevisse went to kneel beside her brother, laid a hand on his, and asked, 'The pain?'

'Whatever Beth gave me has eased it. She promised that I'll probably sleep soon.' He gave Frevisse a smile narrow with the pain he said was eased. 'Best ask your questions while I can still answer them.'

With no point in hesitation, Frevisse said, 'My first is simply how many people knew about this paper before today.'

'So far as I know,' Sir Gerveys said, 'only Edward Helyngton, my sister, and myself. He thought it was something that was supposed to have been destroyed and that no one knew he had it.'

Cristiana nodded in silent agreement.

'Someone had it in Ware,' Frevisse pointed out.

'The prior at the friary there had the sealed packet. He didn't know what it was. More than that, until yesterday Cristiana didn't know where it was. I knew where it was, she had the word needed to recover it, and we were sworn not to share our knowledge until there was need.'

'What if one of you died?'

'If either of us died, the prior would hear of it and see to the other having the packet. He could only give it to one or the other of us.'

She turned to Cristiana. 'How did your husband come by this thing?'

'He happened on it during his duties in the king's household and took it,' Cristiana said stiffly.

'And it was never missed?'

'From what Edward said, it's only a rough writing out of something. Probably a fair copy had been made from it and it was meant to be burned but no one had.' As if suddenly wanting Frevisse to understand, Cristiana said more readily. 'He only took it because he knew how ill he was. He was afraid for me and for our daughters and hoped it would help if there was trouble. You've seen how right he was.'

'I've seen,' Frevisse granted, something like gently, doubting there was anything to gain by upsetting what small, desperate balance Cristiana was presently holding to. Quietly, of both her and Sir Gerveys, she said, 'What it comes down to is that, so far as you know, only you and Master Helyngton knew from where this paper had come and only Master Helyngton knew what it said. Is that the way of it?'

Cristiana and Sir Gerveys both agreed to that with nods.

'And yet Lady Alice came here yesterday demanding to have it,' Frevisse went on. 'How can that be?'

'Someone overheard us talk of it,' Sir Gerveys said with a promptness that told he had already thought on that.

'You neither of you mentioned the thing to anyone else? Not even Ivetta or Pers?'

'No,' Sir Gerveys said.

'No, and neither of them would betray us anyway,' Cristiana said hotly.

'I ask so I can say I did,' Frevisse said. 'When and where did you talk about this paper? Not just here at Baas but before.'

'Never before,' Cristiana said.

'Edward was dying when he told us about it,' Sir Gerveys explained. 'That was the greater matter.'

Cristiana clenched her hands into fists in her lap. 'Nothing mattered then except that I was losing him. Then, afterward, Gerveys went away without there ever being reason to talk about the paper.'

'Here then. Where and when did you talk of it here?'

'The first day,' Sir Gerveys said. 'When Cristiana had just come. In her chamber. We decided then to ask Master Say to help us win Suffolk's help against Laurence in return for the paper.'

'Did you ask his help?'

'That afternoon I told him we had something that would be worth Suffolk's while to have and would he deal with Suffolk for us against Laurence. He said he would.'

'Did you tell him anything more than that?'

'No.'

'Not what this something was, or where it was, or anything?'

'No.'

'Nor anyone else at all? Either of you?'

'No,' Cristiana said.

'We didn't even speak of it to each other again until yesterday when we agreed together to give it to Lady Alice. Or rather, we agreed I'd ask John if we could trust her to deal fairly with us.'

'Where did you talk of it then?'

'In Cristiana's chamber again,' Sir Gerveys said. 'We must have been overheard the first time there, but not yesterday. Besides that the door was shut, Pers and Ivetta were on the stairs outside the chamber. No one could have come close enough to hear us.'

Frevisse thought better of asking if Pers and Ivetta could have heard them; asked instead, 'Where were Pers and Ivetta the first time you talked there?'

Cristiana and Sir Gerveys exchanged questioning looks. He shrugged and said, 'I don't know.'

'Somewhere together, I think,' Cristiana offered. 'They . . .' She broke off with a gasp, pressing a hand to her throat. 'I've forgotten her. She went to Pers and he's dead and I forgot her!' She grabbed Sir Gerveys' near hand into both her own. 'And you! You and Pers were together from when you were first knighted and now he's dead! Gerveys, forgive me, I never thought again about him being dead until now or said I was sorry for it!'

Sir Gerveys reached his other hand to touch her cheek. 'You've enough and more to think about. Don't grieve at a brief forgetfulness. Remember, Pers and I both knew that one or the other or even both of us could well be killed fighting in France or else in Ireland. That it happened here comes to the same. We always knew it could happen. I'm all right.'

Cristiana probably believed him no more than Frevisse did, but pity would not find out Pers's killer, and Frevisse asked, '*Did* you talk to Master Say about trusting Lady Alice?'

'Just before supper,' Sir Gerveys said.

'Did you talk of this paper any other time or place, or with anyone else besides Master Say? Either of you?'

'No,' Cristiana said. 'No one.'

Sir Gerveys rolled his head from side to side on the pillow. 'No one.'

But had Master Say said anything to anyone? Or could they have been overheard? 'When did you talk with him? And where? Both times.'

Eyes closed, Sir Gerveys said, 'The first time was in the garden. Just after Cristiana and I agreed together to ask his help.' Whatever Mistress Say had given him was starting to work; he had begun to grope for his words. 'Then yesterday here in the parlor.'

Willing him not to slip into sleep yet, Frevisse leaned over him. 'Did you tell him where you would go to get the paper? And when?'

'I said I'd fetch it in the morning. I didn't say from where.'

'What of Pers? Could he have told anyone?'

'Pers didn't know we were going anywhere until this morning. Nor he didn't know where until we were on the road.'

'You don't think he might have been deliberately killed because he had betrayed you? That whoever he told maybe wanted to be sure he didn't betray them?'

'How can you ask that?' Cristiana said, furious. 'How can you . . .'

Without opening his eyes, Sir Gerveys shifted a hand he could barely move onto Cristiana's arm and whispered, 'She has to ask. Help her. Remember, they meant to kill me, too. Don't fight her. Promise.'

Cristiana struggled at the words, only finally forcing out, 'I promise.'

'Because I can't,' Sir Gerveys whispered. His breathing evened into sleep. Cristiana leaned over, gently kissed his cheek, then stood up and made a small beckon from Frevisse toward the door, meaning they should leave. In silent agreement Frevisse went with her.

In the hall everything was ready for dinner to be served. Preparations for the royal visit had already taken over the kitchen, so the meal was simple: a green salad of lettuce, cress, fennel, onions, sage, and mint, and last night's roast beef in a garlic pepper sauce. The simpler food was as noticeable as the lack of ready talk at either the high table or along the lower ones. Servants served the meal quickly, everyone ate, grace was said, and the household left the lower tables to go about their afternoon business as if glad to be away.

There had been little talk at the high table and little was said now, except as they rose from their places Alice told Master Say, 'The wagons bringing more pavilions and all should be here this afternoon.'

'If you need aught . . .' Master Say made graceful gesture to show that all he had was hers.

'I know I have but to ask,' Alice answered as gracefully. The royal visit might have been the only matters in their minds. She looked to Domina Elisabeth and asked, 'Would you accompany me this afternoon?'

Domina Elisabeth was more than pleased to do so, and Frevisse was more than pleased to have both her and Alice go – two fewer people with whom to reckon in an afternoon that was not going to be simple.

Then why was she so ready to begin it?

Why hadn't she balked at Alice's order for even a moment?

Because Alice was right. She did have skill at finding things out.

It was not a skill she always used readily, but whoever had betrayed Cristiana and her brother had likewise brought on a man's death, even if they struck no blow themselves, and for both that death and that betrayal they very much deserved to be found out.

Cristiana, leaving Mistress Say in talk with a servant, was started toward the parlor door, but Frevisse said after her, 'Mistress Helyngton, I'd speak with you, please.'

Not stopping, Cristiana said, 'I'll see my brother first.'

Mistress Say turned from the servant. 'Cristiana, Ivetta is come back. She's gone to your chamber.'

Cristiana gave a soft cry of pity. 'Ivetta. Yes. John, would you—'

'I'll make sure all's well with Gerveys,' Master Say said. 'Go on.'

Cristiana and Mistress Say left and Frevisse followed Master Say into the parlor. A nun was not supposed to be alone with a man but it was a rule she had foregone before now when there was need. Sir Gerveys still slept and did not stir when Master Say laid a hand on his forehead. Low-voiced, Master Say said, 'He's not fevered,' and went toward the window, clearly expecting Frevisse to join him.

She did. She regretted she had come somewhat to like Master Say. He was a well-minded, well-spoken man. The affection between him and his wife was open, his kindness to Cristiana apparently unfeigned. But he had not gained all that he had here and his high place in the royal household without ambition. Even granting that the duke of Suffolk had a spy here in the Say household, there was the possibility that Master Say himself might have betrayed Sir Gerveys and Cristiana for the sake of that ambition, to further his place in Suffolk's favor. He could even have set the attack on Sir Gerveys today. That was an ugly thought and she could see no reason why he should, but there might be more layers of ambition and betrayal here than she yet guessed at.

'You have more questions for me?' he asked.

Watching his face as well as her words, she said, 'Sir Gerveys took counsel with you yesterday about whether Lady Alice could be trusted to deal fairly with them.'

'Yes.'

'He'd spoken to you about the paper once before that, though.'

'He'd spoken about having something with which he could deal with my lord of Suffolk, yes. He asked for my help. I said I'd give it.'

'Where did the two of you talk?'

'In the garden the first time. In here yesterday.'

'Did Sir Gerveys tell you he meant to fetch this thing today? That he was going to Ware this morning?'

'He said he would get whatever it was this morning. He didn't say where he would go.'

'Was there any chance you were overheard? Either time?'

'Not in the garden, and in here we kept away from the door and our voices down. I doubt we could have been heard.'

'Where were you standing?'

'Here. At the window.'

'Was it open?' A panel at each end was hinged to swing out and in these days of warm weather they mostly stood open, were open now. 'Could someone outside have heard what you said?'

'No one was likely in the garden then, and even if they were, the window is well above the ground.'

The window was, but that did not mean someone had not been in the garden. As if in answer to Frevisse's unsaid thought, Master Say added, 'It was coming to suppertime when we talked. Every servant should have been busy and accounted for, not free to be wandering in my wife's garden in hope of overhearing something.'

The house servants, yes, but, 'One of the yard servants?'

'Anyone so far from the byre and stableyards would likely have been noted. Besides, why would he have been? No one knew we were going to talk.'

'There were only you and Sir Gerveys here? Not Mistress Say, too?'

'My wife was with the children in the nursery. She came in as we finished.' Easily matching Frevisse's direction of thought, he added, 'Even if anyone had been listening at the door, she would have seen them as she came up the hall.'

She might equally as well have listened outside the door herself. But there was no point in pointing that out, supposing he did not think of it for himself, and Frevisse asked, 'You never said anything to your wife about this matter? Before or yesterday?'

'Given how secret the business was, I didn't see she should be burdened with it without there was need. I told her nothing either time.'

But if she *had* overheard them yesterday, what could she have done with the little they seemed to have said? Sent word to someone that Sir Gerveys was going somewhere this morning to get something? Who would she have told? And why? Master Say could only gain by serving Suffolk in this. Why betray him as well as their friends?

Frevisse stood silent a little while, looking away from Master Say and out the window, able to see from here the pasture and the busyness of men around two just-come wagons near Alice's pavilion there. By the time the king came there after his hawking, in less than two days now, there would be pavilions and food-piled tables, canopies probably, and cushions and very likely some of the Says' chairs. Some several score of people would eat and talk and laugh for an hour or so and then be gone, and within hours after that, a day at most, there would be only pasture there again, with no more than memory to tell anything had happened there at all. Suffolk would have his paper. Cristiana's daughters would be into Master Say's protection. Sir Gerveys would be free to join his lord in Ireland.

And the squire Pers would still be dead.

Whether or not she found out who was behind his death, that would not change.

She gathered up her thoughts and said to Master Say, 'I want to talk to Cristiana now.'

Chapter 16

Cristiana found Ivetta sitting on the chest at the bedfoot, huddled over and holding herself, crying so hard she gave no heed when Cristiana sat down beside her, embraced her, took off her disheveled headkerchief and coif and stroked her hair. Beth brought her something to drink and that finally quieted her wild sobbing, but when she was done with the drink she bent over on her pain again, rocking gently and sometimes moaning, and to all their urging to lie down or speak only shook her head from side to side, refusing.

Leaving her to it but keeping watch, Cristiana and Beth went aside to the window to talk with their heads near together. 'I'd rather keep the stronger syrup for Gerveys' pain, but she can't go on long like this,' Beth said. 'If she doesn't calm soon, I may have to give her more than valerian.'

'Her grief won't be the less when she awakens. It's maybe better to let her live through it to its other side.' If there was an other side to grief. Cristiana had yet to find an other side to her own yet, different though hers had to be from Ivetta's. She and Edward had been deep-rooted together. They had shared years and children and her grief was for loss of all she had had with him. Ivetta and Pers had shared far less, but that must be a whole source of grief in itself. Ivetta was grieving as much for what she and Pers would never have as for what little there had been.

'She's quieter than she was, anyway,' Beth said. 'The man who went with her told me that when she understood Pers was dead, she flung herself to the floor and started to scream and went on screaming until Father Richard dragged her to her knees and told her that Pers needed her prayers, not her screaming. She went to wild sobbing then. Our man got her away only because Father Richard told her nothing could be done with Pers' body until the crowner saw it and ordered her to go.'

They looked at Ivetta still slightly moaning and rocking to and fro. At barely a whisper, Cristiana said, 'I'm so frightened, Beth.' Of so many things now.

Beth laid a hand on her arm, offering a wordless understanding that was more comforting than any useless promise that everything would be well.

Someone scratched at the closed door. Ivetta's head jerked up and Cristiana stiffened, both of them too ready for more trouble. Beth simply went to open the door.

Dame Frevisse was there, alone and with no look of bringing more bad word. Beth stood aside for her to come in and as she did she said in small, pointless courtesy, 'Your stairs here don't creak, Mistress Say.'

'They're too new,' Beth said back with the same courtesy. 'The wood hasn't had to time to begin its shift and settle yet.'

Dame Frevisse looked briefly toward Ivetta, who had dropped her gaze again and huddled down more but not begun to rock again. Quietly Beth said, 'I'll see if she'll lie down now,' and went to her. Dame Frevisse joined Cristiana at the window.

Two women in black gowns, Cristiana thought. Two clots of darkness in a bright room. Two shadow-women, one lost in the shadows of widowhood, the other in the shadows of a holy life. If nuns were holy. Cristiana had had no convent training when she was small, had been taught at home by her mother and the parish's priest and had little to set to any nun's good beside all the fear and anger and humiliation she had had in St Frideswide's. Even knowing her bitterness was unreasonable, she did not care. Her life had so little reason left in it that she was past caring about reason and said uncourteously, 'You want to ask me your questions now.'

'By your leave.'

'By Lady Alice's leave,' Cristiana snapped.

'By that, too,' Dame Frevisse granted. She looked around the chamber. 'This is where you talked with Sir Gerveys both times about this thing?'

'Here. Yes.'

'Where?'

'Here,' Cristiana repeated impatiently.

'I mean where in the room?' Dame Frevisse said patiently back at her.

Cristiana took inward hold on herself. Impatience would not rid her of the woman. Better to help her, for all the good it would do. Then she'd go away. For the sake of that, Cristiana shut her eyes, trying to remember, and said, 'The first time we talked Gerveys was sitting on the chest where Ivetta is.' Except that Beth was gentling Ivetta to her feet now. 'I was in the chair. But it was close to the chest then.'

'How close?'

'Within reach of it.'

'So you didn't need to raise your voices while you talked?'

'We kept them low. Or . . .' Cristiana tried to remember how it had been. 'I don't know that we raised or lowered our voices. We just talked.'

'Was the door open?'

Cristiana thought but had to say, 'I don't remember. It would be shut, I should think.'

'And the next time you talked?'

'I was lying on the bed and Gerveys sat next to me.'

'Which side of the bed?'

'The near side.'

'Was the door open?'

Cristiana tried her memory again and this time was able to say, 'Ivetta closed it as she went out.' She nodded her head with the sudden satisfaction of being certain. 'Pers was there. I heard them speak to each other. So assuredly nobody overheard us that time. Gerveys had Pers on guard there and probably Ivetta stayed with him.'

Dame Frevisse went closer to the window and leaned a little out, then turned and looked to the chamber's other end, past where Beth was persuading Ivetta to lie down on the mattress pulled from under the bed's far side. 'It's the nursery beyond that wall?' Dame Frevisse asked, as if the occasional rise of children's voices did not make that plain.

'Yes,' Cristiana said.

'Were the children there both times you and Sir Gerveys talked?'

'I suppose so. Yes. I remember hearing them.' Cristiana let scorn into her voice. 'You think their nurse or the nursery maid overheard us?'

Frevisse returned dryly, 'Over the children? Or without the children noting one of them was listening at the wall? No.'

Leaving Ivetta lying quietly, Beth came to join them at the window. Cristiana held out a hand to her. Of late she had found herself needing to hold to people more than she ever had. The certainty of someone else's hand helped keep her fears a little at bay. Beth, bless her, took her hand but said, 'Today's too warm for your hand to be this cold, Cristiana. Should you lie down a time?'

She wanted to go back to Gerveys but only said, 'When Dame Frevisse is finished.'

'I think my last questions are for Mistress Say, by her leave.'

'Ask what you will,' Beth said in quiet acceptance.

'What's below us here?'

'The butlery.' Where wine and the better serving dishes and tablewares were kept.

'It's kept locked of course, except at mealtimes?'

'It is.'

'Who has the keys to it?'

'Myself and Master Fyncham, our household's steward.'

'You've no butler?'

'We've only lately become so large a household that we need one. Until now Master Fyncham had been able to see to it all. We mean to find someone shortly.'

Dame Frevisse fell silent, looking down in thought. Cristiana and Beth waited. When she looked up, it was to Beth again. 'Will you give order for your servants to answer whatever I ask them?'

'Of course.'

'I'd talk first to Master Fyncham. Now, if I may.'

'Of course.'

Cristiana wanted to scream at their careful courtesy to each other. What use was their courtesy against death? Edward was dead, and now Pers, and Gerveys could have been, and she had no hope anymore that she'd ever be rid of her pain. Never, never, never rid of her pain and her fear and she was going to die and . . .

She took her hand back from Beth and wrapped her arms around herself, holding herself as bodily together as she was trying to hold her mind, fighting against falling into shattered, sobbing pieces like Ivetta.

A manservant's head and then the rest of him bobbed into view up the stairs.

'Yes, Nol?' Beth asked.

The man bowed while saying, 'That Master Helyngton and his sisters and all are come visiting. Master Say said to tell you.'

Beth dismissed him with, 'Thank you,' laid a hand on Cristiana's arm, and said when Nol was disappeared down the stairs, 'Cristiana, you don't have to see them. You can stay here, if you want.'

'Yes,' Cristiana said. If she never saw Laurence, Milisent, or Ankaret ever again, it would be too soon. But even as she thought that, a second thought came to her and she started for the stairs, saying, 'They've come to take Mary and Jane away again!'

Beth caught her by one arm. 'They wouldn't. Not with Lady Alice here, surely.'

'It's more likely,' Dame Frevisse said quietly, 'that they've heard about the attack on Sir Gerveys and come to learn for certain how badly he's hurt.'

'Whyever they've come,' Beth said, 'you'd best to go calmly if you go at all.'

With effort, Cristiana gathered her scatter of fears into semblance of calmness, said even-voiced, 'Of course,' gently freed herself from Beth, and went.

Frevisse thought Cristiana's rigid back as she left the bedchamber belied her suddenly quiet voice. Mistress Say went with her, but Frevisse paused to look to where Ivetta lay, an arm across her eyes, not stirring. She must be mercifully asleep at last, then. If so, it was one of the day's few mercies, Frevisse thought as she followed after Cristiana and Mistress Say, making no haste to overtake them, so that by the time she was in the screens passage at the stairfoot, they were gone into the hall where – judging by the rise of voices – the Helyngtons already were.

Three Say servants, lingering in the passage to overhear what they could, went kitchenward at sight of Frevisse. She lingered in their place, hearing through the wooden wall Cristiana declare, 'This is no matter of yours. Go away, all of you.'

Both a man and woman started to answer that and Master Say to say something, but Cristiana went on angrily, 'And you, Master Colles. You don't have even their poor excuse for being here. Take your wife and get out of here. No, Milisent, don't tell me what I should do or not do. You and Laurence and your miserable husband have done what you shouldn't and I'll fight you all to have it undone!'

Master Say began, 'Cristiana, have done . . .' as Frevisse went into the hall. Laurence Helyngton, his two sisters, Master Colles, Master and Mistress Say, and Cristiana were clotted together angrily not much beyond the wide doorway, with Laurence Helyngton in the full flow of his anger cutting across Master Say's words with, 'There *will* be fight needed. I'm not giving up my rights in this.'

'Your thefts, you mean!' Cristiana mocked.

'My rights!' Laurence snarled back.

Sir Gerveys appeared in the parlor doorway. What it had cost him to hobble there was not a good thought, and as he leaned heavily against the door to rest, Alice swept past him into the hall. Immediately, Master Say, Laurence, and Master Colles bowed to her and the women made curtsy, a pause before angers would probably flare again, except a small flurry of yellow-gowned child burst past Frevisse and flung herself at the younger of the Helyngton sisters with a glad exclaim of 'Aunt Ankaret!'

Ankaret went to her knees to meet Jane's embrace with her own, exclaiming with matching pleasure, 'Birdling!'

Cristiana started forward with a hand out to snatch her daughter away, but Mistress Say held out an arm, stopping her at the same moment young Mary came past Frevisse, saying in distress as she went to her mother, 'I tried to stop her. I couldn't. I'm sorry.'

Behind her, Mistress Say's little daughter by her first husband hovered in the doorway uncertainly. Cristiana drew Mary close to her, soothing, 'It's no matter. She just wanted to see Ankaret.' But there was no soothing in the hating look she threw at the other woman.

'They haven't come to take us away, have they?' Mary asked her mother with open fear, holding tightly to her. 'You promised they couldn't anymore.'

'They've come to ask after your uncle is all,' Master Say answered with reassuring ease before anyone else could.

'And to see how you and Jane do, too,' Milisent put in. 'You're both still Master Helyngton's wards. He still has say over where you are and all, remember.' The words were to Mary, but Milisent's gloating was at Cristiana as she went on, 'If it seems you're unsafe here, why, of course we'll have to take you away . . .'

'They're not unsafe!' Cristiana cried. She held out a hand toward

Jane, still in the circle of Ankaret's arms. 'Come here, Jane.'

Master Say did not wait for Jane to obey or Ankaret to tighten her hold, simply stepped forward and lifted Jane into his own arms with a smile at her that made Jane smile back while he said, 'Of course they're safe here. It's Hoddesdon where the trouble was and none of us are going to Hoddesdon, are we?' He rubbed noses with Jane who giggled. He set her down with a gentle push toward Cristiana and a look at Laurence. 'Nor are we making trouble here. Are we?'

Alice answered, rather than Laurence, saying in a sweet lady-voice, 'Of course no one's making trouble. Save me of course, bringing the king's visit on you. Master Helyngton, isn't it? And Master Colles. Come, you can see for yourselves how well Sir Gerveys does. Mistress Colles?' she added to Milisent. 'Will you come? And I fear I've forgotten your name,' she said to Ankaret.

She drew them all away with her to Gerveys, still watching from the parlor doorway. Cristiana stayed where she was, her daughters clutched to her. Frevisse saw small nods of agreement pass between Master Say and his wife, and then he followed Alice and the others away and Mistress Say went to Cristiana, put an arm around her shoulders, and guided her and her daughters out of the hall with soft words and soothing voice, gathering up her own daughter as they went.

Frevisse stood aside, out of their way, then drifted toward the others outside the parlor but already too late. Whatever had passed among them had been bitter as well as brief, to judge by Laurence's face as he spun away from Sir Gerveys and started back down the hall, as oblivious of Frevisse as he passed her as black thunderclouds would have been. Lady Alice, Master Say, Milisent, and Milisent's husband came away, too, less openly furious, but Ankaret stayed, and Frevisse was just near enough to hear her plead, soft-voiced, 'Gerveys, you know I won't let any ill come to Jane. I love Jane.'

'What I know, Ankaret,' Sir Gerveys said unsoftly, 'is that you couldn't stop whatever Laurence might choose to do.'

Ankaret opened her mouth to answer him, then sighed instead of spoke, and followed the others away.

Watching Sir Gerveys' face, Frevisse said, 'She has a fondness for you.'

'Far more fondness than I've ever cared to return,' Sir Gerveys replied.

Frevisse could not tell what layers of feeling or meaning might lie behind his words, if any, and offered, 'May I help you back to the settle?'

He assessed her probable strength with a quick look before answering, 'Yes. Thank you.'

She was tall for a woman and not weak. Her shoulder to lean on made Sir Gerveys' hobble back to the settle easier than it might have been; and when he had sat down and swung his good leg up, she helped him lift his hurt leg to lie beside it. Somewhat short of breath with the effort, he thanked her and leaned back into the cushions with a sigh far heavier than Ankaret's had been.

'How does the pain?' Frevisse asked.

'Whatever salve Beth put on it has helped. And whatever she put into the wine.'

His eyes were closed but his face and voice were taut, showing he was nowhere near to sleep. If he had been, Frevisse would have left him to it. Since he was not, she asked, 'Did the Helyngtons truly come here because of the girls, do you think?'

'I think they came here to see how nearly dead I might be. They were surely disappointed to find me not nearly so dead as they'd like.'

'Ankaret would seem to prefer you alive.'

'Having few thoughts of her own, Ankaret holds hard to such as she has. Long before she was married to Master Petyt, she decided I was her knightly hero. I never gave her cause to think she was my damsel – in distress or otherwise – but she's never grown past the hope that someday she might be.'

'But she won't be.'

'She won't be.' Sir Gerveys' certainty sounded complete.

'And Mistress Colles? What do you think of her?'

Sir Gerveys' mouth wryed, as if he had tasted something sour. 'Milisent? My guess is that she's every bit as sharp and nasty as Laurence is.'

'How did the quarrel begin between him and Cristiana's husband? At least, I've supposed there was quarrel that started all this.'

'No outright quarrel, as such. Their fathers were brothers and the Helyngton lands were split between them. Edward's father, as the elder brother, got the larger portion. Laurence wants the properties rejoined. That's reasonable enough in its way, but neither Edward nor Cristiana would be so base as to marry a daughter of theirs to any of

Laurence's sons, whatever the gain, Laurence being what he is.'

'What's Milisent's interest in it all?'

'The trouble it makes.'

'And her husband? What does Master Colles stand to gain?'

'Suppose Mary becomes wife to Laurence's son Clement? In a year or two she'll be old enough to give him a child. With that child the Helyngton lands become joined for once and all again. The baby doesn't even have to live much beyond birth. That it's been born and lived at all gives Clement a claim to the land that will be hard to break, supposing there's anyone interested in doing so. You see?'

He was watching her, to see how much she understood. Frevisse nodded. That was the way the law stood: once a living child was born to a marriage, the husband had claim to the wife's land for his life.

'Suppose then that Mary dies,' Sir Gerveys went on. 'Clement would be a wealthy widower, not yet of full age, his lands and himself still controlled by his father. Milisent has a daughter who by then will be marriageable age. Let her be married to Clement, and eventually Milisent's dower lands will be rejoined to the rest of the Helyngton inheritance, leaving only Ankaret's portion still apart.'

'That only works if Mary dies.'

'Yes. It does,' Sir Gerveys said steadily. 'But I suspect she would.'

He was ascribing a cold calculation to Laurence Helyngton and Milisent that chilled Frevisse. 'I suppose Jane,' she said slowly, 'would be put into a nunnery.'

'As soon as Mary bears a living child it would be the nunnery for Jane,' Sir Gerveys agreed. 'Until then, they'll keep her, on the chance Mary fails to produce that living child. Whichever way it goes, Laurence and Milisent mean to have enough wealth, before it's done, to fund their ambitions.'

'And Ankaret? What does she get from it all?'

'Probably nothing. No matter what they've promised her, that's what she'll get.'

'You're crediting them with a great deal of villainy.'

'Laurence and Milisent had Cristiana declared mad, seized her children by force, put her away where they never meant her to be found, and tried to force Mary into an ugly marriage. What do you think they won't do, having done all that?'

'Do you think it was Laurence who set up the attack on you?'

'I haven't yet thought of anyone else it might have been.'

'It would mean Laurence has a spy in this household.' Maybe the same spy as Suffolk had, selling his services several ways.

'If Laurence had a spy here, he wouldn't have had to come himself to see how I did. More likely would be he had someone set nearby to watch for me.'

'Someone who saw you and Pers leave here and took word to Laurence? How far is it from here to Mistress Helyngton's manor?'

'Not above two miles if you take one of the forest paths across country.'

An easy walk for a fit man. Even an easy run. Laurence could have heard in a half hour or less that Sir Gerveys had ridden out.

'It would have to be two men watching,' Sir Gerveys said. He sounded as if he had been thinking about it. 'One to go to Laurence. One to follow us to know which way we went once we reached the main way.'

'That wouldn't explain how they knew you were only going to Ware and would be coming back, to have the ambush ready for you.'

'True,' Sir Gerveys granted.

Which brought them back to someone here who knew where they were going and that they would return. In silence she and Sir Gerveys looked at that thought for a time before she said, 'It would be comforting to think it was no more than a chance attack by thieves or outlaws.' And added, before Sir Gerveys could, 'Except that thieves or outlaws would have chosen a plain traveler, not two armed and well-horsed men.'

'One of whom died anyway, despite he was armed and well-horsed,' Sir Gerveys said. He closed his eyes and leaned his head back into the cushions. Talking had distracted him a while. Now his face was taut and drawn again, and Frevisse, knowing how grief ebbed and flowed with tidal strength, guessed grief for his lost squire and friend was back in full flow of hurt worse than his leg's pain and with a murmured apology for having tired him, she rose and left.

Chapter 17

Frevisse wanted next to talk to Alice but met Master Say in the screens passage, returning alone from seeing Laurence and the others away. Neither his face, voice, nor manner showed what he might be thinking about them, and Frevisse did not ask. To her question about Alice, he said, 'My lady is returning to her pavilion.' And added before Frevisse could ask, 'Not alone. I've sent a man of mine with her and one of her women was waiting in the garden, she said.'

Frevisse thanked him and by hurrying overtook Alice as she was about to go out the garden's far gate, held open for her and her lady-in-waiting by Master Say's man. Frevisse called out and Alice looked back, said something to the woman and man, and leaving them there, came back toward Frevisse, meeting her in the middle of the garden and asking without other greeting, 'You've learned something?'

Voice pitched for no one else to hear, Frevisse said, 'Nothing that answers very much. You were in talk with Sir Gerveys when the Helyngtons came. Did you learn anything from him that might help?'

Alice turned away. Not merely aside but with her back to Frevisse, as if suddenly, deeply interested in the tall purple bellflowers in the garden bed there. 'No,' she said.

But there had been something and Frevisse asked, 'Then what?'

Alice drew in a deep breath, let it out, and said, her back still turned, 'We were talking around our two sides of the same problem.'

'Cristiana?' Frevisse asked, supposing it had to be her. Or else Laurence.

'The king,' Alice said.

When that made no more sense after a moment's thought than it did before, Frevisse said, 'I don't understand. Why the king?'

Alice hesitated, then said, 'Among the talk you've heard, surely you've heard some against the king?'

Frevisse hesitated in her turn before saying slowly, 'I've heard displeasure at how costly his household has become. And some displeasure against the lords around him.' A great deal of displeasure, and most particularly against the duke of Suffolk, she did not add.

'There's that being said, yes. But there are other things, too. One is that he's childish as well as childless.'

Foregoing protest at that thought, Frevisse asked, 'Is he?'

Alice paused, then said slowly, 'I'm not sure what he is.'

From Alice, who had surely spent as much time at the royal court as anybody, that came strangely; and when she said nothing more, Frevisse only waited. Too much of a land's safety and its people's well-being depended on how strongly a king ruled. She didn't want to hear there were widespread deep doubts about King Henry.

But slowly Alice went on, very plainly feeling her way among the words. 'It's not that he's truly childish. He understands very well, I think, what's happening in the government and with his household and in England and Normandy. The thing is . . . I don't know that he cares.'

'But . . . he's the king,' Frevisse said. 'He *has* to care. It was the duty he'd been born to.'

Alice, who understood that as well as she did, turned around and said steadily, as if she had thought through the words long before now, 'I think caring was worn out of him years ago. He's been king since he was nine months old. I remember Father saying that the lords around Henry from the time he was small were working to bring him up to be the king they wanted him to be. They didn't care about the man he might have been. They wanted him to be the king his father was. The trouble is that he's nothing like his father. He was king before he was ever anything else and I think in some way it's made him not anything at all.'

'Alice,' Frevisse said, warning she had become careless of her voice.

Alice lowered her voice but went on, in need of saying a thing she had kept to herself too long. 'He gives grants and favors to anyone who asks for them and doesn't care whether he's already given the same grant or favor to someone else or that he can't afford to give more away. He lets happen around him whatever happens. He's careless of what the men around him do to his government or about France or about . . . anything. He's careless of the queen and she's just a girl and doesn't understand why. He hides in his chapel or whatever church is nearest. He—'

'He hides?' Frevisse asked. The one unargued thing about King Henry the Sixth was his piety, his devotion to his prayers.

'He hides,' Alice said flatly. 'There's nearly no one dares disturb a king when he's kneeling before an altar. Or even just sitting there. And Henry sits before altars a great deal. On the floor or on a cushion, his hands folded in his lap, sometimes his head bowed, sometimes his gaze on the crucifix. Maybe he's praying all that time. There are those who think so. I think he's hiding from everything people are forever asking of him.'

She said it bitterly, harshly, with the certainty of long thought, nor did Frevisse have anything to set against it except her own unwillingness to believe it. Because if the king was not governing the realm . . . 'Who governs then?' she asked slowly. 'Your husband?'

'My husband and some several other lords with him. The duke of Somerset. The bishop of Salisbury. The bishop of Chichester. But Suffolk mainly, yes.'

'You surely weren't saying any of this to Sir Gerveys.' Whose lord was presently King Henry's heir to the crown and sent to Ireland, as away from the king and out of power as possible.

'He probably knows it well enough,' Alice said. 'And so does York. But, no, I was saying none of that to him. What we were doing, without ever saying it outright, was feeling out if we both feared the same thing.'

'Do you?'

'Yes.'

'And that is?'

Rather than answering, Alice plucked a nearby leaf of balm and stood rubbing it between her fingers, as if taking more interest in its sweet smell than in her answer, until finally she said slowly, answering only indirectly, 'I promise you I would help Mistress Helyngton to keep her children even if this paper were no part of it. I'd see to it she recovered keeping of her lands and all her widow rights. What I fear . . . What I fear is that my lord husband will think Laurence Helyngton and whatever use can be made of him is worth more than justice to Mistress Helyngton, no matter what promises I've made.'

Able to imagine only distantly the pain of being married to someone you no longer trusted, but certain of the pain nonetheless,

Frevisse hid her twist of anger at Suffolk and said with open and utter pity, 'Alice, I'm sorry beyond words.'

But Alice's pain was of no use to Cristiana, and after a moment Frevisse asked gently, 'What are you going to do?'

All Alice's pride and force of will showed as she straightened her shoulders and lifted her head. 'I'm going to do all I can to convince my lord husband, first, that Helyngton is a worthless little man and of no use to him. Then, that my word was given on his behalf and had better be kept.'

Or Alice would not be the only one unhappy in their marriage.

She did not say that but it was in the long look she shared with Frevisse before abruptly leaving with no word of parting.

Left with her thoughts and worry, Frevisse slowly returned to the house. Uncertain what to do next, she was saved from decision when she came into the great hall where the trestle tables were being set up for supper and Master Fyncham, the household's steward, came toward her. He was an older man, always quietly dressed in a plain doublet and surcoat. His duty, under Mistress Say's direction, was to oversee all the varied servants' work that went on in the house, from everything done in the great hall to the keeping of the other rooms to work in the kitchen and bakehouse. In a larger household he would have had various officers under him, each seeing to their own people's duties and reporting to him before he reported to Mistress Say; nor did Frevisse doubt that the Says would come to a household of that size before long. By what she knew and had seen of John Say, she did not think he had reached the end of either his ambitions or abilities.

Of Master Fyncham she knew less, but his bow was respectful as he said, 'Mistress Say has bid me help you in any way I can, my lady. I'm told you have questions for me.'

Still worried for Alice, Frevisse tried to remember what questions she had while asking, 'Is there somewhere we can talk alone?'

'You mean unheard?' Master Fyncham asked. 'Nor overheard?'

'Nor overheard,' Frevisse agreed, appreciating the distinction. To be unheard meant no one else could hear them. To be not overheard meant no one could listen unseen and unknown.

'May I suggest here?' Master Fyncham said. He pointed at a place along the hall's wall not far from where they stood.

Frevisse nodded her acceptance. The servants had finished setting up the tables there, were gone across the hall to set up the others.

With the noise of that and their own talk, they'd not hear anything said quietly on this side of the hall, and when she and Master Fyncham were there she asked without hesitation, 'Did Mistress Say tell you what my questions would be about?'

'I understand her grace the duchess of Suffolk has asked that you find out what you can about this regrettable trouble that's come on Mistress Helyngton and Sir Gerveys. I'm to answer whatever you ask.'

Frevisse hoped his readiness to oblige was matched by his readiness to observe what went on around him and she said, 'From the attack on Sir Gerveys today, it's certain that someone here in the household spied on him and betrayed him. I want to find out whom.'

Master Fyncham slightly bent his head to show he understood and was ready for her questions. Ready with answers, too, she found as she asked him about the household servants: how many there were; how long they had been in the Says' service; what Master Fyncham thought of each of them. There were nine in all – six men and three women.

'But Cook is rarely anywhere but in his kitchen,' Master Fyncham said.

Frevisse agreed they could discount the cook.

They all, including the cook, had come with Mistress Say from her first marriage's household, Master Fyncham said.

Frevisse asked, 'Even Master Say's own man?' Who attended on Master Say personally and particularly, just as one of the maids was especially Mistress Say's.

'No,' Master Fyncham granted. 'I misspoke there. His former man, Symond, died about a year ago. A fever, I fear. Edmund came to Master Say but lately, on recommendation from Master Say's brother.'

'Master Say's brother?'

'Master William Say. Dean of the Chapel Royal.'

Master Fyncham was pleased with that. Frevisse was not. Did William Say of the king's chapel have ambitions that might be served by setting a spy into his brother's household? Not necessarily to spy for himself but for someone higher whom he wished to please? Someone able to help him to higher place than Dean of the Chapel Royal?

'And the children's nurse?' Frevisse asked. 'She of course came from Mistress Say's first marriage?'

'She did.'

The coolness of Master Fyncham's reply led Frevisse to ask more and she soon gathered that Nurse was somewhat his rival and neither she nor the nursery maidservant was included in his count of household folk because she ran the nursery as almost a separate domain from his.

'Did she and the nursery maid both come with Mistress Say?' Frevisse asked. 'With her daughter from her first marriage?'

'Nurse did. The girl was hired here.'

And so knew people hereabout, had ties here that others in the household lacked and had been only the thin wall away from where Cristiana and Sir Gerveys had talked together. How she would have had chance to listen with children and Nurse all around was another question, but at least it was another question.

'And you, Master Fyncham,' Frevisse asked, 'when did you join the household?'

As if taken by surprise at a question directly about himself, the steward's face went almost blank. Then he broke into a smile and answered, 'I was tutor to both Master Say and his brother in their boyhood. When they passed the age for needing a tutor, I became Master Say's clerk and on to being his steward now that he has household of his own.'

Frevisse set aside as unlikely the thought that Master Fyncham was the one betraying his master's trust but, 'What of Mistress Say's steward? What became of him if everyone else came to her new household and you took his place?'

'Master Heton,' Master Fyncham said with affectionate warmth. 'He stayed on to show me how matters were done and which servants were good for what and their weaknesses and all. Then he retired to his daughter's house with a goodly annuity from Mistress Say. We write occasionally. I tell him how things go on here and he tells me how much he enjoys doing very little.'

No angered and dismissed former servant there, then. Not that Frevisse could see how, from outside the household, the man could be making the present kind of trouble. Suborning a servant to do it for him perhaps? Having been suborned himself by . . . whoever was behind all this?

That was stretching possibilities past probableness's bounds and Frevisse let it go and asked, 'Do you know who waited on Mistress

Helyngton in her chamber the first day she was here? Who went to her chamber for any reason? Besides her own woman, I mean.'

For the first time Master Fyncham was perplexed. 'That was . . .' he paused to count, '. . . four days ago. I'll have to ask. Someone will possibly remember.'

'Yesterday, just ere supper, Sir Gerveys talked with Master Say in the parlor. I know Mistress Say joined them there.' And Frevisse dearly wished there was a discreet way to ask if Mistress Say had paused to listen outside the closed door. 'Did anyone else go to – or near – the parlor while they were there?'

Master Fyncham considered that before saying, 'I think not. The high table was being laid then, if I remember rightly, and I was over-seeing it. So, no, no one would have had chance to listen at the door. If that's what you mean?' he added.

'That is very much what I mean.'

Did it help he was clever enough to understand her questions' purposes? Or would his understanding let him slant his answers away from the strict truth as he knew it, either thinking to please her or else to hide something? She could not know, could only go on, though she was fairly well run out of things to ask, left with only, 'Has anyone done anything out of their usual way these past few days?'

Master Fyncham frowned slightly. 'Out of their usual way?'

'Been where they shouldn't be. Done something they usually would not. Or been gone when they were expected to be here. Anything out of the ordinary way by anyone.'

'Young Reignold was gone two days without leave,' Master Fyncham said, 'but he was drunk at the alehouse in Wormley the while and that is *not* unusual.' The steward looked across the hall to where a youth was setting out along the table the thick-sliced rounds of hard bread that would serve instead of plates for lesser members of the household.

'Reignold?' Frevisse asked, somewhat diverted by so grand a name for a servant.

'I understand his mother had ambitions for him,' Master Fyncham said. 'More than he has for himself, I fear.'

If asked, Master Fyncham could probably tell her something like-wise particular about every servant under him and anything about the household's running that she might ask – from how much firewood was used in a day to how many sacks of flour were needed for bread-making in a week to the cost of cinnamon at last autumn's buying of winter supplies. She only wished that he had told her something that helped her toward knowing who in the Says' household was a traitor.

Chapter 18

Frevisse waited until after supper to go on with her questioning. By then everyone in the household knew what she was doing and that Master Say had ordered their cooperation. Some gave it simply enough, answering whatever she asked and making an end of it. Others wanted to tell her anything and everything, and worst of those was the nursery maid, Ellena. Leaving Nurse to settle the children to bed, she was only too glad to stand on the stairs below the nursery telling all about her hope of seeing the world now she was with the Says, 'who'll go to their other manors and even to London sometimes, surely, so finally I'll see more than only Broxbourne, you don't know what it's like to stay in one place and never go anywhere. Oh, but you're a nun, so maybe you do know.'

Only with effort was Frevisse finally able to determine out of all her talk that at the times it mattered she had been in the nursery and nowhere else and had heard nothing from the other room, so she said.

After that, Frevisse spoke with Nurse, blessedly more briefly but to the same end – she had never heard aught through the wall and added she was sorry the children's noise must go the other way readily enough, try though she did to keep them quiet.

Quiet was what Frevisse wanted, but when she had thanked the woman and gone down the nursery stairs, she encountered Cristiana and Mistress Say in the screens passage, going together toward the outer door. They neither of them heeded Frevisse. Mistress Say was intent on pale-faced, distressed Cristiana, and Cristiana intent, Frevisse saw, on following her brother supported between Master Say and Master Fyncham, going out the door above the yard.

Frevisse followed them without considering whether it was her business or not.

Outside, the foreyard was gathered full of blue evening shadows under a yellow sky, the sun only lately sunk from sight beyond a westward stretch of woods. Mistress Say held Cristiana at the top of the stairs with an arm around her waist while the men made their slow way down to where two saddled horses and a groom were waiting. Frevisse moved to Mistress Say's other side and asked quietly, 'Where are they going?'

Not distraught but no happier about it than Cristiana, Mistress Say answered, 'To the church. Sir Gerveys means to keep vigil by Pers' body tonight.'

His squire would have done as much for him if things were otherwise, but given Sir Gerveys' hurt, it was unreasonable. All the protests against it had probably been made already, though, and so Frevisse kept silent, watching the men help Sir Gerveys onto his horse. At his grimace of pain as he settled into the saddle, Cristiana gave a short, sobbing gasp, but he took up his reins, shaking his head to something Master Say said at him.

'John wanted to go with him,' Mistress Say said as the groom swung on to the other horse. 'Gerveys wants him here instead, so Sawnder is going. He'll keep watch on Gerveys and fetch help if need be. Cristiana, all will be right when it's done.'

Despite what it was going to cost Sir Gerveys in his body, he would feel the better in his mind for keeping vigil over his dead squire, Frevisse supposed. It was on Cristiana the vigil would be hardest. Sir Gerveys raised a hand to her in farewell and she waved back, but when he had turned his horse toward the gate, she pressed her clenched hands together to the base of her throat and struggled against sobs as she watched him and the groom ride out of the yard.

Sir Gerveys might have done better to have spared her this, Frevisse thought. Cristiana was not weak. She'd not have held this well together against everything if she were weak, but she needed respite, needed chance to regain her balance and her strength. Frevisse drew Mistress Say a few paces aside and asked softly in her ear, 'Can you give her something to make her sleep tonight?'

'I've already given word for it,' Mistress Say said softly back. 'For her and Ivetta, too. Better for them both if they sleep soundly tonight.'

Better for everyone and a mercy for Cristiana and Ivetta, Frevisse thought, and left them as Master Say and the steward returned up the stairs. Domina Elisabeth had long since gone to their chamber above the parlor. Ready both to be done with questions for tonight and to go to bed, Frevisse went that way, too, hoping Domina Elisabeth would have no questions of her own or want to talk about the day's happenings.

If Domina Elisabeth did, one assessing look at Frevisse changed her mind and she merely said, 'We've badly scanted the Offices today. Would you rather do Vespers and Compline, or only Compline and go straight to bed?'

It was usually Domina Elisabeth rather than Frevisse who scanted the Offices when life became over-full, but this time Frevisse almost answered she'd rather do neither. What she wanted was to be done with thinking for today, to be asleep as soon as might be; but habit was too strong in her and she said, 'Both, if you please.'

That was the better choice. The day's-end comfort of Vespers' and Compline's prayers quieted her with their reminder of all there was beyond the passing troubles of everyday. By the time they came to Compline's soft, sighing end, twilight was drawn well on toward dark and they readied for bed in silence before Frevisse went to slide the shutters across the windows. At the eastward one, she paused to look out at the yellow flecks of torchlight around Alice's pavilion in the field and said a silent prayer for her cousin's good sleep, then another prayer for Cristiana and Ivetta's rest and yet another for Sir Gerveys at his grieving vigil.

Quieted with prayers, she slept well, but all the questions and worries were waiting for her in the morning. As she and Domina Elisabeth walked down the hill to early Mass through a thin mist burning off in a haze of gray and gold, she wished she could simply, for the while, accept the day in its early and uncomplicated peace until after Mass. But she was already turning over in her mind what she had learned yesterday and still finding there seemed nothing there that answered the questions that mattered.

If she could find out Suffolk's spy in the household, she would be better along, she supposed. Especially if he confessed not only sending word to Suffolk but to betraying Sir Gerveys into yesterday's ambush and who had set it. That would answer everything. Unfortunately, she did not see she was anywhere near to learning Suffolk's spy. She'd not even found out how Sir Gerveys and Cristiana had been overheard on that first day although they must have been.

Or else one of them was betraying the other and Frevisse could not believe that. Or Master Say had told Suffolk himself. She must not let go of that possibility, not when she as yet had no sure thought on how yesterday's betrayal had happened either. Since Pers had been keeping guard on the stairs outside the bedchamber, Sir Gerveys must have been heard talking with Master Say. By whom? Mistress Say? Or Master Fyncham? He said himself he was busy in the hall then. Or, again, had Master Say betrayed them? Did his ambition run so high that he'd do a thing so base? But why? She couldn't see what he would gain by it. Or Mistress Say either, working by herself without his knowledge.

Were the two treacheries one person's doing, or were they done separately, by different people?

She needed to find out Suffolk's spy.

If Master Fyncham could tell her who had waited on Cristiana that first day, she would have *someone* then who might have overheard Sir Gerveys and her, rather than the no one she presently had.

As for who had betrayed Sir Gerveys' going to Ware, there was a possibility that would not disappear, no matter how she avoided it: Alice had known Sir Gerveys would go somewhere to fetch the paper. Did she set some of her men to watch for him, follow him, steal it if the chance came?

Frevisse told herself that Alice had no reason to take that trouble or risk.

But she might have. She might have some reason of which Frevisse had no thought at all.

But then why ask Frevisse to find out who was the traitor?

Because she knew Frevisse would try, whether told to or not, and this way she protected herself from suspicion?

No. Frevisse refused to believe Alice was that base.

Except the thought was there, and she knew it would not leave her until she had found out who *was* the traitor. Until then, she would not be free of a doubt she did not want to have.

The twisting of her burdensome thoughts kept her company into Broxbourne. The mist was still thick there in the valley, not yet given way to the just-rising sun. Only the bell-pentice on the church's west gable end showed above the grayness as she and Domina Elisabeth crossed the wide, long village green, and only gradually did they see the gathering people outside the church – far too many for Mass on an ordinary weekday. More folks were hurrying through the mist from the houses around the green, and Domina Elisabeth said, in the same moment that Frevisse thought it, 'There's something wrong.'

They quickened their walk but when they reached the crowd's edge could not see among them and Domina Elisabeth demanded of a man craning his neck to look past the people in front of him, 'What's happened?'

'That knight,' he said, still craning. 'They're saying he's dead. Him and Master Say's man that was with him. Both dead, they're saying.'

Domina Elisabeth and Frevisse crossed themselves. Domina Elisabeth began to draw back, ready to leave, but even while crossing herself, Frevisse went forward. The man, finally looking at her, said eagerly, 'I'll see you through, my ladies,' and began to nudge and shove a way among the other lookers-on with, 'Let the ladies through. Move yourself, Jamy. It's nuns.'

Domina Elisabeth stayed where she was, and when Frevisse came to the crowd's fore-edge, she nearly wished she had stayed with her, rather than see Sir Gerveys sprawled out face-down on the broad, small-graveled space between the crowd and the church door, a single, wide stab wound in his back, with – beyond him, crumpled down close to the church wall, almost against a buttress thrust out from the wall there – the man Sawnder who had ridden from the manor with him yesterday.

Father Richard knelt praying between them. It was probably at his order the crowd was keeping back, but among the excited talk around and behind her, Frevisse heard a woman say, 'It was Father Richard found them. When he was coming to the church.'

'The mist and all,' someone else said. 'That's why nobody saw 'em sooner.'

'That's the fellow that was hurt yesterday,' another woman put in.

And from a man, 'They did for him all the way this time, that's sure.'

Forcing aside the jumble of talk and her own sickened horror, Frevisse forced herself to look straightly at Sir Gerveys. The wound in his back was enough to have killed him, and if it went all the way through him, then most of the blood there had been was soaked down through the gravel, because there was none around him. But why had he been out here? His vigil would have been kept in the church beside Pers's body. How had he come to be outside, in the open, ten feet and more from the church? Sawnder's body was aside from the door, crumpled down as he must have fallen and still in the thick early shadows cast by the just-rising sun. When possible, bodies were left as they were found until seen by bailiff, constable, or crowner. Whoever had the duty here in Broxbourne was surely sent for, would be here soon, but Frevisse, meaning to claim Lady Alice's authority if need be, went toward Sawnder's body.

Father Richard looked briefly up but bowed his head again without speaking, probably supposing she was come to pray with him. She was praying, for both Sir Gerveys and Sawnder, because souls so suddenly, brutally sundered from the flesh were in special need of the prayers they had not been able to make for themselves at their death. But prayers did not keep her from seeing, now she stood over him, how the back of Sawnder's skull was crushed inward, a ruin of brain and bone and black-dried blood hidden until then by the shadows.

From a distance the shadows had hidden, too, the blood spattered across the wall above him, telling he had been killed here, struck a rising blow from behind while facing the wall, Frevisse judged. Someone had come at him silent-footed in the dark, or more probably at a run, to be across the gravel before Sawnder, hearing them, would have had time to turn before they struck him. With a club it must have been, to smash his skull that thoroughly. He had probably been dead before he knew he was dying.

As for why had he been out here when he should have been keeping his watch on Sir Gerveys inside the church, he had maybe come out to relieve himself, or to stretch his legs. Had his murderer been waiting for just that chance to kill him and clear the way to Sir Gerveys? Or – more likely – had they been readying to go in and taken their chance when Sawnder happened to come out?

She realized she was not thinking these were casual murders but that Sir Gerveys had been their certain target and Sawnder merely in the way. After yesterday, what else could she think?

Because her eyes were still cast down as she turned from Sawnder's body, she saw the long scrape marks in the gravel just beyond the stone step to the church's door. Two long scrapes that ran unevenly beside each other from the wide area around Sir Gerveys' body scuffled right down to the hard-packed earth to another scuffled area outside the church door.

She shifted that in her mind. Not to the door. From it. She could only guess why Sir Gerveys had come outside. Had Sawnder after all made some sound, given some warning cry that brought Sir Gerveys to find out why? Or had his murderer feigned a call from already-dead Sawnder to draw Sir Gerveys to his death?

Not murderer, though. Murderers. More than one. The scuffled marks made that certain. They were still there only because everyone but herself and Father Richard were still standing back from the bodies; the first passing feet would rub them out but for now they were easy to read and showed there had been a struggle just outside the church door. Then someone had been dragged – surely Sir Gerveys – those ten feet or so from the door, still alive and not unconscious or there would not be the other marks of struggle where he had died. That meant at least two men, one on each side of him, gripping him by either arm and dragging him rapidly that distance. He must have been dragged rapidly; otherwise the long scrapes would have been more scuffed, like where he had fought again and been killed.

At least two men against him, then, and more probably three at the least. Two to hold him, another to stab.

Sir Gerveys had come out of the church and been seized, or maybe they had gone in after him and dragged him out. Either way, he had fought them at the church door, been dragged, and somehow fought them again, hopeless though it must have been, already hurt as he was and in the dark and outnumbered. The thought of how it must have been made Frevisse both sick and angry. Sick with thought of Sir Gerveys' fear and fury and despair. Angry at whoever had done it to him.

Why hadn't he cried out, either in anger as men did in a fight, or for help? Even in the mist, a shout would have been heard and people would have come, maybe not in time to save him but the bodies would have been found, an alarm raised. Why had there been no outcry?

Intent in her thoughts, she had not noted Father Richard rise to his feet and startled a little when he touched her arm. 'Please, my lady,' he said gently. 'No one expects you to bear this. Withdraw, if you will.'

Her refusal of his kindness was tempered by his horror-blanched face. With feigned womanly uncertainty she said, 'No. Thank you. I'm well enough. But should we . . . could we . . . turn Sir Gerveys onto his back? To leave him lying face down . . . seems . . . wrong.'

What she wanted was to see if there were other wounds in him, but her excuse served well enough; despite no constable or bailiff had come, Father Richard called one of the men from the crowd and between them they gently turned over Sir Gerveys' body. There were other wounds. Two in his chest. One in his stomach. A fourth that looked to be where the sword or long dagger through his back had come out.

Someone had been very thorough in making him dead.

She also saw why he had made no outcry.

A narrow, black bruise circled the front and sides of his neck where something had dug deeply into the flesh. A rope, Frevisse guessed. Guessed now, too, that Sir Gerveys' murderers had taken him from behind and in the church while he prayed beside Pers' body, after Sawnder was dead. If he had heard any footfall behind him, he would have thought it only Sawnder, until the rope went around his neck and strangled off any cry.

Shedding blood in a churchyard was bad enough, but a killing inside a church was a dire thing, a crime worse than plain murder: that even the kind of men there had been here seemed to have shied from it. Instead, they had throttled Sir Gerveys to silence and dragged him from the church to kill him.

The business had not gone all one way, though. Sir Gerveys' dagger, hidden under him until he was rolled over, was still clenched in his right hand and there was blood on the blade. Not his blood either. Hand and dagger had been under his right shoulder, clear of the pooled blood from his wounds and with no blood on his hand at all. The blood on the dagger had to be someone else's, and Frevisse found herself grimly glad that someone among his murderers had not gone unscathed.

A man, his clothing rumpled with hurried dressing but with all the bearing of authority about him, came through the crowd. The village's bailiff or constable, Frevisse supposed, and she faded back, leaving to Father Richard whatever business came now, slipping away not to rejoin Domina Elisabeth but into the church. All was still in shadows there, save for the lamp-glow above the altar at the church's far end and a soft light among the rafters from the rising sun, enough for her to see the bier in front of the rood screen with Pers's shroud-wrapped body on it and the candles guttered out in their tall stands at its four corners. Going closer she saw Sir Gerveys' sword, too, lying on the floor, beside and evenly aligned with the bier. He would have put it in front of him as he knelt in prayer, facing the altar with his back to the door. Come at from behind, half-throttled and dragged backward in the first moment of attack, Sir Gerveys had not even been able to lay hand on his sword.

Frevisse tried and failed to keep from imagining the sudden rope around his neck, his throttled struggle for air and to break free as he was dragged from the church. Only outside, when nearly it was too late, had he been able to grab out his dagger and strike at least one of his murderers, fighting for his life even as he was dying, stabbed and stabbed and stabbed and stabbed again, from behind as well as front, maybe more than one man killing him while others held him. Then they had left him there, lying in his blood; and she wanted them found out and made dead in their turn, never able to kill anyone again. And might God forgive her for wanting that so much.

Chapter 19

The rumpled man and Father Richard came into the church, the priest looking around worriedly for sign of the bloodshed.

'All the killing was done outside,' Frevisse said. 'There's no blood here.'

'You've looked?' the rumpled man asked tersely.

'I can see,' she said. Guessing how little the help of an unknown nun would be welcomed, she was already leaving. Only because she did not know if the man would think of it for himself, she turned back at the door and said, 'Whoever smashed Sawnder's head was maybe badly spattered with his blood. It might be worth giving out word you're interested in anyone seen with blood on them.'

'My good lady!' Father Richard exclaimed, distressed.

But the other man's eyes narrowed in assessment of her as he said, 'That's something I'd thought of, but my thanks.'

'And whatever was used to hit him,' Frevisse persisted, 'if it was a club and wooden, blood doesn't clean easily off wood.'

'If it was wood,' the man said back, 'it's likely ashes in someone's fire by now.'

'Unless they're stupid. They might be.'

The man acknowledged that with a grim twist of his mouth.

'Sir Gerveys wounded someone, too,' Frevisse added.

'It looks he did, aye,' the man said.

'A wound in a man will be harder to hide than a club.'

'It will. I thought that, too,' the man said. 'You were more than praying out there, weren't you?'

Frevisse bowed her head for answer to that and left. Outside, the bodies had been covered and were being guarded by two men. The crowd had begun to drift apart and away to their day's work, but

Domina Elisabeth still waited and asked when Frevisse joined her, 'How could you to look so closely at those men? They were so horribly dead.'

Slowly considering her answer, Frevisse said, 'Sometimes, by God's grace, I see more in such things than most people do. Sometimes, by looking, I find out the murderer.'

'Yes, I know. You've done it other times. But here . . . the blood . . .' Domina Elisabeth broke off. Then, after a moment, she said quietly, 'God's gifts aren't always easy to bear. Come. We'll maybe be needed at Baas.'

They were beyond the green and village, were started up the hill, when Master Say and two of his men came at a fast canter toward them. They drew to the roadside but the men drew rein and Master Say demanded at Domina Elisabeth, 'Is it true? Sir Gerveys and Sawnder, they're both dead?'

'God have mercy on their souls,' Domina Elisabeth answered.

Master Say swore and made to ride on, but Frevisse put out a hand, stopping him long enough for her to ask, 'Please. One question. Did you tell anyone at all that Sir Gerveys and Pers were going to Ware yesterday?'

'No one,' Master Say snapped and heeled his horse forward into a canter again.

It was pity, Frevisse thought heavily, that their being there sooner rather than later would make no difference to Sir Gerveys or Sawnder. She and Domina Elisabeth walked on, the golden morning's warm beauty all around them. The last of the mist was gone from the valley and there was birdsong in the hedgerows and Sir Gerveys was dead and would never see it or any other morning.

Sir Gerveys. Pers. The man Sawnder. All dead because of a secret Cristiana's husband should never have had.

At least Frevisse supposed that was the reason behind their deaths. But Alice now had the thing, whatever it was. Even if the ambush yesterday had been because of it, there had to be some other purpose to Sir Gerveys' death.

Unless . . .

She tried to stop her thoughts from going that way but they were already gone.

Unless someone had wanted to be certain that whatever was in the paper went unknown. Sir Gerveys had handed it to Alice still sealed, but there were ways to open and reseal something without destroying the seal if one had the skill and time enough. Who was to say Sir Gerveys hadn't that skill? And he had had the time yesterday while the thing was in his hands. It maybe didn't even matter whether he had read it or not. That he had had the chance could have been reason enough for someone to decide he should be dead. Had that been the purpose of the attack on him yesterday? To seize the document and kill both him and Pers against the risk they'd read the thing?

Did she believe Alice was that treacherous?

No. She did not. But she could believe someone *with* Alice might be under orders about which Alice knew nothing.

Had Alice told any of her people about her dealings with Sir Gerveys and Cristiana? If she had not, there was still the chance that whoever had overheard them in talk – if someone had overheard them – had passed word to one of Alice's people, under orders from Suffolk.

Or maybe the paper had nothing to do with yesterday's ambush and these murders. There was still the quarrel between Cristiana and her husband's cousins. More than once, Laurence Helyngton had looked as if he wished Sir Gerveys dead. Had he gone past wishing?

If only she knew either the who or the why of yesterday's attack, surely other answers would come. As it was, uncertain whether last night's murders had had anything to do with yesterday's ambush, she did not know which way next to go with her suspicions and questions. What if the ambush and the murders were done for separate reasons by altogether different people? What if Laurence Helyngton was behind one and someone working for Suffolk behind the other? Or could Laurence be working for Suffolk in both matters? Or what if Laurence Helyngton had had naught to do with either one of them? What then?

Again she came back to reminding herself that, little though she liked the thought, Master Say might be less than the friend he seemed to be. If Cristiana's lands and her daughters' marriages were so valuable to Laurence Helyngton, they would be equally valuable to Master Say, a man very capably making his way in the treacherous world of ambitions around the king – a world where the more you had, the better placed you were to lay hands on yet more.

She and Domina Elisabeth were met in the manor's great hall by servants wanting better word than had so far come. Domina Elisabeth

174

could only assure them that, yes, Sir Gerveys and Sawnder were dead. One of the women began to cry, but Domina Elisabeth asked for Mistress Say and Mistress Helyngton and she and Frevisse went on to the parlor, where Mistress Say, pale and tight-lipped, was in low-voiced talk with Master Fyncham. She broke off when she saw them, read their faces without needing to ask more, and said one brief thing more to Master Fyncham, who bowed in answer, bowed to the nuns, and left.

When he was gone, Mistress Say asked, 'There's no doubt?'

'None,' Domina Elisabeth said. 'I'm sorry.'

On the settle where Sir Gerveys had lain yesterday, Ivetta was sitting crumpled and crying in a worn out way, but at Domina Elisabeth's words she gave a louder, more convulsed cry, and began to rock, her arms wrapped around herself. Cristiana, seated alone on the bench below the window, her back to the world outside it, was doing nothing, her hands lying together and unmoving in her lap, a dry-eyed stillness to her face that was worse than any tears. She had raised her head when the nuns came in but now went back to staring at the floor in front of her and said, empty-voiced, out of whatever distant place she was in, 'I want Mary and Jane here with me. I want to be the one who tells them.'

'I'll bring them,' Mistress Say said immediately.

Cristiana's eyes stayed down, her voice empty. 'Only them. I want no one but them. Ivetta, go away with the nuns, please.'

That startled Ivetta into pausing her tears to stare at Cristiana. Using that pause, Domina Elisabeth went to her, raised her to her feet by a hold on her elbow, and started her out of the room. Ivetta did not protest, but Frevisse said, 'I'll stay with Cristiana until her daughters come.' Because she was not sure Cristiana should be left alone.

Mistress Say, following Domina Elisabeth and Ivetta out, agreed with a nod of her head.

Frevisse's hope then was that Cristiana would stay silent, but at the small sound of the door's latch falling Cristiana said without lifting her eyes from the floor, 'How was he killed?'

Because there was small use in trying to keep it from her Frevisse answered steadily, 'He was taken by surprise and outnumbered. He fought back. There are signs of that. He wounded at least one of them before he was cut down. Stabbed from behind and in front. It must have all gone very quickly.'

That last was something of a lie, but there were longer deaths than his had been and Cristiana needed what little comfort could be given.

Cristiana said nothing.

Frevisse waited but the silence drew out, until Mistress Say returned with Mary and Jane. They came in, their eyes large with knowing something was wrong. Cristiana stood up and held out her arms to them and they both ran to her and Frevisse slipped past Mistress Say and out of the room. Shutting the parlor door again, Mistress Say followed her, saying as Frevisse stepped down from the dais, 'Dame Frevisse, wait, if you please.' Frevisse turned and Mistress Say joined her, going on, 'Domina Elisabeth has taken Ivetta to Cristiana's chamber and I've ordered wine taken to them. I'll take some to Cristiana in a while. Then . . .' Her gaze went past Frevisse and with the weight of more worry she said, 'Oh, no.'

Frevisse turned to look, too. Nothing more threatening than a maidservant approaching, wiping floury hands on apron, was there, but sight of her reminded Frevisse of what she had utterly forgotten – tomorrow the royal hunting party would be here. By rights, that should have been all that Mistress Say thought about and did today. Instead she had murders and griefs and distracted servants on her as well.

Given all that, she sorted out with admirable calm the woman's question about the meat pies that were supposed to be baked this morning, moving down the hall while they talked. Frevisse drifted behind them, wanting to know what Mistress Say had wanted with her, but as Mistress Say finished about the pies, Alice swept into the hall past a manservant trying to announce her. Briskly waving aside everyone's curtsies and bows, she said, 'Beth, I've heard what's happened.' She turned her briskness briefly on Frevisse. 'You've been there, I hear. You'll tell me more later. But for now, Beth, we've tomorrow to deal with. With all the present upset, you have hardly hope of seeing to all that needs doing. I'm taking it on myself to send people of my own to Ware and Hertford for everything we'll want tomorrow in the way of food.'

'Bur . . .' Mistress Say began.

'There's ale in plenty to be had in Broxbourne and Hoddesdon, I understand. The barrel of wine I promised you will be here today and with that the matter of drink is taken care of. For the rest, the cook-shops and bakeries in Ware and Hertford should suffice. After all, this is no fine dinner we're giving, only something between these people's hawking and their riding on their way. Meat pies and sweet pastries in quantity and much to drink. That will be enough. And not only do I mean to send for it, I'll pay for it, too. No.' She cut off the beginning of a protest from Mistress Say. 'Having brought this on you at a bad time, I will pay for it. Your share will be to see to everything when it all arrives and that it's served forth in suitable manner tomorrow. All I presently need from you is agreement over what to order. Where can we talk?'

She made to go toward the parlor, but Mistress Say, overwhelmed until then, said, 'Cristiana and her daughters are in there.'

For a bare moment, at mention of Cristiana, Alice faltered, briefly betraying the control with which she was holding her brisk certainty in place, but the next moment her smooth mask was in place again and she turned away from the parlor, saying, 'The buttery, then. That's out of everyone's way.'

She was going as she said it, taking Mistress Say with her. Over her shoulder, Mistress Say said back at Frevisse, 'Master Fyncham wants to talk to you, my lady.'

Without looking back, Alice added, 'Best tell him the change of plans, so he can make the cook happy.'

Left standing alone, Frevisse supposed that if she waited there in the hall Master Fyncham would find her or someone who could tell her where he was, but she was in no humour to wait for anything and followed Alice and Mistress Say from the hall. In the screens passage Alice and Mistress Say were already gone into the butlery. Frevisse went past it and out the rear door to the wooden stairs down to the small cobbled yard between the hall and kitchen where sight of Master Fyncham coming up saved her going down.

He had the harassed look of a man who had been dealing with a cook unhappy over too much to do in too little time, but he was not immediately pleased with Frevisse's word of the changed plans either, saying at her disbelievingly, 'It's to stop? Everything Cook has in hand is to stop? None of it's going to be needed?'

Frevisse saw the double danger of telling a cook that not only was everything thus far planned now changed, but that everything thus far done was no longer wanted, and she said hastily, 'Just say that nothing else should be started. Finish what's in hand and then wait to hear what Lady Alice and Mistress Say decide.'

Master Fyncham looked hardly happier with that, but since it let him shift trouble away until later – and maybe altogether to Mistress Say – he said willingly enough, 'Wait here, pray you,' and returned down the stairs and across the yard to the kitchen. Soon thereafter Frevisse heard what sounded like a heavy pot-lid crashing down on a heavy pot, and immediately after that Master Fyncham came from the kitchen in haste, across the yard and up the stairs and past her without pause. She followed him into the screens passage where he shut the door between them and the kitchen yard, drew and released a long breath, and said, 'Done.' He settled his ruffled dignity, gathered his thoughts, and asked, 'Do you mean to go on with your questions from yesterday despite today's grievous trouble?'

Hiding her surprise at his thought she might stop, Frevisse said only, 'Yes.'

'Then . . .' Master Fyncham began, but they were at the foot of the stairs to Cristiana's bedchamber and as he spoke her door opened and a servant with an empty tray came out and started light-footed down the stairs. 'Nol,' Master Fyncham said, 'I was just about to speak of you.'

A cheery-faced young man, Nol sobered at the sight of Master Fyncham and came more slowly to the stairfoot while Master Fyncham asked, 'You served Mistress Helyngton and her brother in her chamber the day she first came here, didn't you?'

Nol went from sober to wary, and well he might, Frevisse thought. To be suddenly questioned about a man who had just been murdered was very good reason to be wary. But after his pause, Nol remembered to bow to her and answered, 'Aye, I did. I took them wine, I think. Like I did just now to that Ivetta. She's in a bad way.'

'You remember that day, though?' Frevisse asked. 'When Mistress Helyngton first came here?'

'Oh, aye, I remember,' Nol said, beginning to be brightly confident again.

Frevisse wished she was. What was she supposed to ask him? Did you happen to listen outside the chamber door? Are you the duke of Suffolk's spy? Did you betray Sir Gerveys yesterday? She settled for, 'Tell me how it was. You went up to their room . . .'

She left that hanging and Nol's eagerness took over. 'Aye. I went up the stairs, that Ivetta right on my heels: Thought she'd go right over the top of me, the way she hurries, you know. I nipped quick to stay ahead of her and went in.'

'You *knocked* and went in,' Master Fyncham said.

'I didn't, I don't think,' Nol said. 'The door was standing open and . . .' At Master Fyncham's look, he reconsidered and said quickly, 'I must have knocked. I did, surely.'

Before that could go farther, Frevisse asked, 'How did they seem to you when you went in?'

Nol paused to think about that. 'Worried, I'd say. Tired, too. Her anyway. Is he dead, her brother, the way they're saying?'

'He's dead,' Frevisse said. 'Yes.'

'Sawnder, too. That's bad all around.' Distress took over Nol's face. 'How'd it happen? Nobody—'

'We'll know more when Master Say returns,' Master Fyncham said. He looked at Frevisse, but she slightly shook her head; she had no more questions for Nol just then, and Master Fyncham dismissed him with, 'That's enough for now. See if there's any help you can give in the kitchen.'

Nol screwed his face into a mock distaste at that but bowed and left, and behind him Master Fyncham said, 'I fear he talks more than he listens, does young Reignold. A young man with ability enough but making no effort to put it to good use.'

'Reignold,' Frevisse said. She'd have known Nol was only a slighting of his name if she had troubled to think about it. 'You said something about Reignold yesterday. In the hall.'

'Did I?' Master Fyncham sifted through his memory. 'I did, yes.'

'You said he was gone, drunk, for two days.'

'In Wormley. In the alehouse there. The alewife finally sent to ask he be removed, he was in the way. He was brought back sodden. If he does as much again, I'm not sure we'll keep him.'

'When was this?'

'When?' Master Fyncham searched his memory again. 'He went missing just after Mistress Helyngton came. He had his half-day off and didn't come back. It was two days later the alewife sent to be rid of him.'

Frevisse hoped she hid her hot glow of triumph. If this Nol's half-day was added to his two other days, he had been gone almost three days. Time enough for what she thought he might have done. 'I need,' she said to Master Fyncham, 'someone to ask more closely about his days in Wormley. Someone who'll question closely and find out certainly whether he was truly there or not. Not from the alewife but others. And if he wasn't there, did he hire a horse somewhere?'

'You think Nol has something to do with all that's been happening wrong here?'

'There's chance, yes. But don't say that to anyone. Not before we know more.'

'Assuredly. I'll see to it. I'll go myself. The household will hold itself together that long. If you'll make it well with Mistress Say?'

'I'll make it well,' Frevisse promised.

Master Fyncham gave a firm nod and left, leaving Frevisse to hesitate at what to do next. If Nol was Suffolk's spy, that was one question answered, with maybe more answers to come from it. But this was too soon to hang all her hopes on it and she went up the stairs to Cristiana's chamber, stopped outside the shut door and listened, able to hear Domina Elisabeth urging Ivetta to lie down, to rest. Frevisse knocked and went in.

Domina Elisabeth was standing near the window. Ivetta was pacing the room's length, hands wrung together, tears and grief still marring her face. As she turned at the far wall and began to pace back, Frevisse asked, 'Ivetta, the servant who was just in here, have you seen him before this?'

Ivetta stopped where she was, staring at Frevisse as if the question confused her.

'The man who was just in here,' Frevisse insisted. 'Did you know him?'

'The man?' Ivetta groped through her grief. 'He's one of the household.'

'Have you seen him here, in this room, before today?'

Ivetta looked at her blankly. Frevisse tried again.

'The day Mistress Helyngton first came here, she and Sir Gerveys talked in here together. Only the two of them. That man brought them wine. He went up the stairs just ahead of you and then left again. Do you remember?'

Ivetta finally took hold on what she was being asked. 'That man. That day. No. I didn't see him go up the stairs. I *heard* him, is what. Heavy-footed as a plough-horse he was. It was going down he passed me going up. I don't remember he brought any wine.' She looked suddenly surprised, then her eyes narrowed and a flush of anger covered the mottling of her tears on her face. 'There was the other time, too. When Pers and I . . .' Her tears rose again. 'Pers and I, we saw him skulking at the foot of the stairs here two days ago. When Mistress Helyngton and Sir Gerveys were talking in here then. Pers went after him to see what he had to say for himself, but all he said was he was wondering what *we* were doing on the stairs. Pers thought it was more than that, though. Pers thought he was hoping to spy and said he'd keep an eye on him after that. Only he . . . Pers . . .' She gulped on returning sobs and said with a burst of fierceness, 'You ask that fellow some questions! You ask him *hard*.'

'Pers went after him,' Frevisse said, unready to leave her to her tears, just yet. 'But you stayed at the door, yes?'

'What? Stayed? Yes. Right there. He never got near, he didn't. He never . . .'

Ivetta gave up and collapsed in heaving sobs on the chest at the bedfoot. Domina Elisabeth went to pat her shoulder. Frevisse stayed where she was, considering that if Ivetta was to be believed, Nol might well have heard what passed between Cristiana and Sir Gerveys the first time they talked here together but neither he nor anyone else could have heard them here two days ago. That meant it must have been Sir Gerveys' talk with Master Say afterward that was overheard.

Or that it was Master Say who had betrayed them.

Chapter 20

Frevisse came down the stairs from her talk with Ivetta troubled by her thoughts. She did not want to ask the questions she needed now to ask of both Alice and Master Say, because even if she heard answers that freed them from her suspicions, she was afraid she might likewise hear the lie behind the words. Voices could treacherously give away what someone meant to keep hidden. What if she heard a lie behind either Alice's or Master Say's voice? What then?

But Alice had set her to this. She had to believe in Alice. And Master Say? If she were honest with herself, she had to admit she didn't want to find him treacherous. Given a choice, she would rather lay everything on Laurence Helyngton.

But if she could find no way someone had overheard Sir Gerveys in talk with Master Say . . .

In the screens passage Mistress Say was just coming from the butlery. If not happier, she at least looked less desperate than earlier as she said, 'Dame Frevisse, my lady of Suffolk was just saying she would talk with you.'

'Frevisse,' Alice said from the butlery doorway. 'If you please,' and drew back into the small, windowless room where the daily supply of wine and ale was kept under lock and key, and there were shelves of the household's platters, plates, cups, and goblets of everyday use and the locked chests of greater valuables. Alice in her gown of finest linen and her cauled headress with soft trailing veil was so ill-matched to the workaday place that Frevisse paused in the doorway. Alice, able to see her face by light of the shallow oil lamp burning on the narrow desk set to one side of the room, asked impatiently, 'What is it?' Then added, without waiting for answer, 'Come in. Close the door. We'll be as private here as anywhere.'

Frevisse obeyed but said as she did, 'I was only wondering how long it's been since the duchess of Suffolk was in a butlery.'

'Two weeks ago at Ewelme,' Alice said with asperity. The manor she had inherited from her father. 'Discussing with Master Gallard if we had wine enough on hand to last until the autumn wine fleet comes from Gascony. Would I were there now, with naught to think about but how the harvest is going, rather than all this.' She stood up. 'What have you learned? Anything of use?'

Frevisse matched her asperity. 'It's very likely your spy here is a servant named Reignold, usually called Nol. It also seems *un*likely he knew Sir Gerveys was going to Ware.'

Alice waited for more. When nothing more came, she demanded, 'That's all?'

'Yes.'

'But you suspect . . .' Alice left a gap for Frevisse to fill.

'Yes,' Frevisse said. 'I suspect.' And did not go on.

'What?' Alice demanded. 'Say it.' And then, sharply, 'I already know it. Ask it.'

'Did you tell anyone that Sir Gerveys would go somewhere to collect this paper? Or set someone on to watch him when he went?'

'I did not. Not either of those things.'

'Did Master Say tell you about his talk with Sir Gerveys that evening? That Sir Gerveys would be going the next day for the paper?'

'Master Say told me nothing about it. No one did. I didn't know when Sir Gerveys would go, or where. Nor did I speak to anyone at all about what passed in the orchard with Mistress Helyngton.' Alice's voice sharpened more. 'Nor – before you ask it – did I have anything to do with the murders last night. Once I had the document, Sir Gerveys was no longer a concern of mine.'

Returning sharp for sharp, Frevisse challenged, 'He was someone's concern. Someone who maybe feared he had read the thing and had to stop him from ever telling what it said. Someone not willing even to risk the possibility he'd read it.'

Eyes and voice cold, Alice said, 'Yes, that has to be considered, doesn't it? But I haven't even read the thing myself. Look.' She slipped her right hand into the close-fitted wrist-band of her gown's left sleeve and brought out the packet Sir Gerveys had given her yesterday. She held it out. 'I haven't even opened it. My lord husband *ordered* me not to open it,' she added with a bitterness perhaps more betraying than she meant it to be. 'Do you truly think I'd order a man's murder – two men's murders – for any reason, let alone for a thing I haven't even read?'

Frevisse went very near to her and said at nearly a whisper, urgently, 'Alice, not you. But someone could have come here with you already ordered to murder if there was need.'

Alice went deeply still. Except her eyes widened. Then she closed them and pressed a hand over her mouth.

'Always remembering,' Frevisse said, watching her face, 'that the order may have been to kill *anyone* who might have read the thing, not simply Sir Gerveys.'

Eyes still closed, Alice said, 'God forgive me.'

Cold clenched around Frevisse's heart. There were some answers she did not want to hear, but she asked nonetheless, 'What?'

Alice opened her eyes, lowered her hand, and said in a voice as cold as Frevisse felt, 'God forgive me for what I thought just then. That my husband could have ordered such a thing. That he could have sent someone with me with order to make sure anyone who might have read the letter had no chance to tell what it said. For just that moment I believed it possible.' She looked down at the packet in her hands; turned it over; turned it over again; then held out a hand to Frevisse and asked, 'Might I use your knife?'

Meaning the short-bladed knife carried in a small sheath in the pouch hung from Frevisse's waist, mostly used at meals. Most people had them, but Alice was too fine a lady to be troubled with a belt pouch, and Frevisse silently handed her own to her. Equally silent, Alice slid the blade under the packet's cord, slit it, then slid the blade under the wax seal, breaking it and letting its pieces and the cord fall to floor.

'Since I was more than halfway to believing my husband could have given such an order,' Alice said, handing back Frevisse's knife, 'I mean to see what has us all so frighted.' She began to unfold the packet.

This was Alice as Frevisse had mostly known her – a woman clear of thought and quick of decision. And finally she understood why Alice had seemed not herself here. These few days past she had been more than merely worried. She had been afraid.

For her husband? Or *of* him?

Alice let the packet's cloth wrapping fall to the floor, too, only the small-folded paper that had been inside it in her hands now. She unfolded it to the black-inked writing on it and began to read. Unable to see the words, Frevisse watched Alice and by the oil lamp's soft glow saw the stark deepening of every line of Alice's face, aging her out of her carefully kept middle years into seeming of the woman she would be if she lived to grow old. Her beauty was still there, kept by her bones, but laid over it, etched into it, was . . . grief. Grief first. Then anger. Made the worse by Alice letting neither of them loose.

Instead, she seemed to draw them inward, where their burning must have been scalding her heart, if her eyes, when she looked up from the paper to Frevisse, were anything by which to judge. 'He's betrayed us,' she said. 'He's betrayed the king and us and everyone.'

'Who?'

'Suffolk. And the duke of Somerset. The two of them together.' Stiffly, carefully, Alice began to fold the paper closed again. Her voice stiff and careful, too, she said, 'Shall I tell you what it says?' But the anger was beginning to burn through her control. She did not wait for Frevisse's answer but went on, bitter and harsh. 'It's a rough writing out of an order to Somerset in France. He's the king's governor of Normandy. Of all our towns and castles and fortresses and troops in France. This orders him to set Sir François de Surienne . . .' With hands that trembled now, Alice unfolded the paper again and read, 'set him to that Breton business we agreed to ere you went into France, that an end may be made once and for all to this.'

She stopped. Frevisse waited, but Alice only stood staring at the paper, until Frevisse asked, 'What does he mean by 'an end'? An end to what?'

Alice looked up from the paper. 'To the French war. That attack on a border town in Brittany this last March – the attack and the sacking afterwards that broke the truce so badly there was no mending of it – it wasn't some piece of over-bold foolishness by Surienne, the way the first reports told it. He's been one of our best captains of mercenaries for years. He was even made a Knight of the Order of the Garter two years ago. I never understood why. Now I do. They were readying him – my husband and Somerset. Even then they were readying him for this.'

'I don't understand,' Frevisse said, though she was beginning to.

'That breaking of the truce,' Alice said. 'It was deliberate. Surienne attacked that town by surprise, captured it, stripped it of everything worth stealing. The French demanded apology and reparation from Somerset as the English governor of Normandy. Somerset refused to do anything about it. Nor was he ordered to it, the way he should have been, by the king. Or my husband. Finally King Charles, as he was bound to do, began to attack our border fortresses in return. You have to know this much about it, surely.'

'I knew the truce had been broken and that the war had started up again.' The way the war had been starting up now and again for the past twenty years and more, so that this time had not been worth any more thought than the other times had been.

'The war started up again because we broke the truce *on purpose to start it up again*. Surienne's attack was meant to goad the French into attacking us, and they have, and Somerset is doing nothing to stop them. I didn't understand why. Nor would Suffolk talk about it.' Alice made as if to pace but there was no room for it, and she went on angrily and with growing despair, 'I don't know the tally of how many fortresses and towns we've lost by now. In a matter of weeks, Frevisse. Weeks! After all these years of laying claim to the French crown and fighting to get and hold Normandy, Somerset has been all but *giving* everything back to the French. He and my husband. They planned it. That's what this paper tells me. That they planned it, all of it. Surienne's attack and everything that's happened since then. They've wanted for years to be done with the war and this is their way of doing it.'

'But why? Why break the truce? Why end the war by losing it?'

'Because losing it is the only way we can be done with it. We're never going to win it.'

'But we had the truce. And the king's marriage to Margaret of Anjou to make it good . . .' A French princess who had brought nothing to the marriage but the hope of peace and the promise of an heir to the throne. Except that there was no heir yet. And now there was no peace either. 'We've held Normandy for decades. Why lose it?'

Alice's voice hardened. 'Holding Normandy costs money. When the war was new, when towns were being taken and sacked and lands were being seized, there was plunder in plenty. Enough to mostly pay for the war and make men rich into the bargain. But everything has been stalemated for years now. The money goes out for holding onto Normandy but no money comes in from it. The king's honor requires we hold what's left of his kingdom in France, but the king's household has taken to spending more money on itself than comes into it and who's going to tell king or queen or any of the lords around them – including my husband – that the money has to go into the French war instead?'

The words, long-dammed and now unleashed, were pouring out – far more than Frevisse wanted to know and surely far more than Alice ought to be saying but bitterly, angrily, Alice went on, 'Do you know why Parliament wouldn't give any money to the war this year? Because for years they've watched almost everything they give go into the royal household's pleasures, not the war. When the duke of York was governor of France, the King and his Council rarely sent him enough of the money he was promised to pay the soldiers and for supplies and all. He paid for things as best he could, much of it out of his own lands and money. I promise you that Somerset is not about to make that sacrifice. Not him nor any other lord. Instead, he and my husband have set up to be done with Normandy as fast as may be. They mean to save themselves the trouble and expense of the war by *losing* it, and never mind the dishonor and betrayal in what they're doing.'

Alice ran out of breath and words together. Frevisse looked down at the paper clenched in her rigid hand and said gently, as she would have handled a wound, 'Alice, that's much to take from the little that's there. It says none of that . . .'

'Put everything I haven't understood of what's happened these past few months together with what it *does* say and suddenly there's sense where there wasn't any,' Alice said fiercely, 'I promise you, it says enough. It even says it several different ways. They must have been trying out ways to say it without putting it straight into words. Suffolk and whoever else was there. There's more than only his hand here. That's what this is – their trial and error at giving the order for betrayal. They didn't dare send it through a messenger by word of mouth or put it in clear words, lest it was captured on the way. But once they'd done it, why did they have to be careless with this?' She shook the paper, hating it and angry at their foolishness. 'Why did they have to leave this lying where someone could find it?'

A discarded piece of paper that should have been burned but was not and instead became the thing on which Cristiana had hung her hopes of her daughters' safety and brought on – probably – the deaths of three men.

Weary with the weight of it all, Frevisse said, 'Likely each of them thought someone else had seen to destroying it.'

Sounding weary, too, with the kind of weariness that comes with defeat, Alice said, 'But no one had. And now what am I going to do?'

Chapter 21

Frevisse had no useful answer to Alice's desperate question. Even if there were enough on that paper to prove Suffolk's treachery, anything Alice might do against him would come back on herself and their children. Let him be found guilty of treason and he would be sentenced to death and everything he owned stripped from him – nobility, properties, reputation. He would be dead and his family dishonored. His destruction would be theirs. And even if Alice risked that, even if she – or someone – denounced Suffolk, would it be of any use? He was presently all-powerful in the government. Who in England had anything like sufficient power to bring him down now that the duke of York was sent away to Ireland?

Alice's place and power came through her husband. Frevisse had none at all. What could they do that would change anything for the better? But there were lives being destroyed in France and countless people betrayed. To say nothing, do nothing . . .

'The king,' Frevisse ventured. 'If you could tell . . .'

Alice unhesitatingly shook her head against that. 'No. He . . .' She broke off, shaking her head more, rapidly refolding the paper and thrusting it back into her sleeve. 'No. I have to think.'

She pushed past Frevisse, seized open the door, and left. Frevisse, slow with thought, picked up the cloth that had been around the paper, folded it and hid it up her own sleeve while pushing the cord and wax seal aside with her foot, out of sight under a chest sitting along the wall. Better no one knew the packet had been opened.

Still slowly, still thinking, she blew out the oil lamp, turned to leave, and found Mistress Say in the doorway.

Uncertainly, Mistress Say asked, 'Lady Alice . . .?'

'She's just gone . . .'

'Gone out. I know. She passed me without a word. Is there something more wrong?'

'About tomorrow? No. She's gone to set everything in hand,' Frevisse said quickly, coming out of the butlery. And added, to take the talk away from Alice, 'How is it with Cristiana and her daughters?'

'She's told them about Sir Gerveys. They've cried. The girls have. Not Cristiana.' That lack of tears worried Mistress Say as much as it did Frevisse. Grief turned inward instead of let out could be a deadly thing. 'She wants to go to her chamber with them. I came to be sure she'd not meet Lady Alice on the way.'

'Domina Elisabeth and Ivetta are still there, I think.'

Locking the small room's door with a key from among those hung from her belt, Mistress Say said, 'It might be a comfort to her if your prioress prayed with them.'

'Has Master Say returned?'

'Not yet.' Mistress Say's worried frown deepened between her eyes. 'Nor sent any word.'

'Will he bring Sir Gerveys' body back here, or will Cristiana go to the church, do you think?'

'Cristiana means to go nowhere. She says she'll stay in her chamber and keep Mary and Jane with her there until this is over, until she knows they'll be safe. By your leave, my lady.' Mistress Say left her, going back toward the parlor.

Glad to be alone and not wanting to meet Cristiana, Frevisse went along the screens passage and out the foredoor, down the steps, and along the yard to the garden. As she had hoped, no one was there and she settled herself on the turf bench along one wall, alone with her thoughts, little though she presently liked them.

There was nothing she could do about the secret now burdening Alice, and with the rest, no matter how she sorted and sifted and arranged what she knew, she saw no answers. Because nothing else seemed of any use and she had missed all the day's Offices since Prime, she tried to pray, both for the good it might do and to free her mind from her thoughts' useless circling. And sometimes answers came to her while she prayed.

None did this time. She was unable even to hold her mind to the prayers themselves, and she was grateful when a servant brought food, and drink to her on a tray. He said that since there was no dinner in the hall today, Mistress Say had thought she might want to eat out here alone. Frevisse sent back her thanks, ate and drank without much noting what, and was something like glad, as she finished, to see Master Fyncham come through the gateway.

The midday sun was pleasantly warm along the turf bench and she beckoned him to join her there, saying as he bowed to her, 'Sit, please you. You found out something?' For he looked very much like someone pleased with himself.

He sat and said, 'Nol was *not* in Wormley that while. He paid the alewife to lie for him.'

'She told you that?'

'She did. It seems she told him she'd lie for him so long as there was no trouble about it, but "If you're here asking about him," she said to me, "then there's trouble and, no, he wasn't here." I found out, too, whom he hired a horse from. What they told me agreed with what the alewife said – that he was gone about two and half days. He left in early afternoon of his half-day off and came back at evening two days later and spent the night drinking at the alehouse after paying the alewife to send her lying complaint about him along to here the next morning.'

Frevisse gave him well-deserved thanks and asked, 'Do you know where Nol was last night?'

Master Fyncham began, 'In the loft where the servants' – then he saw what lay behind her question and trailed off uncertainly – 'sleep.' He recovered. 'Or he should have been. I'll ask the other men.'

'Another thing. Has he been away from the manor any other time since Mistress Helyngton came here? On his half-day or even for only a few hours?'

'He hasn't, no. He's been under my displeasure and close watch since his supposed while in Wormley. He's been nowhere except here. Unless,' Master Fyncham said grimly, 'it was at night, and about that I shall ask, too.'

As he rose to his feet, Frevisse warned, 'We don't want him frighted into running.'

'I'll take care,' Master Fyncham assured her briskly.

'I want, too, to send a message to Lady Alice. I need to write it and have a servant take it.'

'Yes, my lady.'

Frevisse thanked him again, he left, and she was left with the satisfying certainty that this Nol was Suffolk's spy and had taken word of the paper to Suffolk. What part he had had in Pers's and Sir Gerveys' deaths was still to be found out. He likely had struck no blow himself, but had he passed word to someone else who had?

To someone else in Suffolk's pay? Or to Laurence Helyngton? But then Laurence might well be in Suffolk's pay, earning Suffolk's regard and satisfying his own anger against Sir Gerveys at the same time.

It would tie together so many ends if that proved true.

Except that Suffolk might well protect Laurence if Laurence was his man in this. What would happen to Cristiana and her daughters then? Alice had surely promised their safety in good faith, but what good faith was in her husband?

That thought kept Frevisse uncomfortable company into the afternoon. A servant came with the pen and ink and paper she needed to write to Alice. When she had done, he took the message and sometime after that Master Say returned home. Hearing horses in the yard, she went to look, saw Master Say dismounting, and followed him into the house, needing to pause at the stairfoot to let men carrying down the tabletops, trestles, and benches from the great hall go past her, on their way to load them onto two wagons waiting to haul them to the field for tomorrow's use. When finally she was able to go up and inside, she found Master Say in the parlor, telling his wife and Domina Elisabeth how the crowner's arrival had kept him in Broxbourne.

Sent for because of Pers's death, the man had found himself with two more and, 'I stayed to give what help I could,' Master Say said. 'Everyone who lives around the green has been questioned, but no one heard anything, let alone saw aught. The mist and darkness took care of that. We found out as best we could what travelers were at the inns in Broxbourne last night, questioned those still here, and sent men after those already gone to be sure who they are and if they know anything.' His discouragement was open. 'I doubt they will.'

'One of the murderers was wounded,' Frevisse offered.

'The crowner has sent men to question herbwives, apothecaries, and doctors from here to Waltham, Ware, and Hertford in hopes someone has been treated for a dagger wound. If it was only slight, though, we won't find anything out that way. And priests,' Master Say added. 'Priests are being asked, too, on the chance it was bad enough to kill the cur. That's our best hope.'

'What's been done with Sir Gerveys' and Sawnder's bodies?'

Mistess Say asked.

'Sawnder's cousin is seeing to his. I thought Cristiana . . .'

A servant appeared in the doorway. 'Lady Alice, sir,' he said and moved quickly aside, barely out of Alice's way as she swept passed him, swept a look at them all rising to their feet, and declared, 'Master Say, I've come to talk to one of your servants. A man named Nol. Send for him.'

Master Say, just straightening from his bow to her, bowed again. 'Of course, my lady. Edmund, tell Nol he's wanted here.'

As the servant started to leave, Alice added, 'I've two men of my own in the hall. They'll go with you to see that he comes.'

With the servant gone, Master Say asked tersely, 'What's amiss, my lady?'

As tersely back, Alice said, 'You've a spy in your household, set here by my husband. Dame Frevisse found him out for me. Now I want to question him.'

Master Say started to say something but thought better of it. Alice moved to the middle of the room. The gracious friend and guest were gone from her manner. She was altogether the duchess of Suffolk, possessed of power and able to use it. She turned to face the door, waiting. In silence the rest of them waited, too, Master Say with a hand on his wife's shoulder; Domina Elisabeth looking questioningly at everyone; Frevisse careful to meet no one's gaze.

Wherever Nol had been, he was soon found. He came into the parlor boldly enough, despite Alice's two men behind him. He surely had small doubt why he was there and less when the men took places on guard either side of the doorway, but he put on a brave front, trying to look as if he was clear of any thought why he was there.

'You,' Alice said, wasting no time on subtlety. 'You're a spy here for the duke of Suffolk.'

Probably ready for clever word-play while he tried to find a way out of however much trouble he was in, Nol froze at the blunt accusation, then gathered himself and said steadily, 'Yes, my lady.'

'You took word to him that Mistress Helyngton and Sir Gerveys had a secret they would sell to him.'

'Yes, my lady.'

'How did you find that out?'

'I listened outside the room where they were talking. They said they had something that would ruin the duke of Suffolk.' He seemed to have decided that, once begun, he might as well hold nothing back. 'I didn't hear more than that. That woman Ivetta was coming, so I finished going up the stairs as loudly as I could and claimed I'd come for a tray.'

And that was why Ivetta had not seen him when she came along the screens passage, Frevisse thought. He had been already on the stairs, listening.

'You then went to my lord of Suffolk with word of what you'd heard,' Alice said. 'Is that how you always got word to him when you had something to tell?'

'No, my lady. There's someone comes through Wormley at set times. I meet him and tell him if there's anything to tell.' He shifted an uneasy look at the Says and away to Alice again. 'Not that there's been anything to tell, but I've told him that, too. But this was something that seemed shouldn't wait until he came. So I went myself.'

'And were well paid, I trust,' Master Say said coldly.

Even wariness could not keep the gleam of coins out of Nol's voice. 'I was.' But he had the grace to add, 'It wasn't like what they said had anything to do with you, sir. It was all them and against the duke of Suffolk.'

'Who else did you tell?' Alice demanded.

Nol's answer came as quickly as Alice's demand. 'No one. I never told anyone else at all.'

At the doorway one of Alice's men moved suddenly, barring the way. Past him, Cristiana said, 'I want to come in.'

Mistress Say looked to Alice for permission.

As Alice hesitated, Cristiana said, 'Ivetta heard in the kitchen you were questioning someone.'

Alice nodded at her man and he stood aside. Cristiana came in. Her dreadful calm was still on her – dreadful because it was the calm of someone facing a thing so terrible she did not dare to feel it; so terrible that when she finally felt it, the pain might tear her into pieces. Frevisse wondered how long it would be until she could no longer hold back that pain. And what would happen when finally it broke free in her.

Mistress Say met Cristiana and led her toward the settle with an arm around her waist, saying, 'You shouldn't be here. You shouldn't be up at all. At least lie down.'

Her gaze fixed on Nol and her words as stiff as her body, Cristiana said, 'Lying down hurts.' She slipped from the curve of Mistress Say's arm, sat down on the settle's edge, and asked, still looking at Nol, 'This is the man?'

'He overheard you and Gerveys talking, yes,' Mistress Say said gently. 'He's the one who told my lord of Suffolk about you.'

'And then you killed my brother,' Cristiana said at Nol. 'And Pers and the other man.'

'No!' Nol said that quickly, not to Cristiana but at Alice and Master Say. 'I swear I'd nothing to do with that!'

'If not you,' Cristiana said, 'then who? You didn't have time to tell Suffolk himself they were going to Ware, but you could have told someone here.' Her gaze flicked toward Alice. 'Or Laurence Helyngton.' She stood up and her voice rose with her. 'You told him, didn't you, and when he only killed Pers the first time, you told him Gerveys would be in the church last night so he could kill him then. Or you killed him yourself?'

Nol was no fool. He understood the danger he was suddenly in and cried, 'No!' again at Alice and Master Say. 'I never did that! I swear it! I've never had anything to do with Master Helyngton or any of them!'

'How very honorable of you to spy for only one person at a time,' Alice said coldly. 'Supposing we believed you.'

'It's true, though! I'll swear on the Bible or anything else you ask me to that I've had nothing to do with anybody's murder!'

'Who else would it have been?' Cristiana said at him. 'How many treacherous curs can there be in one place?'

Alice, looking at Nol with the cold regard she might have given a piece of rotten fruit, held up a hand for Cristiana to be silent and Mistress Say gently made her sit down again, while Nol said, both sullen and ill-eased, 'All I did was tell my lord of Suffolk about what I heard. That's all I did. Naught else.'

'So you say,' Alice acknowledged mildly. 'It will be interesting to hear what you say when asked about it somewhat differently.'

She slightly moved one hand. Her two men stepped immediately forward and took hold on him, one of them twisting his arm up behind his back, not all the way to pain, Frevisse thought, but enough that Nol went rigid, knowing what could come next. Watching him, Alice asked Master Say, 'Is there somewhere among your outbuildings where my men can keep him under guard tonight? Until there's time to deal further with him?'

'I'll show them where,' Master Say said.

'Master Say!' Nol pleaded at him. 'Don't let them! You—'

Master Say coldly cut him off. 'Apparently, Nol, I'm not your master, merely someone who paid you wages while you served my lord of Suffolk.'

Before Nol could find answer to that, Master Say went past him and out of the room, and as her men began to shove Nol around to follow him, Alice said to them, 'You know what's to be done with him. See to it.'

Both men answered, 'Yes, my lady,' and the last sight Frevisse had of Nol was his frightened face turned back as if to make some final plea as they shoved him out of the room.

Mistress Say was half-lifting Cristiana to her feet, telling her, 'Now you must come and lie down in bed. You shouldn't have come.'

Cristiana let herself be led away. Domina Elisabeth, after quick looks at Alice still standing hard-faced in the middle of the room and at Frevisse with her gaze fixed on Alice, silently followed.

Behind her, Frevisse rose, went and closed the door, turned to Alice and said, keeping the words flat, free of accusation, 'Torture is illegal.' Allowed by law only to make an accused plead either guilty or not guilty so that his trial could go forward.

Alice looked at her and said as flatly back, 'I gave no order for torture. They'll hurt him a little tonight, then leave him to think about it. He'll be far more ready to talk in the morning.'

'Alice, I gave him into your hands. The fault will lie on me, too. On my conscience, if nothing else.'

'It will not. The fault of whatever happens to him lies on that man himself.'

'Alice,' Frevisse said, not trying to keep grief from her voice.

'Frevisse,' Alice said harshly back, almost mocking her. 'I need to know how treacherous this man is. I need to know who else he's sold this secret to.'

'How would it matter who else he's told? You were the one who opened and read the thing. No one else.'

'I have to know who else knew about it. I need to know how far this treachery goes.'

No, that was not what Alice needed, Frevisse realized sharply. What Alice needed was to learn whether or not her husband had ordered these three deaths.

But while Frevisse tried to find something to say, Alice, maybe misunderstanding her silence, said, 'Frevisse, this Nol is nobody. Set against two kingdoms and a war, he's less than nobody. He's in the way of things that need to be known. I can't let him stay in the way.'

Coldly, the words away before she thought to stop them, Frevisse answered, 'Let us exalt the kingdoms of the earth – Mankind's creation – over God's creation, Mankind itself.'

Alice started to answer that but stopped, tightly shut her mouth, turned sharply away, and left.

Chapter 22

G rief lay leaden in Cristiana. Grief for Edward. Grief for Gerveys. Grief for everything that had been her life and was gone past ever having back. Grief. And the certainty that now there would never be an end to sorrow, to grief, to pain. Grief. And the wish that she were dead instead of Gerveys,

Gray and heavy as she now was with grief and constant pain, why couldn't she be dead instead?

Gerveys was dead and no one seemed to care except herself. Tomorrow maybe they would all care again, but today the only thing on everyone's mind but hers was the king's hawking along the river, the king's feasting afterward here at Baas, and the day's bright weather was cruel and everyone's pleasure in it more cruel.

And she was cruel, she knew, in refusing to let Mary and Jane go out with Nurse and the nurserymaid and little Betha and the baby Genofeffe and a servingman, to watch the hawking from the slope above the river meadows and the feasting from a distance with the crowd of village folk there would surely be. Cruel, yes, but not so cruel as to risk them away from her.

Sitting on the chest at the foot of the bed with her arms wrapped around herself and holding very still against the pain, Cristiana watched them sprawled on cushions on the bedchamber's floor sullenly playing fox-and-geese with Ivetta on a gameboard brought from the nursery. For all that they had cried for their uncle yesterday, today they were angry and hurt at being kept in here and safe. Even Mary, who should have understood better. But they wanted to see the king and queen.

Cristiana had seen both king and queen as lately as two years ago when Edward had last taken her to London. King Henry was a tall young man with brown hair and brown eyes and the grave air of a child watching the world from a distance. Queen Margaret was a pretty-faced girl-woman in a beautiful gown. Cristiana had no care to see either of them again.

Just now she had no care to see anyone ever again except her daughters.

Except Laurence, if she could see him dead.

The nun said there was no way yet to tell who had killed Gerveys, but that was foolishness. Who else had it been but Laurence?

Laurence, who was out there in the bright day among the gentry come to wait upon their king and queen and keep company among the courtiers. Laurence with his claim to Mary and Jane still unbroken. Laurence.

Pain throbbed in her, adding the raw goad of its fear to all her other fears. She wanted to call Mary and Jane to her, take them in her arms, hold them, feel them warm and alive and safe with her. Mary with her little-girl body and her little-girl ways but her womanhood not far away and too often now a worry in her eyes she should be too young to have. And Jane, sturdy and determined but still so little, still so unknowing of so very much. If Lady Alice failed to keep her promise, what would happen to them, given back into Laurence's hands? They were all that was left of her life. To know that her love could not keep them safe grieved her beyond almost any other grief, hurt her beyond any other pain.

Everything hurt. Everything in her life was come down to pain, to fear.

To hating Laurence.

Jane lifted her head from the gameboard as if she had heard something. Then she scrambled to her feet and ran to the window, too small to see out but trying to pull herself up to the sill. Mary, almost as quick to her feet, joined her, gave her a boost, and braced her so they could both look down into the kitchen yard from where Cristiana could now hear a bustling and excited voices.

'They're starting to carry out food!' Mary said. 'The hawking must be done.'

'Nearly done,' Ivetta corrected. She was climbing to her feet, too, and Cristiana saw by the wetness on her cheeks that she had been crying even while she played with the girls. With a small pang of guilt, Cristiana admitted to herself how little thought she had given to

Ivetta's grief since yesterday. But her own grief was so much the greater, so much the worse than Ivetta's could be. Edward was gone, and now Gerveys, and she still had no surety her daughters would be safe. If anyone should cry, it should be her.

And yet since yesterday no tears had come to her, as if they were lost under the weight of all her griefs, her fears, her pain.

Ivetta had joined the girls at the window, was saying, 'Word must have come to have everything out and ready for when the king and queen and everyone ride up from the river.' Tears or not, she was excited, too.

That forgetfulness of grief – Ivetta's and the girls' – hurt Cristiana. Like the fair, bright day, it was wrong. And yet . . .

Cristiana stood carefully up. It was maybe not at them she should be disappointed but at herself. Wrapped in her griefs and fears, was she beginning to forget how to be kind?

As she joined Mary and Jane and Ivetta, the open uncertainty with which they looked at her gave weight to her worry and made her almost glad to say, 'Would it be better if we went to the garden and watched from there?'

Mary and Jane bloomed into instant happiness and started for the stairs, Ivetta hurrying after them, trying to tidy their gowns and hair as they went. Cristiana, following more slowly down the stairs and along the screens passage, felt the house's emptiness around her and was glad to see the outer gate to the road was shut and there was a man on guard atop the gatehouse. John was too sensible a man to leave his house open to thieves while everyone was busy and gone elsewhere, had probably even set up for a constant change of guard so that none of his men would miss out too long on the day.

The girls and Ivetta were well ahead of her. By the time she reached the garden door, they were to the garden's far side, crowded to the gate there. Beyond them, Cristiana could see servants passing on their way from the kitchen to the pasture – Lady Alice's people as well as John's and probably more from the royal household, too. She could remember when such things had greatly mattered to her, when she would have wanted to know how all was being seen to and done. Now her thought had no feeling to it. Was she going to lose all feelings except fear and grief?

Even sight of Dame Frevisse seated on the turf-topped bench along the garden's north side where the sun fell pleasantly barely stirred feeling in her. It seemed the nuns were among the things about which she had ceased to care, and instead of avoiding her, she went toward Dame Frevisse, who stood up at her approach and might have said something but Cristiana demanded, 'Have you found out anything about my brother's death? Did they make that man tell what he knew?'

'I've not heard that he's said more than he did yesterday,' Dame Frevisse said evenly.

'What have they done with him?'

'He's still here under guard.'

'He has to be made to tell that Laurence murdered my brother. That Laurence did it or had it done.'

'Very possibly,' Dame Frevisse granted. 'But we have to be certain.'

'*I'm* certain.'

'I know.'

Goaded by the nun's quietness, Cristiana challenged, 'You'd rather it was Laurence than your cousin, wouldn't you?'

'I'd rather have the truth,' Dame Frevisse said back, ungoaded. 'For Sir Gerveys' sake as much as anyone's.'

And in the nun's face Cristiana saw what she had wanted to see in someone else all day. Sorrow. Not simple, soon eased unhappiness, but sorrow. Deep-set sorrow that would be held in heart and mind with prayers and memories, not let to slide into the back of forgetfulness as soon as might be.

And quietly Dame Frevisse said, 'I think I failed to tell you yesterday how sorry I am for your brother's death. He has my prayers.'

And Cristiana had her pity. Cristiana felt it enwrap her, cool against the heat of her unshed tears. Cool and . . . sustaining, like a hand held out to steady someone in danger of falling; there because it was needed.

Why the nun's pity mattered, Cristiana did not know. Or her sorrow. Time was that she had wanted nothing from the nuns but for them to go away. But some of the tightness around her heart unclenched a little, and with a quietness that surprised herself, she said, 'Thank you.'

'They're coming!' Mary called from the gate. 'We can see the horses! Hurry!'

Cristiana turned from Dame Frevisse and went to join her daughters. Ivetta crowded aside to let her come close behind the girls, and she put an arm around their waists and tried to feign enjoyment with them as they exclaimed at the several score of riders now cantering up the long slope of the shallow stream valley in a rainbow-array of gowns and surcoats, sunlight shining and glinting off their horses' bright-brassed harnesses.

'Oh, please,' Jane begged. 'Let's go nearer. We won't see anything. There'll be people in the way!'

There was a great gathering of common folk from nearby villages and countryside strung and clustered all along the slope and closing behind the riders as they passed, following them toward the gaudy gathering of pavilions and awnings in the pasture below the house, already encircled by more people kept back by a line of guards. Jane was right: there would be little seen from here once the royal party dismounted. But among those who would be around the king was Laurence. Like John and Beth, he was there among the riders, and probably Milisent and her dull-eyed husband Colles. They were there and Edward was not. . . .

The fresh rise of her grief was forestalled by Mary asking where King Henry and Queen Margaret were among the riders. Because the riders were drawing rein beside the pavilions Cristiana could answer that easily. As the servants came forward to take the horses and the riders dismounted, there was a tall man in green around whom everyone else moved like water flowing around an island in a stream. Cristiana pointed him out and added, 'The woman with him, in green, too, that's Queen Margaret,' in a wide-coifed headdress and a gown whose sleeves trailed nearly to the ground.

Jane, disappointed, said, 'They're not wearing their crowns.'

'Not for hawking,' Mary said disdainfully.

Quickly, before Jane could make an insulted reply, Cristiana said at random, 'There's Master Say, I think.' Because the guards were keeping a gap in the crowd for the servants to come and go, the food-laden tables and people moving around them could be narrowly seen from the gateway, and Cristiana went on to pretend she recognized various neighbors and great lords there, diverting Mary and Jane while her mind lurched back to her heart-hurting thought of Edward.

He should have been there and he was not. Not there or ever anywhere again. Or Gerveys. He was gone, too. They were gone and only pain was left. . . .

She realized she had slid into silence, that Mary and Jane were looking questioningly up at her, and she fumbled for something to say, pointed and said, 'There's Mistress Say. I remember the gold-tawny gown she was wearing this morning. Wave to her.'

To encourage them, she waved, too, never supposing anyone over there would note them, and no one did, but some of the servants returning from the field for more food did and waved. The girls waved back at them, but Cristiana let her hand fall to Mary's shoulder and stared past them toward the pavilions. Somewhere Laurence was waiting his chance to beg the king's favor. She knew as surely as she knew the sun was shining and hatred scalded through her. Edward was dead and Gerveys was dead and Laurence was there, talking, eating, laughing, waiting his chance. . . .

'Please, Momma,' Jane begged, tugging at her gown. 'Couldn't we go nearer? Please?'

Mary added her plea. 'Please, Momma?'

Cristiana looked down at their upturned faces, hardly able to see them through her blind fierceness of hating Laurence. But she forced her own face into a smile and kissed them on their foreheads and said, pointing away, 'Oh, look what they're doing now,' though they were doing nothing more than they had been – standing around the tables, eating, drinking. But Mary and Jane looked and Cristiana ignored Ivetta's stare at her. Ivetta was nothing in this. No one was anything in this except Mary and Jane.

Her thoughts cleared by the scald of her hatred, Cristiana looked at the stark, plain shape of things with a terrible clarity. Her love had not been able to keep either Edward or Gerveys safe. Neither would her love keep Mary and Jane safe. Nor would promises from Lady Alice or John. Promises were weaker things than love. If love was not enough, what good were promises? Her pain's promise was the only sure promise, promising that she would die and Laurence would be left alive with his unslaked greed.

He must not be.

But with the same hate-brought clarity that she shaped that thought, Cristiana knew she must be done with hate or she'd go to Hell. To Hell and not to Heaven where Edward was. Unless she wanted to spend Eternity without Edward, she would have to want Laurence's death only in the same way she would want the death of any evil man – not with hatred but only for justice's sake.

She stared down at the top of her daughter's heads. They were her only love left in the world and love had to be her guide and guard now. Not hatred. Love. The only burning she must have in her was her love for Mary, for Jane, for Edward, for Gerveys. Whatever she did, it had to be done only in love, never in hatred, because only in love would she ever be again and forever with Edward.

Chapter 23

Frevisse supposed it was to the good that Cristiana had loosed her fears enough to come this far with her daughters and Ivetta. Watching them across the garden, she was able to hear Mary's and Jane's delighted exclaims and, once, their pleading to go nearer. She saw Cristiana kiss them and set them to watching again, and then saw Cristiana go very still. So strangely still, with such a deep-set quiet in her face as she stared away toward the royal gathering, that Frevisse went on watching her.

There had been too much quiet in Cristiana since yesterday.

And then Cristiana turned and said something to Ivetta, turned back to her daughters and said something to them, then moved them gently out of her way and went out the gate. They both protested, but Cristiana only bent and kissed them over the gate, cupped a hand tenderly along each girl's face while looking into their eyes and saying something. Then she turned and walked away, falling in behind several servant-women carrying filled platters toward the gathering.

Cristiana had done it all so simply that Frevisse sat looking for a while longer at the emptiness where she had been without much thinking about it before – with the first, small spark of alarm – she wondered *why* Cristiana was going there.

Very probably to plead in person for the king's favor and mercy. He was known for giving both to almost anyone who asked.

But. . . .

Frevisse stood up and went toward the gate. Mary and Jane hardly glanced at her but Ivetta looked around with tear-reddened eyes. Frevisse took her by the arm and drew her back from the gate, to ask low-voiced and beyond the girls' hearing, 'What did Mistress Helyngton say to you?'

Ivetta repeated somewhat blankly, 'Say to me?'

'Just now. Before she left. What did she say?'

'She said . . .' Ivetta seemed confused by the question. 'I don't know.'

'You do. She just said it. You can't have forgotten. Tell me.'

With effort, Ivetta gathered her wits. 'Yes. Well. She said something like it was time to make an end. Then, like I'd said she mustn't, she said, "I must." Only I hadn't said anything because I didn't know what she meant. "I must," she said and away she went.' Ivetta was agrieved about that. 'After telling us all morning that we couldn't, then she did.'

'What did she say to Mary and Jane?'

'To Mary and Jane? That she loved them, of course. She always says that when she's going away.'

Ivetta was beginning to be annoyed at being questioned. Not caring, Frevisse demanded, 'Does she have any weapon on her?'

Ivetta stared at her. 'What?'

'Does she have a dagger on her?' Frevisse said roughly. 'Some weapon? Anything?'

'She has my Pers's dagger. I brought it back with me after . . . after he . . . it was all . . . all . . .' Ivetta stumbled over returning tears.

Frevisse tightened her grip on Ivetta's arm. 'She has it now? You're certain?'

'She made me give it her after Sir Gerveys . . .' Ivetta gulped on a sob, fumbling for words. 'She said she'd never go without weapon again. She slept with it under her pillow last night. She—'

'She has it *now?*' Frevisse insisted.

'Hidden up her sleeve. In its sheath. She said—'

'Stay here,' Frevisse ordered. 'Keep the girls with you. No matter what happens, keep them here. Or take them inside. Do not let them come after me.' She was leaving even as she said it, at the gate pushed Mary and Jane aside, went out, and shoved the gate firmly shut behind her, pausing only to order, 'Stay here,' at them for good measure before she started after Cristiana.

She could see her too far ahead among the scattered servants going to and coming from the pavilions. In her plain widow's garb, she blended easily with the servants, would probably pass with no trouble between the guards. Frevisse hesitated either to shout or run after her. If Cristiana purposed nothing more than kneeling to the king to plead for his well-known mercy, it would be wrong to hinder her. What Frevisse wanted was to make certain that was all she meant to do – to overtake her, ask her, make certain of her – and with her longer stride she closed on her along the slope, was barely a dozen yards behind her as Cristiana past the guards unnoticed.

Frevisse passed with almost equal ease. One of the guards made as if to speak to her but she gave him a purposefully arrogant stare and he let her go on – being a nun was sometimes useful in unexpected ways. Ahead of her, the servants Cristiana was following were nearly to the edge of the crowd spread among the pavilions and food-laden tables. Frevisse would have called out then, but in the time Frevisse took to draw breath, Cristiana went suddenly aside from the servants, around them and away into the crowd.

Cristiana made her way among the talking, laughing, eating, drinking men and women all around her without the slightest fear that anyone would see her, heed her, stop her. Fear, as well as thought, had left her when she left the garden. The only thing left to her was the need to do. She was air and light and simple purpose, and as she had known she must, she found Laurence easily.

He was standing in talk with several other men on the edge of where the crowd was thickest, beside a white-cloth-covered table untidy with the remains of food. Milisent was beside him and her unpleasant husband beside her, but their backs were to Cristiana and she barely noted them or the other men. Her gaze was fixed on Laurence, and she paused, her arms folded in front of herself, hiding her right hand as she slipped it into the tight-fitted left sleeve of her undergown, to the hilt of Pers's dagger waiting in its sheath along the inside of her forearm. Happily, he had favored a narrow blade, easily hidden there. She had wanted Gerveys' dagger, because it was his, as well as for the comfort of it, but the crowner had it. That had mattered then. Now it did not. Any dagger would serve for what she had finally, in the garden, understood she had to do. And she slid the dagger from her sleeve, and holding it still hidden by her crossed arms, went forward and slipped past Milisent, so suddenly in front of Laurence that he broke off in mid-word of whatever he was saying, staring at her and unready as all in one half-instant she drew back her right arm, grabbed his shoulder with her left hand, and with a strength she would have had for nothing else drove Pers's dagger into him, below his ribs and slanted upward to come at his heart.

In some cold corner of her mind she must have planned that blow, but at that moment it seemed simply there, the way that Laurence's surprise was simply there as he stared downward at her fist thrust against his belly around the dagger's hilt. She knew she had struck true, against no bone, and his surprise was joy and balm and blessing across all the raw wounds he had made in her. He made to clutch at his belly where the pain must be starting, and she jerked the dagger out of him and stepped back, aware that around them people had begun to yell, some falling back, others grabbing for her, and without time to stab again, she swung wide and high, slashing the dagger at Milisent's throat. She missed: Milisent had begun to back away, screaming, but the sudden bloody line that opened across her face from cheek to forehead was triumph of a kind.

Then a blow drove into her side below her wide-flung arm and she staggered sideways; but in some cold other corner of her mind she had known that would come, did not mind, and yet was surprised that her legs had ceased to hold her-up, that she was falling. . . .

Frevisse searched with rising urgency among the talking, shifting crowd, saw Cristiana and moved toward her, was almost in reach of catching hold on her when Cristiana went suddenly forward, slipping past a woman and in front of a man Frevisse only too late saw was Laurence. She started to cry out to Cristiana and in warning but the half-made cry was lost in a sudden shouting and a backward shove of people. Against them, she shoved forward, in time to see Master Colles drive a dagger into Cristiana's side, staggering her sideways with the blow's force.

Laurence was on his knees, bent over on himself. Milisent was screaming. People were shouting, some of them pushing to get further away, others crowding forward to see what was happening. Cristiana began to fall. Someone among the men pressing forward saw a man down, a woman shrieking with blood flowing from her hands pressed to her face, another woman falling, and Colles with a dagger in his hand, and did what instinct told him – had out his own dagger and struck at Colles.

Frevisse saw Colles's look of surprise as he took a single staggered step, then dropped to his knees, and – still looking surprised – slumped forward and sprawled across the trampled grass. Above him, Milisent, blind with blood and pain, went on screaming. Frevisse, at last reaching Cristiana, went to her knees beside her, arms stretched out over her body to keep men's feet away, but the shoving and shouting were making a circle clear of the bodies now. She was able to turn Cristiana onto her back, slide an arm under her shoulders, and lift her a little, saying her name.

People were taking still-screaming Milisent away. Someone shoved at Master Colles with a foot and said, 'He's dead,' while two men turned Laurence over. He was alive but his body arched upward with pain and his strangled moan was bubbled with blood.

Cristiana's eyes opened. White-faced and wide-eyed with pain and fear, she whispered up at Frevisse, 'He's not dead?'

'He won't live,' Frevisse said. She looked around at the staring circle of faces and ordered, 'For mercy, get a priest here.' Because Cristiana was not going to live, either.

But Cristiana's fear had gone, leaving only the pain as she whispered, satisfied, 'If he's dead. Then they'll be safe.'

'They'll be safe,' Frevisse said strongly, wanting to be sure she heard. 'They'll be safe now.'

'Not for hatred . . .' Cristiana broke off on a moan and her body twisted with pain. Frevisse held her more closely. Cristiana steadied from the pain. 'For love,' she forced out, short of breath. 'Tell them. For love.'

'For love,' Frevisse assured her. 'You did it for love. Not for hatred. For love. I'll tell them.'

More pain took Cristiana's body. Laurence was still now. Dead, Frevisse thought, and so did the priest finally there, because he paused over Laurence's body only long enough to sign it with the cross before coming to Cristiana. To judge by the gold and jeweled cross hung on his chest by a thick gold chain, he was maybe one of the king's bishops, but it was his priesthood that mattered now, not his lordly rank. As he knelt beside her, Cristiana gasped, 'My sins. Confess me.'

He signed the cross above her and began the necessary prayers. Frevisse went on holding her. Around them the crowd had thickened into a wall of staring faces but the babble of voices had fallen away to silence as people understood what was happening. In that silence the bishop leaned close over Cristiana for her to whisper her confession in his ear, too low for even Frevisse to hear. It was enough that she got the words out and he gave her the absolution and final blessing that cleansed her soul and freed it to go heavenward. But it was to

Frevisse Cristiana finally looked, finally whispered, 'My daughters.' Then the life went out of her and her eyes went empty and Frevisse was left kneeling with blood on her hands and blood on her gown and Cristiana gone.

Chapter 24

Night was thickly come, the hour for bed long past. In the parlor, the deep darkness was held back to the room's corners and in long shadows among the ceiling beams by candles arrayed on stands beside the settle and beyond the chairs. The yellow light lay gently over the faces gathered there, but the faces were too few and there was nothing gentle in the grief on Mistress Say's face or Ivetta's, nor anything gentle about the weariness lined into Master Say's as he laid a thick-folded parchment heavy with a wax seal on his wife's lap and said, 'It's done,' before he sank down onto the long seat of the settle beside her.

He was still dressed as he had been when he rode out to the royal hawking this morning, but had ridden far more miles than he had purposed then. King Henry and his company had ridden on to Buntingford for the night, as they had intended. Master Say, who had not intended to, had ridden with them and now had ridden back, having made some manner of explanation to the king for the killings done almost in front of him this morning.

Only this morning?

From where she sat alone in the shadows at the shuttered window, Frevisse tried to make the day take on a shape that made sense but this morning seemed to have happened in someone else's lifetime. And yet every moment of it kept playing over in her mind, an all-too power-ful nightmare that would not end with some welcomed awakening. Cristiana was dead. And Laurence Helyngton and Colles. And Milisent was scarred for life across her face.

But here and now Mistress Say laid her hands on the parchment on her lap and asked, 'Their wardships and everything?'

'Their wardships, the keeping of their lands, their marriages. All sealed with the king's privy seal. The girls are ours. They're safe.'

Master Fyncham came quietly into the room, bearing a tray with goblets that he offered first to Master Say, who took the nearest one with ready thanks. While he drank deeply and Master Fyncham went silently on to everyone else, Mistress Say said, 'I don't know if word was sent after the king, but when the crowner viewed the bodies, he found a day-old dagger-thrust through Henry Colles' left arm.'

Master Say stared into the darkness, slowly taking that in before he finally said, 'So he's the one Gerveys stabbed, surely. He didn't dare not be at the hawking, lest questions be asked, but it must have cost him something in the way of pain not to show he was hurt. Good.'

'The crowner took it further than that,' Mistress Say said. 'He had Laurence's men gone over. One of them had a wound as fresh as Colles' and he turned appellant and told everything. By what he says, Laurence wasn't at Gerveys' killing or even the attack on the road, but he did set Colles on to do both. The man said Colles frighted him, he enjoyed the killing so much.'

'Master Say,' Frevisse said from the shadows, 'what of the man who killed Colles?'

'Pardoned by the king,' Master Say answered. 'He saw three people hurt and a man with a dagger in his hand, all within twenty feet of the king, and he struck in the king's defense, as he thought.' Master Say rubbed a hand over his face. 'It simplifies matters anyway, having Colles dead.'

'And Milisent alive,' Ivetta said with weary, bitter satisfaction from where she sat huddled in a chair at the edge of the candles' wavering light, clutching a wine goblet. 'She can answer what questions there still are, she can.'

Master Fyncham, the wine served, went to stand in the shadows beyond Ivetta, waiting to do whatever else might be needed.

Master Say slumped back on the settle. 'Where's Cristiana?'

'In her room here,' Mistress Say said quietly. 'Ivetta watched by her into early evening. Domina Elisabeth is with her for now, and Dame Frevisse will pray the night beside her.'

'Mary and Jane. How are they?'

'Sleeping, I hope. They've cried all they can for today, I think. They understand she's dead. After we'd readied her body, they saw it. But it's all too much for them at present. Tomorrow will be worse for them.'

'The funeral?'

'Tomorrow in the afternoon.'

'She and Gerveys together?'

'That seemed best. There's room to bury her beside Edward, and Gerveys beside her. Somewhere has been found for Pers, too.'

All the flat and necessary details that followed death and helped lead the living step by step into life as it would be now. But at mention of Pers, Ivetta, who like Mary and Jane had cried herself out some-time during the afternoon, began to rock forward and back, moaning softly.

Master Fyncham stepped forward and poured more wine into her goblet, probably sharing Frevisse's hope that she would soon drink herself to quietness And sleep. But Mistress Say's thin, tight hold on herself slipped, too, and she clutched her husband's hand, clinging to him while she asked with a sorrowing need to understand, 'How could Cristiana bring herself to this? How could she?'

The desperate why of Cristiana's killing they all knew. Master Say had already said it most simply just after her death, while helping Frevisse to her feet and turning her away from Cristiana's body, 'I know her, yes. And him. He'd threatened her daughters. She was afraid for them.'

Frevisse did not know who had asked him that but it was a woman with a French-tinged voice who said, 'For her children. Yes, that I can understand,' and Frevisse had lifted her gaze from Cristiana's body to the woman standing beyond it. The queen. Frevisse had met her once, not that Queen Margaret would remember it nor did Frevisse care. But this was her first near sight of the king, standing there beside his wife. A tall, thin man with a long, still face and dark eyes, staring down at the blood and bodies.

Then, mercifully, Alice had taken her from Master Say and away to one of the pavilions where Mistress Say, tears streaming, had found them and, later, Domina Elisabeth. None of them, then or later, had needed to ask why Cristiana had done it, but now, with despair, Mistress Say cried, 'How could she have brought herself to it? And there. With the king there. Didn't she understand the danger of that? If Colles hadn't killed her, someone else was as likely to, the way they killed Colles. What was she thinking of?'

Ivetta, still rocking back and forth and with the words thick with grief and tears and the wine beginning to take hold, said, 'It's probably what she hoped for. That someone would kill her. It's what she wanted, most likely. Surely.'

'No.' Mistress Say's protest was sharp. 'She'd never hope that. Leave Mary and Jane like that? She never would.'

Ivetta stopped rocking, pulled herself straight in the chair, and said on a sob, wine and sorrow both at work in her, 'She was going to have to leave them anyway. She was going to die. That's how she could bring herself to do it. Because she was dying.' Ivetta pressed a hand between her breasts. 'It was back before her husband died, when the pain first frighted her, she told me about it. That her mother had died that way. Of a canker in the bone eating her away. But there was her husband to worry over, and I think most times she let herself believe it wasn't happening. You know how we do with things we don't want to think about. But down deep, where the pain was coming from, she knew it was going to be worse before it was done and would kill her at the last. So she likely hoped somebody would kill her, too. That's what I think. Because it would be better if they did. Mary and Jane would be safe with Master Helyngton dead, and if someone killed her, then she wouldn't have to be afraid of the pain anymore, see.'

They were all staring at her, probably remembering – as Frevisse was – how often Cristiana had been openly in pain. Mind-pain, they had all thought, grown from her over-wrought griefs and fears, and some of it had been, surely. But much of it must have been more, and her mind-pain made all the worse by the certainty of her own death closing on her and the fear that she would die not only in pain but without her daughters safe.

Quietly Master Say said, 'That much fear and that much pain. I can see, then, how she did it. God have mercy on her soul.'

With matching quiet, Frevisse said, 'She left it to God whether she would die then or have to live to a worse death. He gave her the mercy of dying then. Surely he'll have mercy on her soul, too.'

They all made the sign of the cross on themselves and Ivetta took a deep drink of wine before saying fiercely, 'At least Laurence Helyngton is dead, too, and that's good. He's why they're all dead. My Pers . . .' She broke off with a heaving sob and hunched over again, gone back to her grief.

'At least with Colles and Laurence dead, and Nol dealt with, it's all ended,' Master Say said, trying for some satisfaction. 'Did Lady Alice have Nol taken away or am I to send him after her?'

'He's still here,' Mistress Say answered. 'Dame Frevisse asked her to leave him.'

Frevisse had hoped the matter of Nol would wait until the morning, but Master Say turned a questioning look toward her and she answered, 'It isn't ended. Nol wasn't the only one here who betrayed Cristiana and Sir Gerveys.'

Ivetta's new sobbing stopped on a gulp. Along with everyone else, she stared at Frevisse and in the candleglow and shadows Frevisse looked back at them all. The Says. Ivetta. Master Fyncham. All of them as much in need of sleep and being done with the day as she was. But as steadily as if her mind and heart were not dragged down under the weight of her own grief and guilt, she said, 'Nol was Suffolk's spy but he never had chance to know Sir Gerveys would go to Ware. When Cristiana and Sir Gerveys talked of it, Nol never overheard them. Both he and Ivetta say Pers was with him then. Nor did Pers know where they were going until their horses were being saddled. The only people who knew Sir Gerveys would go to Ware before he went were himself, Cristiana, and Ivetta.'

'Me?' Ivetta said as if short of breath.

'You. You were outside Cristiana's chamber when she and Sir Gerveys talked. You could easily have overheard them.'

Ivetta stared at Frevisse, her mouth hanging open. Then she closed it, swallowed, and said, 'I didn't. I wasn't near the door. I was farther down the stairs. With Pers. We were talking.'

'Pers saw Nol skulking at the stairfoot and went to talk to him,' Frevisse said. She abruptly shifted her heed to the steward still standing in the shadows. 'Master Fyncham, as part of your duties you know where the house servants are and what they're doing? To be certain they're earning their wages and not wasting their time, yes?'

'Yes, my lady.'

'You therefore usually know if they're where they should be when they should be, and if they're not?'

'Yes, my lady. Usually,' Master Fyncham said steadily.

'Three evenings ago, the evening before Pers was killed, do you remember if anyone was missing from where they should have been, before or during or after supper? Particularly after supper.'

After a moment's consideration, Master Fyncham said, 'No. Everything was in order that evening. Everyone was here and doing what they should have been doing.'

'Do you remember if you saw Ivetta anywhere then?'

Ivetta had cramped around in her chair to look, along with every-one else, at Master Fyncham, but she jerked around at that to stare at Frevisse again. Gazing thoughtfully down at the back of her kerchiefed head, Master Fyncham considered the question before finally saying, 'She was at supper. I don't remember her after that. But she was not within my concern, for me to note or not note, you understand.'

'Where were you that evening, Ivetta?' Frevisse demanded at her.

'Here!' Ivetta said. 'Where else would I be?'

'Where here?' Frevisse pressed.

'With Mistress Helyngton. With the children in the nursery.'

'When we ask Nurse about that in the morning, will she say you were there?' Frevisse asked.

Ivetta's eyes flicked down and up and from side to side, seemingly in search for what to say next. Frevisse did not give her chance to find an answer but stood up, moved toward her, said, 'There's no use in telling me you were with Pers then. Master Say's man Edmund told me he played at dice with him after supper for a good hour or more in the hall that evening. If you weren't with Cristiana and you weren't with Pers, where were you?'

'Walking,' Ivetta said. 'In the garden. In the orchard, I mean.'

'Alone?'

'Yes. All alone.'

'All alone.' Step by deliberate step, Frevisse came closer to her with every word. 'After supper. In the orchard.'

'Yes!' Ivetta's voice shrilled up. 'I was . . . I was . . . I had a headache and . . . and . . .'

Frevisse cut off her flailing for words. 'You were walking but not in the orchard. I've been told it's two miles to the manor of Highmeade. A half hour's good walk. A half hour's walk to Laurence Helyngton. A half hour's walk back. You needed to be gone hardly more than an hour. An hour and a little more to go and come back from telling Laurence Helyngton that Sir Gerveys was going to Ware in the morn-ing to get something valuable. Something that the duke of Suffolk very much wanted?'

She was standing over Ivetta by then, and Ivetta was pressed back-ward into her chair, her hands gripped together around the wine goblet, her head bent sharply back to stare up at Frevisse. On short breaths she gasped out, 'What? I wouldn't. I couldn't. I didn't know.'

'You're the only person who could know. Cristiana and Sir Gerveys told nobody he was going to Ware. They talked of it only to each other and in her chamber, where there was no one else to hear them. Except you on the stairs outside the door. Then, the first chance you had, you slipped away to tell Laurence Helyngton.'

'Why . . . I wouldn't . . . why would . . .' Ivetta let go of the goblet with one hand to push herself straighter in the chair by one of its arms, her protest growing stronger. 'Why would I do that? I didn't!'

'I don't know why you did it,' Frevisse said. 'But you did.' She kept her eyes set on Ivetta's, and Ivetta, trapped, stared back as Frevisse went coldly on, 'So tell us why you did it. Tell us so we can understand why you betrayed Cristiana to her worst enemy. Why you betrayed Sir Gerveys. Why you sent Pers to be killed. Sent Pers to die from a sword thrust through him. To die—'

With a gasping scream, Ivetta dropped the goblet and covered her ears with both hands, bending over to hide her face, crying out, 'Stop it! Nobody was supposed to be killed! There wasn't supposed to be a fight! They were only going to make Sir Gerveys give it to them! They were only going to take the thing!'

She had probably truly believed that but the stupidity of doing so made Frevisse insist even more harshly, 'Why? What did Laurence want it for? Did you even know what it was?'

'No! I still don't! I just knew it was something he could use to buy the duke of Suffolk's favor he wanted so much. They were just supposed to take it!' Her voice scaled up into a wail and broke on a new rush of tears.

No one moved to comfort her.

'Why?' Frevisse coldly insisted again. 'Why did you tell him about it?'

When Ivetta only went on sobbing, too lost in her own hurt to answer, Master Fyncham stepped forward and laid a hand heavily on her shoulder in firm reminder that she had been spoken to and had to answer. Tear-smeared and far gone in sorrow for herself, Ivetta raised her head and said on a half-whimper, pleading to be understood, 'It was for my boy. He's a priest stuck away nowhere. I want better for him. When they were trying to make Mary marry that Clement, Master Helyngton swore that if I helped them, then he'd help me. I didn't. I wouldn't. But this was only a paper or something. I thought maybe it would be enough. He said it was. That he'd help my boy. But he swore there'd be no killing either!'

'And you believed him?' Master Say protested disbelievingly.

'I didn't have anything else to believe in, did I?' Ivetta wailed. 'There was nobody else going to help my Nicholas, was there? Not Sir Gerveys with his duke of York and going away to Ireland and taking Pers with him. Not Master Say. He'd get the girls away from Master Helyngton but that wouldn't have done anything for my Nicholas, would it? It had to be Master Helyngton or nobody and he said he would!'

Now it was Mistress Say who protested, 'Ivetta, how could you think to let him have Mary and Jane? How could you mean to do that?'

Ivetta was beginning to be sullen at all their doubts. 'Mistress Cristiana was going to die and not have them anyway. Master Say would stop that Laurence. I knew that. So if I could do something for my Nicholas, I had to, that's all. Don't you see?'

Frevisse saw. Protected by a muddle of excuses to herself, Ivetta had chosen ambition for her son over Cristiana's need.

'It was that Master Colles,' Ivetta said with angry misery. 'He laughed when Master Helyngton said nobody would be hurt. I should have known then. It's his doing it all went wrong.'

There were a great many reasons besides Colles why so much was gone wrong, but Frevisse did not bother to point them out. She had not planned her sudden attack on Ivetta, had meant to leave accusing her until tomorrow, but the words had come on an uprush of anger, and now that it was done, she was not surprised by how easily Ivetta had broken. She saw that the woman had no depth of thought or strength. She did whatever seemed immediately needed, followed her soonest thought, probably never held to a longer course than whatever she saw lying just in front of her. This time her shallow thinking had cost five men's lives and Cristiana a bitter death. That the death had been a quicker death than Cristiana would otherwise have had might someday be a comfort to Frevisse. Just now it was not.

'Master Fyncham,' Master Say ordered, 'lock her away some place for the night. I'll give her over to the crowner to be questioned tomorrow.'

As Master Fyncham took her under one arm and raised her from the chair, Ivetta protested, 'I didn't do anything! Not against the law!'

'You'll tell what you did so the sheriff will better know what happened,' Master Say said coldly.

His coldness – or maybe the looks on all their faces – silenced her. Beginning to sob again, she let Master Fyncham lead her away, and only when she was well gone did Frevisse ask, 'What will be done with her?'

Master Say made a small, discontented sound. 'Little can be done. She'll be questioned about what she did and what she knows and then, if I have my way, she'll be sent to live with her son in that place in the Huntingdonshire marshes and serve her right. I won't have her anywhere around here, that's certain.'

Weary with sorrow, Mistress Say asked, 'But why, when it was too late to have this hateful paper, did Colles kill Gerveys? And poor Sawnder? There wasn't any use to it then.'

'To have Gerveys out of the way?' Master Say guessed. 'To end his interfering?'

Among the day's nightmare swirl of memories Frevisse had a clear one of Colles's face as he killed Cristiana. It had been alight with pleasure. He had looked a man come suddenly alive at the chance to kill. And because she was so tired, Frevisse said, when otherwise she might not have, 'Or he did it simply because he wanted to. For the pleasure of having Gerveys dead.'

Mistress Say stood up abruptly. 'I have to go to bed.'

Master Say rose, too, but stiffly, his hours of riding telling on him, and said to Frevisse, 'My lady, if you'll see to the candles, please?'

Frevisse made a small nod that she would but asked, 'What will you do about Nol?'

'Nol.' Master Say seemed to pull thought of Nol out of some far corner of his mind. 'Yes. Nol. I think I'll send him to Lady Alice with a letter of what we know now, and tell him not to return. Let him make his way in the world with Suffolk's favor. Or, better, with no one's at all.'

He took a candle from the nearest stand and followed Mistress Say through the shadows to their bedchamber. When the door was shut behind them, Frevisse took another candle for herself, blew out the rest, and left the parlor for the high-roofed blackness of the hall. Not bound for her own bed, she had to go the hall's length, the candle's light small among the huge shadows. The close walls and low ceiling of the screens passage and the stairs up to Cristiana's bedchamber were better, and the bedchamber itself was brightly lighted enough, candles burning at the four corners of the bed where the long, still form of Cristiana's body lay in its shroud.

Kneeling in prayer on the bed's far side, Domina Elisabeth looked up when Frevisse came in but did not speak and for that Frevisse was grateful. Just now there was nothing she wanted to say to anyone or for anyone to say to her. She and Domina Elisabeth merely bowed their heads slightly to one another, Frevisse knelt beside the bed to take up the prayers for Cristiana's soul, and Domina Elisabeth rose and went to the mattress waiting on the floor across the room. Head bowed, hands folded together, Frevisse waited through the quiet sounds of her removing and folding and setting aside veil and wimple and outer gown; waited while she lay down and settled; waited until the steady breathing soon told she slept. Waited then for prayers to come but they did not. She was alone with the night's deep quiet and the deeper quiet of Cristiana's body on the bed and wanted to say her own prayers for mercy for Cristiana's soul, but nothing came to her. Only plain *Requiescat in pace*. Rest in peace. Which was insufficient to the great need crying in her not only to pray for Cristiana but to find a way past her own guilt for Cristiana's death.

No one else was ever likely to see her guilt, but she knew and that was enough. Knew she had understood too little and had left too much until too late. Knew she had had everything sorted down to near certainty of Ivetta's guilt by this morning, but had chosen to leave accusing her for later. Had chosen to wait until the already over-busied day was done because Ivetta would still be here then and nothing more would happen before then. She had thought. And had been most terribly wrong.

But if she had spoken out this morning, would it have kept Cristiana from what she did? Or only burdened her with one more bitter grief? As it was, she had been spared knowledge of Ivetta's betrayal. And the death her disease would have finally given her.

Frevisse supposed that time would come when she might weave some shred of comfort from that; but there would never be comfort against knowing her own guilt in having given too little heed to Cristiana these past days. She had not troubled to see how far Cristiana was gone into despair, how at the end of her strength she was to endure any more; and because she had not seen, two men's souls were surely gone to hell and Cristiana had died with hardly time to make her own peace.

But Cristiana *had* made that peace. From her last words, Frevisse could even find hope that she had killed Laurence not so much in hatred for him but for love of her daughters.

Was it better to have killed for love rather than in hate? Frevisse did not know, could only hope, and with a sigh out of her depths of sorrow and regrets, she turned to Compline's prayers. Despite the hour was probably nearer to Matins, she wanted Compline's prayers. They were meant to bring the heart and mind to peace after a day's troubles. Even such a day as today. But the prayers that came to her first were from Matins after all. *A vinculis peccatorum nostrorum absolvai nos omnipotens et misericors Dominus.* From the chains of our sins set us free, almighty and merciful Lord. *Miserere nostri, Domine, miserere nostri. Fiat misericordia tua, Domine, super nos, quemadmodum speravimus in te.* Pity us, Lord, pity us. Let your mercy, Lord, be on us, as we have hoped in you.

The words wound around her mind and into her heart, giving her, if not the peace she needed, then the beginning of what might some-day be peace.

Because beyond today was Eternity and the vastness of God's Love.

Author's Note

What happened in Normandy that summer of 1449 is told in detail by French chroniclers of the time – Enguerrand de Monstrelet and Jean de Waurin among others – but in less detail by English contemporaries and usually in even less detail by modern historians. To follow the latters' example, suffice it to say that after more than a hundred years of warfare in France, the English in a matter of months lost almost everything the war had gained them.

On the other hand, the French chroniclers and the documents in the treasure-trove *Letters and Papers Illustrative of the Wars of the English in France During the Reign of Henry the Sixth, King of England* (edited by Joseph Stevenson for the Rolls Series, 1864) detail Somerset's refusal to negotiate over the broken truce despite the king of France's repeated attempts to do so and Somerset's orders to various English-held fortresses and towns to offer no resistance, simply to surrender. *Letters and Papers* also has the report written by Sir François de Surienne – the man whose attack on the Breton town broke the truce – to the king of France (Joan of Arc's King Charles VII, once the Dauphin) of how Suffolk and Somerset set him on to do it. They had tried to put all the blame for the English losses on him as a scapegoat, so he had escaped and with this report was making personal peace with the French. This element of self-interest of course casts doubt on anything he might report against Suffolk and Somerset, except for the corroborative evidence of Somerset's own letters to the French king and his well-chronicled failure to resist the French sweep into English-held territory.

Charges of treason were made against Somerset in England for years afterward, but he was never prosecuted for his utter dereliction of duty in Normandy. In fact, following the duke of Suffolk's death in the following year, Somerset took his place as head of the royal government. For reasons I fail to understand, most modern histories of the Hundred Years' War not only brush past these events but go on to treat the ensuing charges and outcry against Somerset as unjustified political maneuvering by the duke of York and others.

John Say – Sir John Say, as he became – of Broxbourne and his wife Elizabeth are real. In the anti-Suffolk polemics of the next year and so he figures as a villain by association and I had thought to use him as my villain in this book. Researching his overall career and life, however, I found him less a villain and more a highly competent man who seems to have served the crown of England rather than other men's political ends. There is even evidence of the affection between him and his wife in the epitaph still to be seen on her grave: 'Here lies Dame Elizabeth Sometime Wife to Sir John Say Knight daughter of Lawrence Cheyne Esquire of Cambridge Shire a Woman of Noble blood and most noble in good manners which deceased the xxv day of September The year of our Lord MCDIxxiii and interred in this church of Broxbourne awaiting The body of her said Husband whose Souls God Bring to Everlasting bliss amen.'

The manor of Baas remains, though nothing of the Says' manor house itself. Gone, too, is St Augustine's church as it was in 1449 except for the ancient font. All else was built anew not long after this story, paid for by . . . John Say. He is buried there, his grave and damaged tomb brass still to be seen. Should you go there, you will likewise see that one Richard Goodhirst – Father Richard in the story – was priest at St Augustine's sometime in the mid-1400s. For a detailed study of John Say's life and career, there is J.S. Roskell's *Parliament and Politics in Late Medieval England*, vol. 2, The Hambledon Press, 1981.

All other non-noble characters in this story and the events around the Says and Broxbourne are fictional, save that King Henry VI did ride by way of Waltham and Ware to Cambridge and Ely in August 1449.

A minor point is my use of *butlery* in place of the more common term *buttery*. Butlery, the older form of the word, was still occasionally used in the 1400s and better conveys the room's purpose.

A less minor point concerns the use of torture in late medieval England. Common enough as a legal device in earlier centuries, it was illegal by this time, except in such a situation as Frevisse cites in the story. Like police brutality in our own time, it surely occurred; but only later, with the rise of the Tudors and the Renaissance in England, did torture again become an established, accepted, and extensive part of the English legal system.

Again, my particular thanks go to Sarah J. Mason and Bill Welland. It was because I've been very happily a guest at their home in Broxbourne that 'Sir John Say of Broxbourne' caught my attention and set me on the path taken by *The Widow's Tale*. Because my health prevented another visit there during the first drafts of the story, they generously sent me information and pictures and maps of the area, Bill even venturing out to take photographs around Baas so I could better envision the lay of the land, changed though it surely is after more than five hundred years. When I did finally go there, I found I needed to change nothing, they had so well provided me with facts and details.

Certainly not least among their many kindnesses, they have phoned me so that I could hear the bells ringing at St Augustine's church across Broxbourne's green from their home.

Z677073